"Highly entertaining . . . kept my interest all the way through."

—*Deadly Pleasures Mystery Newsletter*

"A page-turner . . . first-rate entertainment."

—*Publishers Weekly*

"Spare and tense . . . a hard-boiled mystery fan's delight. . . . A top-drawer example of the nineties private eye school of writing."

—*Romantic Times*

"Fast action and a believable, appealing cast of characters . . . prepare to be shocked again."

—*Booklist*

"This suspenseful novel offers ample evidence why the Dave Garrett mystery series is so popular."

—*Southwest Times Record*

"The Dave Garrett series is a real find. Garrett is a strong but credible character that will wear well with readers long after 'December' is gone."

—Jeremiah Healy, author of *Rescue*

"Fast-paced. . . . Don't miss this one."

n Times

NEIL ALBERT

CRUEL APRIL

A Dave Garrett Mystery

SIGNET
Published by the Penguin Group
Penguin Books USA Inc., 375 Hudson Street,
New York, New York 10014, U.S.A.
Penguin Books Ltd, 27 Wrights Lane,
London W8 5TZ, England
Penguin Books Australia Ltd, Ringwood,
Victoria, Australia
Penguin Books Canada Ltd, 10 Alcorn Avenue,
Toronto, Ontario, Canada M4V 3B2
Penguin Books (N.Z.) Ltd, 182–190 Wairau Road,
Auckland 10, New Zealand

Penguin Books Ltd, Registered Offices:
Harmondsworth, Middlesex, England

Published by Signet, an imprint of Dutton Signet,
a division of Penguin Books USA Inc.
Previously appeared in a Dutton edition.

First Signet Printing, April, 1996
10 9 8 7 6 5 4 3 2 1

Printed in the United States of America

PUBLISHER'S NOTE
This is a work of fiction. Names, characters, places, and incidents either are the product of the author's imagination or are used fictitiously, and any resemblance to actual persons, living or dead, events, or locales is entirely coincidental.

Absent friends—

Ray Chrobot
1943–1993
Dos vedanya, comrade

Jean Krainck 1934–1994
and her infinite grace and courage

John Ebersole, M.D., Captain, USN (ret.)
USS *Nautilus*, USS *Seawolf*
1925–1993
On permanent patrol

Author's Note

My deepest thanks to all of those who helped bring this book to a conclusion—my agent and friend, Blanche Schlessinger; Sergeant McGrath of the Marcus Hook Police Department; Dr. Michael Rakosky; the Lancaster County District Attorney's Drug Task Force; and Marilyn Thomson of the Blue Lion Inn. A particular debt of gratitude is owed to my editor, Danielle Perez, for all her help and encouragement through all the versions of the manuscript. Last but not least, thanks to my friend and resident firearms expert, Lynne Boyer.

On a serious note, the kidnapping of Tara Leigh Calico described in Chapter Fifteen is all too real. Anyone with any information about this case should contact 1(800) VANISHED or Sergeant Garvey of the Valencia City, New Mexico, Sherriff's Office at (505) 865–9604.

Chapter One

Tuesday 10:00 P.M.

I picked up my second Wild Turkey and looked at my reflection in the glass. It didn't tell me much. There was a hint of a smile around the mouth, but my face was faceted by the ice, distorted by the glass, and colored by the dark golden glow of the bourbon. I wondered how many people were studying themselves in bar glasses around the country at that very moment. There was a line from an Ingmar Bergman movie, or maybe it was from the Bible—something about how humanity sees through a glass, darkly. I thought of how much bourbon I'd dumped into my poor liver in the last twenty-five years. Middle-aged thoughts. Maybe it was that I had a whole new reason to worry about my health.

I took a sip and let it roll around in my mouth. "I didn't expect to find the hundred and one proof stuff in an airport bar," I said.

Most of the people who tend bar at the Philadelphia airport are either college students picking up vacation money, or black women from Chester or Philadelphia exhausted from working two and three jobs to keep their families together. But this one was a grandfatherly Italian with a big smile and thick horn-rim glasses.

His head bobbed, accepting the compliment. "I special order it. Buncha the TWA pilots get together every Friday night, they like it." He leaned over the bar. "So, you meetin' your girl?"

"It's that obvious?"

"A man don't look that happy waiting to pick up his momma." He pointed at my hand. "And you ain't wearing no wedding ring."

"You're good. You ought to be in my line of work."

"Whadya do?"

I looked at my drink again. "I used to be a lawyer. Center City. Now I'm a private detective."

"No kiddin'? So what's it like, bein' a private eye?" He was a good bartender. If he was curious about why I wasn't a lawyer anymore, he didn't let it show.

I shrugged. "I used to feel sorry for myself sometimes, when I was a lawyer, about how hard I had to work. I work harder now and get paid a hell of a lot less."

"You catch crooks, like in the movies?"

"The cops get paid to do that. I mostly do investigations. Missing persons cases. Take statements from witnesses. Surveillances, things like that."

"That how you met your girl?"

"You're relentless." I smiled. "What's your name?"

"Tony. Glad to know yuh."

"Dave." We shook hands over the bar. When I pulled my hand back it smelled faintly of aftershave.

"Her name's Kate," I said after a moment.

"Irish?"

"Oh, yes. Red hair and green eyes. And a real redhead's complexion. She lives in Miami, and she has to put on gobs of sunblock before she can go outside."

Tony pulled out his wallet and handed over a picture of a round-faced woman with short, frizzy hair, standing in front of a small brick row house. Her body hid most of the house. She could have been anywhere from sixty to eighty.

"Your wife?" I asked.

He beamed with pride and tapped the picture with a stubby forefinger. "Thirty-seven years we been together, six children, three grandchildren."

I handed back the picture. "Kate doesn't look anything like that. She's straight up and down. Has to run around in the shower to get wet." I almost added that when she unzipped her pants they fell right down to the floor.

I could see him struggling with the concept of a woman like that being attractive, and failing. "You two—getting married?"

Tony had a knack for asking good questions. "Maybe. I'm not sure. Things have been happening pretty fast between us. Tonight will be the first time I've seen her in a couple of months."

He shrugged. "Things happen fast, slow—if it's right, it don't matter. Angie and I, we have three dates, all with chaperones, then we decide to get married. We were just a couple of kids. And look at us now. Say, Dave, you got any kids?"

"No. She has two from her first marriage. They're both in college now."

"College? Boy, none of mine made it that far."

"Education runs in the family. She teaches English at a community college down there."

"Smart lady." He hesitated before he asked his next question. "Say, if you don' mind me asking . . . how old is she?"

"I'm not actually sure," I admitted. "I think just about my age, forty-four."

"Angie was a grandma by the time she was forty-seven. You know, it's nonna my business, but you want to have a family, you better start pretty soon."

"I'd like that," I admitted.

He tapped his chest with an open palm. "Take it from me, when you hold your own child for the first time, there's nuttin' like it, nuttin' in the whole wide world." He paused for a moment and shook his head. "Nuttin'."

I took a long sip of my drink and let him enjoy his memory. "When I got divorced," I said, "I figured that was it for me, as far as getting married or having kids, I mean. This is like something falling out of the sky for me."

He became very serious. "Dave, you can't take it that way. It won' last."

"How do you mean?"

"I'm seventy years old this next August, and let me tell you one thing I found out. Life ain't no lottery and there ain't nuttin' free worth havin'. You only get to keep what you earn."

"That's an interesting philosophy."

He spread his arms wide, gesturing around the bar. "I'm just a guy stretching out his Social Security a little. I ain't no philosopher. But I know what I know."

"Don't you believe in just plain good luck?"

"For small stuff, sure." He shook his head sadly. "But *family* . . ." His voice trailed off and he rubbed an imaginary spot on one of the glasses. "So, she as excited as you are?"

"I talked to her from the Miami airport just a couple of hours ago. Yeah, she sounded excited." I looked down at my glass, which was nearly empty. "But there's some complications."

He gave a rich, robust Italian laugh. "The two of you are old enough to be grandparents, you hardly know this girl, and you say there's *complications*?"

"She's still married."

Tony was very much the South Philadelphia Catholic family man. "Oh."

"They've been living in the same house, but separate

lives, if you know what I mean, for a long time. They were planning to divorce when the youngest got out of college."

"Same house?" he repeated.

"It's not as uncommon as you might think," I said. "When we first met she told me she was divorced. It was only later that I got the whole story."

Tony started wiping the bar, which was already spotless. "Dave, I like you, but I gotta say this. You two have to come from behind. You started with a lie."

I was startled. "I thought you would say that God will forgive."

He leaned closer, as if imparting a secret. "God don't run the whole show. Things happen that got nuttin' to do with Him."

"Like whether you earn things?"

"Yeah." He held my eyes for a moment, then his expression relaxed and he was just a jolly bartender again. "Hey, Dave, sorry to get so serious on you. This isn't like me, getting so personal. One on the house, okay?"

I held my hand over my glass. "Thanks, but I have to run. Her plane's due in right now."

"Sure you ain't sore? It was none of my business, sayin' what I said."

"No. It was good to have somebody to talk to."

He put his hand on my sleeve. "Dave, will you do me a favor?"

"What's what?"

"Bring her by. I'd like to meet your lady and wish her well."

"Okay." I collected my coat from the chair next to me and stood up to go.

"Dave, one more thing?"

"Yeah?"

"My wife and I, we'll light a candle for you and your girl this Sunday."

"I'm very touched, Tony. But I'm not Catholic, and she's about as lapsed as you can get."

"Tell you somethin', I don't think He really cares."

I found the gate just as the plane pulled in. A vendor across the corridor was selling oversize Mylar balloons. I bought one that said Welcome Home in big pink letters and found a spot right at the head of the stairs. Welcome Home seemed a little silly—she'd never even seen my apartment—but it was either that or Bon Voyage. Besides, if things worked out it would be her home from now on. Our home.

The door to the ramp opened and a stream of suntanned passengers came through. Most seemed to be college students coming back from spring break. Seeing them made me realize that if Kate and I had met in our early twenties, we could have kids this age already. It could be one of our kids coming up the stairs.

I saw a pale, slender woman with short red hair, but when I looked more closely I saw that she was younger than Kate. Then came some tired businessmen and some equally tired businesswomen, most of them burdened with luggage that looked heavy. The men and the women all seemed hot, miserable, and homesick. Welcome to the era of equal opportunity, I thought, where gender is no bar to ulcers, heart attacks, nervous exhaustion, and alienation from one's family. Well, I thought, why not? Men always thought it was worth having. Why shouldn't women think so, too?

Four huge college boys, all broad shouldered and blond, came up together. They looked like the linebackers from a small school, breaking training. They all wore T-shirts that appeared to have obscene sayings, but they went by too fast for me to read them. Next was a young couple, a little bit older. Maybe grad students. The girl had a fine set of hips and she knew exactly how to move to show them off. Long brown hair piled up on top of her head. It was the kind of hairdo no man could look at without wanting to unpin it and let it fall down on a pillow. The boy was trailing behind, managing an armful of carry-on bags and enjoying the view.

Some more college students went by, and then a few older couples. Retirees moving up north for the summer, I guessed. It was easy to tell the ones who were still in love and those that weren't. After the old folks was another rush of college students—evidently the retirees had been holding things up. Then no one for a minute, then a few more retirees. Then no one at all.

After a couple of minutes one of the flight attendants, a short brunette wearing too much makeup, came slowly up the stairs. A black bag on a little baggage cart trailed behind her like a faithful dog. She looked hardly older than the college students, but she was barely putting one foot in front of the other. I wondered how long she'd been working.

I caught her eye but she didn't stop until I sidestepped and blocked her path.

"Excuse me. My—fiancée was on board and hasn't gotten off."

Her face was impassive behind her makeup but her eyes were bleary. "Sir, all of the passengers have deboarded."

"That can't be."

"It's part of my job to check, sir. There's no one on board but the flight crew."

"She has to have been on the flight," I insisted.

She closed her eyes and rubbed her temples, but her voice stayed level. "Perhaps she missed it, sir."

"She called me from the airport in Miami just before boarding."

"Perhaps the flight was overbooked."

"Well, was it?"

"I don't know. And even if I did, I can't give out any passenger information."

"Would you mind if I went on board, just to make sure?" I asked.

"I've already checked, sir. Even the lavatories, we always do. There's no place to hide on an airplane."

She was right about that. "Can you please—"

"Sir, all I can tell you is that there's no one on board. Perhaps she never was aboard."

"Look, I know you're tired, but I'm really worried about her. Would it be such a problem if I went down and took a quick look?"

She shook her head in a way that left no room for argument. "The airline would be fined and I'd lose my job. You don't have any security clearance and you're not a passenger. For all the FAA knows, you want to plant a bomb."

I hadn't thought of that. "Look, miss—"

"I'll tell you what I'll do for you, sir. I'll go back and check one more time, okay?"

"I'd appreciate it very much."

She left her bag with me and disappeared back down the ramp. About five minutes later she came back, shaking her head. "Sorry, sir. There's nothing I can do."

"Please, miss. I need your help."

"Did she have a reservation? I understand the flight up from Miami was full."

"Yes, she had a reservation."

"If the flight was overbooked, maybe she accepted an offer for a free ticket or something and she'll be on a later flight."

I shook my head. "She would have called."

"Well—did she have checked baggage?"

"I'm pretty sure."

"The one thing I can tell you is, check baggage claim. If a passenger voluntarily gives up their seat we try very hard to make sure the bag doesn't go without them. If the bag is there, well, I don't know what to tell you."

It was a sensible suggestion. "Thanks for your help. Very much." She nodded at me and disappeared into the crowd.

By the time I found the right carousel, the bags had all been unloaded and reclaiming was in full swing. The college students were shoulder to shoulder around the carousel, pointing and shouting at their friends as familiar bags traveled past. The four linebackers hogged one side of the carousel all by themselves. The older people mostly hung back, except for one tiny woman who'd cleared a prime space for herself with the aid of an umbrella and a no-nonsense attitude. She reminded me of my mother. As I watched she hefted four enormous suitcases off the carousel and shouted for Myron to hurry up with the hand cart.

As the crowd began to thin, the rest of the older passengers began to come forward to claim their bags. I saw the pretty grad student—if that's what she was—and some other familiar faces, but not the thin woman with red hair. I only saw a couple of the business travelers, but then I remembered that most of them had carry-on bags. Then the retirees thinned out, leaving four items behind.

I moved up and took a look. The first one that came by was a torn athletic bag with a University of Pennsylvania address on the label. The next was a big dark leather suitcase with side straps and a brass nameplate. I couldn't catch the name, but the address was Camden. The third was a large cardboard box with the airline's logo advertising its contents as diving equipment.

The last one was a gray cloth suitcase, packed to bursting. I'd seen it before, in her room in Lancaster. And the tag had Kate's name and address.

I watched the bag circle slowly around till it was out of sight. I realized I was still holding on to the balloon. I let go and let it bounce off the ceiling twenty feet above. I wouldn't be needing it now.

Chapter Two

Tuesday 11:00 P.M.

My next stop was the American Airlines' ticketing desk, which was nearly deserted. I wound up facing a short, balding man with reading glasses who looked like he'd slept in his uniform. "Yes, sir. Can we help you?"

I flashed my "Citizen of Philadelphia" badge and hoped he'd never seen a real detective's shield. "My name's Garrett and I'm a detective. I'm working on a possible missing persons case involving a passenger of yours. Her name is McMahan. Kate McMahan."

He pushed his glasses up on his nose, which I took as a sign of interest. "You say she's missing?"

"She apparently boarded your flight from Miami but never got off. It landed about forty-five minutes ago. Her luggage is here, unclaimed."

"Would that be flight 637?"

I looked at the copy of her itinerary she'd faxed up. "Yes, it would."

"Let me check something." He lowered his head and tapped at his computer keys for a moment. His glasses slid back down his nose. "Ah. Here you are, sir. I may have an answer for you. That flight had a scheduled stop in Harrisburg."

"She said—I'm told it was a nonstop."

He smiled thinly. "We prefer the term 'direct,' sir. There's no change of planes, just a quick stopover."

"It doesn't show on her travel papers."

"That's right, sir." He cleared his throat. "Since there's no change of planes." He smiled some more, and pushed his glasses up again.

I began wishing that everyone would be less polite and a little more helpful. "Could she have gotten off in Harrisburg if she wanted?"

More tapping at the computer. "If she wanted to, yes, sir. But she didn't."

"Huh?"

"Her ticket was used all the way through—Miami to Harrisburg, Harrisburg to Philadelphia. We collected boarding passes from her in both cities."

"So how can she not be here?"

"We can only tell you that her ticket was used, not who used it." He shrugged. "I don't know what else to tell you, sir."

"She wasn't bumped off in Miami?"

"No. If she had been, her ticket wouldn't have been used."

"Could she have flown to Miami, gotten off in Harrisburg, and given her ticket to someone else to finish the flight?" I asked.

"Well, I suppose. But why?"

"That's a very good question," I said. "When's your next flight to Harrisburg?"

"Just a moment . . . at this time of night the commuter shuttles have stopped . . . flight 1721, in two hours."

"Thanks, but I can drive it faster." As I turned away, he nodded at me and his glasses fell down again.

I had two options—three, if you count going home and

waiting for something to happen. One was to drive to Harrisburg, and the other was a call to Kate's house. And who would answer? Kate? Sorry, dear, I lost my nerve at the last minute. What if her husband answered? What would I say to him? What if I reached one of her children? Kid, if your mom isn't with you, then she's vanished—but don't worry about it, okay?

No, it wasn't time to call.

I found an airport snack shop that was still open and ordered the largest coffee they had, to go. Then I hurried to the parking garage and unlocked my Honda Civic. March had been a hair-raising month, and the poor car had taken the brunt of it. The entire passenger door was new—its predecessor had stopped most of a load of double ought buckshot. The door's exterior had been painted white, to match the car, but the interior was green, not beige like the rest of the car. The driver's door had a hole the size of a .357 round. I'd plugged it with a cork, covered it with some body putty, and touched it up with a can of spray paint. At night, from certain angles, it didn't look too bad. From a distance, that is. I hoped it would stand up to an hour and a half of sustained turnpike driving.

Traffic was heavy on the Schuylkill Expressway all the way to City Line—apparently a basketball game had just finished at the Spectrum. The other cars were full of people; sometimes whole families, sometimes just men, and their only care in the world was making it home before they fell asleep. Home to a refrigerator with a couple more beers, a color TV, and maybe a bed with a willing partner. I sipped at my coffee, which was already turning cold. It's easy to feel very alone if you give yourself the chance.

I decided to stop feeling sorry for myself and concentrate on getting to Harrisburg as quickly as I could. The Expressway brought me to King of Prussia, a small crossroads town best known as the home of a gigantic shopping mall. I cleared the toll booth, made the wide right hand circle that brought me on to the westbound side of the turnpike, and pressed the pedal to the floor. The Civic responded gamely, and I edged her to a shade over eighty. The new door vibrated and the wind whistled through both windows, but she hung together.

I don't know what I expected to find in Harrisburg—wherever she was, there was no reason to think she was there. The smart money said she was back in Miami, that she and her husband had had a last-minute reconciliation. That, right now, while I was straining my eyes and pushing my rattletrap through the night, the two of them were having a bubble bath somewhere, all was forgiven, and sooner or later she was going to have to get up and call Dave what's-his-name, but that could wait till the champagne was gone. . . .

But maybe not. Could her husband hold her in Miami against her will, trying to talk her out of leaving? Possible, but if anything Kate had said about their marriage was true, they'd already been married ten years too long. He was wrapped up in his business, and, she suspected, a couple of girlfriends. No, it didn't sound like a recipe for the act of a desperate husband.

I flashed by the Ephrata exit, a little more than halfway to the Harrisburg airport. Kate and I had met not far from there, just two months before. Four days together, and nothing but phone calls since. Whoever thought up phone sex should get a medal. . . .

So why shouldn't she get on the plane in Miami? I couldn't think of a reason, not even a bad one. Unless I was willing to assume that Kate was a completely different person than the one I thought I knew, that she was capable of changing her mind without warning. Okay, so she gets to the airport, confirms to me she's taking the plane—and then what? She takes the plane. She probably didn't know the plane stopped in Harrisburg, but so what? So she finds out the plane is making a quick stop. Either she sits tight for a few minutes, or she gets off to stretch her legs. But either way, she finishes the flight. What could possibly make her get off in Harrisburg and not reboard?

Make her get off. Try it another way—why would someone want to *make* her get off? My hands started to sweat on the steering wheel as I struggled to keep my thinking logical. It seemed crazy, a fantasy fueled by fatigue and speculation and a mixture of caffeine and booze, but at least it accounted for the facts. But who would want to stop Kate except her husband? It made no sense. But the reason it made no sense wasn't because of anything inherently illogical—it was silly only because I couldn't think of the motivation. That wasn't the fault of the theory; it was my own lack of imagination.

Maybe a third party was involved. Someone who wanted Kate, and who wanted to make his move in Harrisburg instead of Miami. That explained a little—except for a few details like who, how, and why, that is. The Florida State Board of Higher Education might be unhappy to be losing a good community college teacher, but it didn't seem like a sufficient reason to me. Even *I* thought I was coming up with stupid ideas. I stopped for a second cup of coffee at a turnpike rest stop and then pushed on.

For years, the Harrisburg airport had been a traveler's purgatory. It was a former air force base, and the terminal was cheerless, grimy, and inconvenient. But finally, after years of promises and probably a few payoffs, the new terminal was finally opened. It was a handsome structure, curved and sweeping, with a facade of glass and steel. Most of the lights were out when I pulled up, and the full moon was reflected dozens of times over.

The ticket counters on the first level were deserted, but a coffee shop on the second floor was still open. Sitting at a tiny white plastic table in the rear were three men wearing American Airlines uniforms. Their caps were off and their neckties were all pulled loose from their collars.

"Excuse me, gentlemen."

They looked up. The pilot was a slender, mild-looking man with thinning gray hair and a pencil mustache. He looked like the accountant I'd used when I'd been a lawyer. It was hard to imagine him handling a thousand tons of metal at hundreds of miles an hour. I had assumed that all pilots looked like John Wayne. The other two—I assumed they were the flight engineer and the co-pilot—were much younger, young enough to be his kids.

"Yes?" the pilot said.

"By any chance did you fly in from Miami this evening? Flight 637?"

"Every inch of the way."

I dragged up a fourth plastic chair and sat down. I wasn't going to wait for an invitation, especially when I was afraid it wasn't going to be coming. "My name's Garrett. A friend of mine was on that flight. We were supposed to meet in Philadelphia, but she never made it there. She's about forty—"

The pilot held up his hand. "Save your breath, friend. The plane was packed. None of the standbys made it on. When we landed nearly everybody deplaned. There were two hundred people milling around the gate. She could have had two heads and nobody would have noticed."

"So no one checks to see if the person who got off is the same ticket holder who reboards?"

"If the flight is nearly empty they try to keep an eye on things. People sometimes steal tickets around the terminal and try to get free flights. But when we're busy like tonight, they just herd them back on.

"And if no one complains, that's it?"

"That's right."

"One more thing, if you don't mind. If you flew up from Miami, how come you didn't finish the flight?"

"We're running close to our maximum hours for the

month and they need us to fly back to Miami tomorrow," he explained patiently. "The time in taking her down to Philadelphia and back would have left us short."

"So the cabin crew that went from Harrisburg to Philadelphia was new, too?"

"Oh, yeah."

I remembered how the flight attendant had phrased her answers. No, she'd never said she'd come up from Miami herself—she just said she thought that the flight had been full. "So where's the cabin crew from the flight up? Maybe one of them remembers something."

He looked at his watch. "I'd say they're about ready to land in Chicago."

"Oh. I see."

"I'm sorry, mister, but unless you happen to see her around the terminal, I think you made a trip up here for nothing."

"I'm starting to think so, too. Thanks."

I scoured every public space in the terminal. I only found a few people, cleanup crews mostly, and none of them remembered seeing her. I checked the security office—no messages for me and no reports of any unusual activities. I left my card with the officer on duty, just in case.

I sat down on a concrete bench just outside the terminal. The seat was cold and it chilled the base of my spine, but I didn't move. I watched the clouds drift by in front of the moon and slowly blot out the light. Rain for tomorrow. Was it going to be raining where Kate was?

It was that time in the middle of the night when things slow down and all your defenses against fear and despair start to crumble. In the last three hours I'd accomplished exactly nothing, and for all the good I was doing, for her or myself, I might as well have stayed in the bar. I felt scared and foolish and most of all, useless. If she needed me now, I wasn't doing anything to help.

I looked around, wondering what to do next. Airports are never entirely deserted, no matter how late. A couple of food service trucks were unloading, and every once in a while a car would pull into the parking lot. Then a bus came and went. No one got off or on.

A bus. Ground transportation. Cabs. I looked around. Way over to my left was a taxi stand. Parked in the darkness between two overhead lights, almost invisible, was a battered Yellow cab. It was worth a try.

The driver was a young black man with two gold earrings and an odd haircut that made the top of his head look flat. I approached the driver's window, which was down. "Where yous goin'?" he asked.

"Nowhere. Just need to ask you a question. You been out here all evening?"

"Off and on. It been slow."

"Here about three, four hours ago?"

"Around then, yeah."

"I'm looking for someone. She was on a flight that stopped here. American Airlines. She may have gotten off."

His eyes narrowed and he straightened up in his seat. But there was nothing in my questions that ought to cause him to pay any particular attention. "What time you say?"

"The plane probably landed here about ten, maybe nine-thirty."

"And what'd she look like?"

"Thin, short red hair, about forty-five, very pale skin."

He shrugged. "Could be lotsa people."

"You'd remember her hair. It's flaming red, almost orange."

I saw the hint of a nod before he caught himself. "Who are you?"

"I'm a detective from Philadelphia, and she's a friend of mine."

"Why you lookin' for her?"

"Does that make a difference?"

"This lady—she in trouble?"

"Not that I know of."

He looked down. "I ain't seen her, man."

I looked at him. "I think you did."

He raised his eyes and tried for a smile. "Hey, man, no, I didn't."

"I bet you were here when that plane landed and you saw her go right past here."

His mouth became tight. "Lotsa people go past."

"But this one you remember. Why?"

"Ain't none of my business."

"It's mine."

"Man, I can't get involved, you know?"

"Involved in what?"

"Whatever this business is. Ain't my problem."

He saw the look on my face, but before he could react I shot my left hand through the open window and grabbed his throat. I squeezed hard. He tried to pry away my fingers, but I just tightened my grip. Whatever was in that man's head was my only link to Kate. "Don't even think of hitting the horn, friend." He nodded frantically. "You going to play ball with me?" He nodded again. I released the pressure on his neck, just a little.

He breathed deeply a couple of times and swallowed. "Who *are* you, man?"

"I'm somebody who doesn't want any harm to come to that lady."

"I see lotsa things in my job, you know. Things you keep quiet about. Hookers, drug deals, man. Stuff gettin' loaded and unloaded that don't look like it's got no paperwork, you know. But I stay clean. I don't wanna get involved, you know?"

"You're not involved. No one's going to know where I got this."

"I don't know, man."

I tightened my grip again. He was better prepared for me this time, and he was able to get both hands on my fingers, but they held tight. Slowly I pushed him back until the back of his head was buried in the headrest. He wriggled his head and upper body but I held him pinned. Finally he ran out of air and nodded.

I relaxed long enough for him to get just one breath and reapplied the pressure. I put my face down next to his. "Now give."

"The lady—one you said—she come out—with another lady and a guy. The first lady and the guy—get into the back of this van. Second lady goes back inside the terminal."

"You see any luggage?"

"No."

I relaxed the pressure a little more. "You sure the first woman was the one I'm looking for?"

He nodded. "That hair? Red like a fire engine? Yeah, that's why I took notice."

"Describe the other woman."

"I didn't get much of a look, honest. She was behind the skinny one. She was white, that's all I can say."

"The guy?"

"Big, kinda rough lookin'. He was a Spanish dude."

"Ever see either one before?"

"No, sir."

"How close were they standing to her?"

"Pretty close."

"See any weapons?"

"No."

"Was either of them close enough to have a gun or a knife pressed against her?"

"Both of 'em."

"What about the van?"

"It pulled away right after they got in. Dark color, no windows. Kinda dirty, though. Muddy."

"Make, model?"

"Sorry, mister."

"Any writing on the side?"

"Not that I seen."

"Anything else?"

"No, sir."

"I'm going to let go now. If I find out you've been holding out I'm going to be back and I'm going to fuck you up."

"Yessir."

"You got anything else to tell me?"

"That's all I know, honest."

I headed for my car.

Chapter Three

Wednesday 4:00 A.M.

It was a fast trip back to Philadelphia. At that hour, the odds of running into a state trooper were less than the chances of being struck by lightning. I had only a few tractor-trailer rigs for company, and none of them was in as much of a hurry as I was. My Civic continued to grind through the miles without complaint, though she did need a couple of quarts of oil when I stopped for gas at the Valley Forge rest stop.

While they were taking care of the oil I stretched my legs and went looking for some more coffee. The counter was closed, but I found a vending machine that sold me something hot and dark. When I finished it I felt more awake, so I suppose I got my money's worth.

I looked at the line of pay phones just inside the door. I could have called Miami two hours earlier, from Harrisburg, but I hadn't. I didn't care about the time of night but it was too important a call to make on the spur of the moment, before I had a chance to think this through. Now I wished I had just picked up the phone in Harrisburg. After turning it over for the entire drive back, I still hadn't the slightest idea of what I was going to say.

I found a bill changer and threw quarters into the pay phone like a strung out gambler feeding his favorite slot machine. I knew the number by heart—Kate and I had talked almost every day. I wondered when I'd be talking to her again. A couple of seconds, a couple of days, never?

I counted six rings before someone picked up. After a pause I heard a masculine noise that might have been "Hello."

"Frank McMahan, please."

"That's me," he yawned. "You know what time it is?"

"I'm sorry, but it's an emergency."

There was a pause and I heard the rustle of bedclothes. "What's going on?" His voice was still thick with sleep.

"Don't hang up, this is important. This is Dave Garrett. In Pennsylvania."

"Garrett? The detective?"

"Yeah. Look—"

He was awake now, and his voice was sharp. "What the hell are you calling here for?"

"I'm sorry—" I began.

"You don't know what sorry is, bud. You think this is funny, don't you? Steal a man's wife, a man who never did a damned thing to you, break up a family—you just don't—"

"Frank, she's missing."

"No shit."

"No, I mean really missing."

"What are you talking about?"

"She never got off the plane in Philadelphia."

"This is some kind of joke."

"I'm not kidding. She wasn't on the plane."

He paused for a moment. "Well, how does it feel to be stood up, huh?"

"I guess that depends if she's down there or not."

"Of course not," he snapped. When he spoke again, it

was halfway to a normal tone of voice. "Really, she's not up there?"

"No, they checked the plane and she wasn't on it. She may have gotten off before Philadelphia."

"You're lying to me, Garrett."

"So I could get to have the pleasure of talking to you?"

That slowed him down a little. "Jesus. Hold on. Let me get myself a drink."

He was only gone from the phone for a moment. I wondered if he had a bottle at the side of the bed. "So tell me what's going on," he said.

"Let me ask you a couple of questions first. When did you see her last?"

"Well, our daughter Annie took her to the airport. They left a little after seven."

"Did Annie see her get on?"

"Security's tight at the airport. Unless you're a ticketed passenger they don't let you past the metal detectors. But Annie waited there till the plane took off, and Kate never came back."

"What kind of mood was she in?" I asked.

He hesitated before he answered, as the possible responses got in the way of one another. "She was looking forward to seeing you again," he said at last.

"I want you to know, Frank, that when she and I met, she told me she was divorced. I wouldn't have ever gotten involved with her otherwise."

"You knew later, didn't you? And it didn't stop you, did it?"

"No. Or her, either."

"Well, at least I got you to admit it." His speech was slow and deliberate. I wondered exactly how much he'd had the night before. "She was everything to me, you know."

"She told me that the two of you . . . each had your separate lives."

"Fuck you."

"Well, that's what she told me." Silence. "Is it true?"

"Why should I tell you?"

"Because it's important to me and it might even be important to finding her."

"I never said we always got along on everything, and it's none of your goddamn business anyway."

I decided to stick to the case, if I could. "Did you know the plane had a stop first? Before Philadelphia?"

"A stop? I thought it was straight through."

"So did Kate. And I. But they had a stopover in Harrisburg."

"Where's that?"

"The south-central part of the state, about eighty miles west of Philadelphia. Anyway, I found a cabdriver who says he saw a woman matching Kate's general description leave the terminal with another woman, and a man. The woman who looked like Kate and the man got into a van and drove off. Kate's baggage is in Philadelphia, unclaimed."

"So who were they?"

"Damned if I know."

"How did they get her to go along?"

"I don't know. Maybe they didn't even use force. Where are your kids?"

"Both of them are right here."

"Well, maybe they tricked her somehow, telling her that one of the kids was hurt or sick or something. Maybe they told her they were from security and there was a problem they needed to see her about."

"Sounds like you don't know much."

"No."

"So, what are you going to do about it?"

I avoided his questions. "Can you think of anyone who would want to harm her? Or anyone who'd want to get at you through her?"

"No. I'm just a contractor. I can even get along with the damn unions when I have to."

"Who made her reservation?"

"I don't know. Either Kate or Annie. Probably Annie—she's working part-time as a secretary at a travel agency."

"So three people would have known when she was leaving."

"At least. There could have been more."

"What do you mean?"

"Some of our friends knew she was leaving last night. If someone wanted to know the exact flight they could have asked, or called the airlines to see who flew to Philadelphia."

"Have there been any threats, by phone or mail or anything, against any of you?"

"No, of course not. Now, what do we do? You're supposed to have the know-how."

"Sorry to disappoint you, but I've been a detective for only two years and I've handled exactly one kidnapping." I was sorry I'd used the word—it had a way of focusing things that I didn't like. No, the best way to think of it was just as a disappearance. But a disappearance from where? Maybe she never made it out of Miami. Maybe the scene at the Harrisburg airport was a stunt to get everyone to look in the wrong place. Hell, maybe it never happened at all—maybe they just gave the cabbie a hundred bucks and told him to tell that story if anyone asked. Or maybe something really happened at the Harrisburg airport but it didn't have anything to do with Kate. . . .

"Garrett? Do we call the cops?"

"Not just yet." I decided to keep my speculations that she might have disappeared from Miami to myself. "I don't think they'll take it very seriously unless we have something more."

"What more could we get?"

I avoided a direct answer because I didn't have one. "I

know what they're going to say. A woman feels caught between two men, lots of pressure, decided to get away on her own for a few days, and think things through. They'll say she's sure to turn up somewhere. And most of the time they're right."

"That's bull."

"That's not the point," I explained. "But that's how they're going to want to look at it, and we don't have much to convince them otherwise."

"What would the cops say about the two people in Harrisburg?"

"If they ever existed. If that was Kate. If it really was forcible."

There was silence for a while as he mulled it over. "Huh," he said at last.

"Stay by the phone." I gave him the number of my home answering machine, and also my office number. "I'll be in touch if I find anything out. And you call me if something happens down there."

"What could—oh, I get it." Neither one of us wanted to think about the possibility of a ransom demand. It was a way I didn't want my thoughts to run. "Garrett?"

"Yes?"

The line was quiet for a long moment before he spoke. "We were together a long time, you know. Two great kids."

"I know."

"Hell, it wasn't always hearts and flowers, but—listen, don't fuck this up."

"I'm giving it my best shot."

The parking lot was covered with a heavy frost that sparkled in the moonlight. I walked back to my car, my hands in my suit pockets to ward off the cold. April is a funny month in Pennsylvania—it's as much late winter as early spring. A light snowfall or two is nothing unusual, and sometimes the western mountains get a first-class past-ing as late as the end of the month. No matter what else happens, it's seldom warm at night, and never at four in the morning.

It was still dark when I reached the Philadelphia airport, but the day was already beginning. Shuttle buses were running from the parking lots and hotels, and one lane was taken up by a line of food service trucks waiting to unload. I found a space in short-term parking and headed for baggage claim.

As I expected, after all this time Kate's bag was no longer on the carousel. A skycap directed me to the unclaimed baggage desk, an enormous room separated from the public corridor by a half door. Luggage of every description was everywhere—trunks, suitcases, cardboard cartons, surfboards, disassembled bicycles, skis, guitar cases—just about anything that could be crammed into an airplane.

"Hey! Anybody home?"

"Back here!" a female voice responded. "Inna minute!"

I waited, and after a while a large black woman in a rumpled white blouse and black skirt appeared from behind a crate half the size of a pickup truck. She had on a badge, but if her outfit was supposed to constitute some kind of uniform, it didn't succeed. She wiped her hands on her skirt and looked at me. "Yeah? What can I do for you?"

"Friend of mine left her bag. She was on American Airlines 637 out of Miami, via Harrisburg. One bag. Name tag said Kate McMahan."

She blinked and looked at me with interest. More interest than the question justified. "What's your name?"

"Garrett. Dave Garrett. I'd like to pick it up, please."

She wrote down my name in a small notebook. "You got your claim check?"

"Sorry. No."

"Where's the passenger then?"

There was something in her eyes that gave me a sudden attack of honesty. "That's a good question. I'm looking for her, as a matter of fact."

"What's it to you?"

"I'm a private detective, and she's my fiancée. Her bag was here—I saw it on the carousel—but she never made it. I don't know if she got off in Harrisburg or if she ever got on at all."

"Tell me, we got us a full moon out there?"

"Pretty close," I said.

"It's been a full moon kind of night. Lotsa strange stuff tonight. What's the bag look like?"

"Gray cloth, pretty big, and packed tight. Had her name on a tag, Kate McMahan, Miami."

She looked me up and down and rubbed her chin. "You said you saw the bag? What time?"

"When the bags were all unloaded it was still there. About eleven, give or take."

"Mister, there's something funny going on. That bag was brought in here 'bout eleven-thirty. I remember 'cause I was here by myself. They bring in the bags from the old flight just before a new flight uses the carousel, to keep it clear of old stuff. And a lady came by and claimed it jus' a couple minutes later."

"You're sure?"

"Sure I'm sure. I remember 'cause I'd jus' started doin' the paperwork on it. I was glad she saved me the trouble."

"She have the claim check?"

She put her hands on her hips and nodded. "Nobody gets *nothin'* without no claim check."

I believed her. "What did she look like?"

"Taller 'n me, skinny, red hair, kinda pale. Didn't say nothin' I can recall." She looked at me. "What your lady look like?"

"Forty-five, very thin, short red hair, green eyes."

"I didn't take no notice of her eyes, and I ain't much of a judge of age, but she didn't look too well."

I felt my throat tighten up. "How do you mean?"

"Oh . . . I don't know. Her color didn't look too good."

"She's naturally pale," I said. "Anyone with her?"

"Nobody." We were real quiet right then.

"You're sure she didn't say anything? Anything at all?"

She shook her head. "Jus' the usual."

"Did she seem scared, or worried?"

"Nothin' I took notice of. Maybe in a little bit of a hurry, but most folks are, you know. This ain't a place people like to hang around."

"When she left which way did she head? Out the main doors?"

"No, over to the left."

I looked. The corridor ran straight, with nothing on either side, and seemed to dead-end. If there were any signs, I couldn't see them. "What's down there?"

"Hall takes a left, and then you get to the rental car counters."

"She ask directions?"

"No. Not from me, anyways."

"Thanks very much." I needed a good night's sleep and a day of hard thought to think this one out. But there was only time for a quick cup of coffee.

Chapter Four

Wednesday 6:00 A.M.

I held my coffee cup and looked out the terminal window. To the east the sky was turning light gray and the stars were fading. The earliest of the early bird commuters were already starting to come in. By evening they'd be back, looking as tired and dispirited as the business travelers I'd seen last evening. Another day's wear on the body, another day of not seeing your kids growing up. But right now it was morning and there were places to go, people to see, deals to make, a whole world to run, the poor dumb bastards. Thinking about it would have made me tired if I wasn't so tired already.

I sipped my coffee and tried to collect my thoughts. There were three basic possibilities, with some alternatives. One, Kate could have landed here, avoided me somehow, claimed her bag, and gone almost anywhere. At this point she had a six-hour head start. She could be anywhere from California to England, and every hour widened the circle. I couldn't imagine why she'd do that, but I couldn't say it was impossible, either.

Two, Kate could have gotten off in Harrisburg, either on her own or against her will. Again, no idea why. And possibility number two gave her almost a nine-hour head start.

Three, she could never have boarded the plane in Miami. If her husband was telling the truth, no one saw her get on. And I believed him, not because I especially trusted him, but because if he was involved in anything it would be in his interest to tell me a story that would keep me from even thinking about Miami. If he had a role in what happened—whatever it was—he'd want to throw me off the scent by assuring me she'd been on that plane.

Miami. She goes to the airport, goes to the gate . . . and why not get on? Hell, she has to get on. Her claim check shows up in Philadelphia five hours later. She either took that flight, or another flight that left within a short time. One way or the other she made it up here, or at least her claim check did.

The claim check . . . The person who picked up the bag headed straight off for the rental cars. As far as I knew, Kate had only been to the Philadelphia airport once, and that was to catch a flight out. She wouldn't have known where to look for a rental car, and there were no signs. Sure, she could have asked someone, but she'd never been to the unclaimed baggage department before, and people don't usually ask for directions to two different places at the same time. You do your business at the first and then get directions to the second.

I could think of only one reason why the person who picked up the bag would avoid me. Because she wasn't Kate McMahan.

I finished my coffee and saw that my hands were starting to tremble. I'd only been up one night and it felt like three already. In the marines, on maneuvers, I'd gone as long as fifty hours without sleep, but I'd been twenty-two then, not forty-four.

The Philadelphia airport has a rental agency area with half a block of counter space. Fortunately for me, few of them were busy at six in the morning. Even more fortunate, after a couple of minutes' checking I found that most of them had been closed at the time the bag was picked up.

I worked my way down the row to the Alamo desk. Approaching from unclaimed baggage, it was the first of the major agencies. Hertz and Avis had bigger counters, but they were farther down. If the person I was looking for had something to hide, she'd want to clear out as soon as she could. Especially, I realized, if she'd seen me hanging around the baggage carousel.

I waited my turn in line. The counter was black plastic, and came to the middle of my chest. For some reason someone had brightened up the counter with a couple of vases with yellow lilies. They didn't exactly make me feel like I was at home. On the other side of the counter, at waist level, was a battery of monitors, fax machines, and computer keyboards. The clerk was brunette, with her hair pulled back, but the effect wasn't nearly as nice as the long-haired grad student I'd seen get off the plane the night before. This one's hair was pulled in a tight bun that said, Stay clear. Her uniform was buttoned to the neck. Under the makeup she could have been anything from a sourpuss twenty-five to a well-preserved forty. "May I help you, sir?"

"I hope so. Were you here last night about eleven-thirty?"

"Uh-huh."

"I'm looking for someone who may have rented a car at that time. Maybe from you and maybe from one of the other agencies. She—"

"What's your business with her?"

I thought of trying the Citizen of Philadelphia badge again, and then thought better of it. "I'm a detective, looking into a possible missing persons case."

"Can I see some identification?"

I handed over my identification card. She looked at it and handed it back without changing expression.

"A woman came through here with a gray cloth suitcase around eleven-thirty," I said. "Medium to tall, pale, short red hair."

"How old?"

That was a good question. "I don't know exactly. If the woman is the person I'm looking for, she's about forty-five. If the woman with the suitcase wasn't her, she could be almost any age."

For the first time she showed an expression, a mixture of puzzlement and annoyance. "If it wasn't her, why do you care?"

"Because the woman with the suitcase had the missing person's claim check. She may know where she is."

"I can tell you something, but it won't do you any good."

"Try me."

"There was a woman a little like that, with that kind of suitcase. I remember it because she was having trouble with it."

"Trouble?"

"She couldn't get the hang of carrying it, and it looked heavy. That's the main thing I remember. Usually when a woman has a heavy bag and she's alone, she has a cart."

"What did she look like?"

"Washed out."

It was vague enough to fit how Kate might look after a long flight. "How old was she?"

"Early thirties," she said flatly.

"Sure?"

"No more than thirty-five."

"Couldn't be forty-four, forty-five?"

"No way."

"Did she rent a car?"

"Sure. Right here."

"Great. You get a driver's license when you rent, right?"

"Sure do."

"Can you give me the name and address, then?"

"Nope. Company policy says customer has privacy."

I leaned forward until our faces were close together. "Look, the woman I'm looking for, she's my fiancée. Something has happened to her, I'm certain. I'm starting to think she's been kidnapped. Whether it happened in Miami or Harrisburg or here, I don't know. But whatever is going on, my only hope of finding out is to follow that bag and that woman."

"Nope," she repeated.

"If you were in my shoes, you'd want someone to give you a little slack."

The corners of her mouth tightened. "Well, I'm not, sir."

"Can't you call someone and see if you can get authorization?"

"They're not in till nine."

"She's already been missing for eight hours. Every minute counts."

"Then come back at nine, sir." She looked over my shoulder at the growing line behind me. "And unless you're going to rent a car, you'll have to excuse me. This is going to be a busy day. You want a car, sir?"

"No. I want the name and address."

"I've already told you no. Now step aside."

"You don't really give a shit, do you?"

"You want me to answer that? Sir?"

I stretched out my arms to either side, blocking the access of the people behind me, and held onto the edge of the counter with both hands. "Just what do you think that accomplishes?" she asked.

"You married?"

"That's none of your business."

"I'm forty-four years old and this is as close as I've ever

been to getting my life in some kind of order. If you have any idea what that means to me, you'll help me."

She looked at me with her impassive, professional expression, and for a moment I was sure she'd made up her mind to call security. Then she leaned closer and dropped her voice. "If I give you what you want, will you promise not to tell where you got it?"

I nodded.

She punched at the keyboard for a moment. I heard a clattering noise, and then a printout began emerging from a printer somewhere under the counter. When the noise stopped she tore off about a third of a page and handed it over. Most of the information was meaningless to me, but I saw what I wanted: Marjorie Kuwalchack, 440 Bentwood Drive, Allentown.

"Thanks," I said.

She kept her eyes down on the keyboard. "Don't mention it," she said. "Please." It was probably as much of a joke as she ever made. I gave her a smile and moved on.

Chapter Five

Wednesday 7:00 A.M.

I strapped myself into my seat on the USAir Shuttle to Allentown and gulped down the last of a doughnut. The flight attendant went through her usual speech and no one paid any attention, including me. In my lap was the scrap of computer paper, now creased and smudged, and I looked at it with all the pride of a new father. It might be eight hours old and lead me into nothing but trouble, but it was a lead and I thanked my good fortune for it. A line from English lit came to me—"A poor thing, but mine own."

I fingered the slip of paper and thought about what I was going to do. I closed my eyes for a moment, trying to concentrate. The next thing I remembered was the bump when we landed in Allentown. I hardly felt refreshed, but at least my eyes weren't aching.

The Allentown-Bethlehem-Easton airport was surprisingly modern, but the low ceilings and chocolate-colored walls gave it a cramped, depressing feel. It was a good deal larger than I'd expected—and busier, too—I had to wait through a line ten people long for my turn at the Alamo Rental Car desk.

The clerk was a thin, dark-complexioned man, Pakistani or Indian, as far as I could tell. Somehow, in Allentown, I'd expected a Pole or German. "Yes, sir? Can I help you?"

"Yes, please." I put on my mildest smile and handed him my slip of paper. The Dave Garrett Improvisational Theater was about to commence. "My wife rented a car at your Philadelphia office early this morning, and—well, things are getting a little screwed up, with both of us being on the road at the same time, we're both on the go, and I just want to make sure that we're not sitting around with one too many cars, if you know what I mean." I smiled, and he smiled back. From the way his smile didn't get all the way to his eyes, I could tell that he hadn't the slightest idea what I was talking about.

"You want to know if car turned in?"

I smiled again. "Please."

He consulted the computer. "Yes, sir. Car check in here, four this morning. All paid, thankyouverymuch."

"Great. Do—ah—you remember seeing her?"

"I no duty then, sir."

I decided to press my luck. "You know, I talked to her after she rented it, she said it drove real well. Could I rent it myself?"

"Sorry. We busy. No time to clean up, check out."

"I don't mind. I'm sure she left it in good shape."

"You sure, sir? We have guarantee clean car, new Honda, new Tempo—"

"No, I'd really like that one, if you don't mind. I'm sure it's fine. After all, I know my wife." My face was starting to ache from holding the smile.

He studied me for a moment. It was obviously a demented request, but if he could save the trouble of having it cleaned between customers, why not? He nodded and turned to the paperwork.

Fifteen minutes later I was in their rental car pickup area, going over a blue Pontiac Grand Am with lipstick-rimmed cigarette butts in the ashtray. A lot of them. Either the woman was a heavy smoker or she had something to be nervous about. I didn't like that part. A map, folded and recreased to show the area between Allentown and Philadelphia, was on the passenger's seat. No writing on the map, and no stamp to show where it came from. Some mud on the floor on the driver's side, but none in the back or on the passenger's side. The trunk was empty.

The man at the checkout gate was helpful with directions and even gave me a map. Within a couple of minutes I was fighting the rush hour traffic on Route 22 heading toward Allentown. If the area was dying for lack of jobs, which was what we heard down in Philadelphia, it wasn't affecting the level of traffic. I crept along for nearly three miles before I found what I was looking for and could get off.

I found a discount drugstore in a small strip mall where I bought some talcum powder, a pocket notebook, and a pair of cheap nonprescription reading glasses, the kind that only magnify. Back in the car I dusted my temples with powder till they were gray, and tried on the glasses. I got just the effect I wanted: a little bookish, and on the other side of fifty. Definitely not threatening. I practiced my bland smile some more.

As I drove I glanced through my library of business cards. It was too early in the morning to be Mark Mendehlson, life insurance salesman, and there was no plausible reason for Donald Cody, accountant, to be paying a call. Or Charles Gilcrest, hair stylist, for that matter. But Jerome Goldman, from Equifax, was another matter. Jerome had always worked well for me. He was a hard-working credit investigator, fatherly but businesslike, and everyone respected him. He always managed to convey how boring and thankless his job was, in a way that won sympathy and cooperation. Since the real Jerome Goldman was an unmitigated jerk, I'd always felt I was doing him a favor by improving his public image.

The road wound through a series of suburbs, gradually taking me both uphill and upscale. The grimy red brick houses of the forties on quarter-acre lots gave way to ranchers on half-acres, and then to big mock Colonials and Cape Cods.

Just before the crest of the hill I turned onto Bentwood. At first glance it seemed a street with no houses at all; on either side all I could see was trees. Then I saw a couple of mailboxes and realized that the houses were set well back in the woods.

The Kuwalchack mailbox was near the end of the street, just before a cul-de-sac. I turned down a long driveway that curved and eventually brought me out in front of a large modern house sprawled over the top of a small hill.

I mounted the wooden steps and crossed a porch that was wide enough to be a deck. The front entranceway was a set of cedar double doors that must have been eight feet wide and ten feet high. On the side of the door was a keypad for an alarm system. A tiny pile of fresh sawdust lay in the corner formed by the door trim and the top of the keypad box. I rang the bell and waited.

A short, deeply tanned woman with reddish blond hair opened the door. "Yes?"

"I'm Jerome Goldman, from Equifax, ma'am." I handed her my card. "Could I speak to Mrs. Kuwalchack for a moment, please?"

She looked at the card and then at me. Her face said she was forty but her hands said sixty, give or take a couple of facelifts. "That's me."

"As I'm sure you know, my company investigates credit applications." I decided to vary my usual speech. "If credit is extended to the wrong people, the rest of us wind up paying for it, of course." I glanced at the interior of the house behind her, and she followed my look. The expression on her face told me that she'd had damn well enough of paying other people's bills.

"Come on in, Mr. Goldman, and have a seat."

We sat on uncomfortable sofas facing each other in an entirely white room the size of a basketball court. Except for the sofas and a coffee table between, the room was empty.

She spread out her arms across the back of the sofa. If she was trying to display the results of her latest breast lift she was succeeding admirably, but there was nothing flirtatious about her voice. "So what does the insurance company want from me, as if I didn't know."

"Know?" I repeated stupidly.

"I really shouldn't be talking to you at all, Joe says."

"Why is that?"

"He thinks we should let our lawyers handle it all. You know what he said? 'Why keep a dog and bark yourself?' "

"I'm sorry. I'm not following you."

She looked at me with suspicion. "Well, you're here about the theft, aren't you?"

For once, my mind worked in real time. "Well, that's part of it. When was that, again?"

"Monday night, between seven and midnight." She sounded like she was used to telling the story, and she probably was. "Joe and I were out to dinner, and when we came back the door was ajar."

"Where were your driver's license and your credit cards?"

"In my purse in the front hall. I hadn't bothered to take it, 'cause Joe was driving."

"Has the purse been recovered?"

"It never left the house, but the wallet inside, with my cards and license, was gone."

"What else was taken?"

She shrugged. "I gave the company a list. The furs, the jewelry, Joe's coin collection, his guns. That's about it."

"No appliances? TVs, stereos, things like that?"

She shook her head. "They knew exactly what they wanted and they didn't leave any fingerprints. The police were here for hours and couldn't find a thing. Left the place a mess with all their fingerprint dust. It took a crew a full day to get it even halfway clean again." She gestured around the gleaming room with disapproval. For myself, I would have felt safe eating right off the floor.

"Who's the detective assigned to the case?"

"Lieutenant Bonowitcz."

I made a note of the name in my notebook. "We've had a report that someone using your driver's license and one of your credit cards rented a car in Philadelphia."

Her voice turned icy. "I get a bill for it, you're hamburger, honey."

"I'm sorry, ma'am, I'm just doing my job."

"I know, none of you people make the rules. But—"

It was time for Mr. Goldman to make the grand gesture. "Ma'am, I promise you, those bills aren't your responsibility. We'll either collect them from the thief or absorb the loss."

"Really?"

"I personally guarantee it. Now, which department is Lieutenant Bonowitcz with?"

I'd pressed my luck a little too far, and Marjorie was no fool. "You didn't know anything about the theft, did you?"

"Not as much as I should."

"Who are you?"

"Like I said, I'm an investigator." I waved the notebook in the air as proof of my status.

"The last one had a briefcase."

We locked eyes. "I'm sure he did, ma'am."

She started to say something. Then she stiffened and took her arms off the back of the sofa. A big man with white hair, wearing slacks and a sweater, was coming through the front door. He moved awkwardly, his hands jammed in his pockets, and he kept his head down like a man expecting trouble. He stopped when he saw her and tucked his chin in tighter. Somehow, as big as it was, the room didn't seem large enough for both of them. "Who's that?" he demanded.

Whatever doubts she had about me, she wasn't about to share them. "The man from the investigation agency, about the theft, Joe."

He didn't ask to be introduced. "How many times you people going to keep coming out?"

"It's a major loss, sir," I said. "And there's a connection to some other crimes."

He stepped forward, his arms folded across his chest. "One of my guns in a shooting?"

"Nothing that serious. Just the use of your wife's identification and a credit card."

"You start hounding us about bills that aren't ours, you—"

"Take it easy," she interrupted. "It's all taken care of."

"That's what you're always saying and it never is."

"It's under control, Joe."

"Yeah, sure. It's a goddamn bowl of cherries, right?"

"Lower your voice," she said coldly. "If you'd follow through on something for once instead of flitting around here and—"

"You never do a damned thing but sit back and—"

She jerked her head in my direction. "At least I know when to keep my mouth shut."

They were locked in some old sad domestic dance, and this particular number sounded like it might go on for hours. I cut it off. "Have you been having other insurance problems?" I asked.

Her head snapped in my direction. "What—makes you think that?"

"You both seem pretty upset about a routine burglary,

especially where everything's insured. Was there anything taken that's not replaceable?"

She looked at me, and then away. "I don't feel like answering any more of your questions."

I turned to the husband on the theory that he might be cooperative just to spite her. "Who knew you and your wife were going out that night?"

The question bothered him. "Well, no one, I don't think."

"You set the alarm before you left?"

"Yes—uh, no."

I glanced over my shoulder in time to catch Marjorie shaking her head no at him. I decided to change my approach. "How new is that alarm system?"

"I can't remember," he insisted.

"It looks pretty new to me."

"Well," he said, "it's a few months old."

"How come you put it in?"

"Just, oh, general security."

"Come on. You want me to call the alarm company and find out what you told them?"

He drew himself up to his full height, but I was getting to him. "Who are you to talk to me like that?"

"Just answer the question."

He dropped his eyes. "Well, we had a problem, sort of."

Marjorie stood up. "That's just about enough from you, Mr. Goldman. Now get out."

I kept my eyes on her husband. "What was taken the first time?"

"I really shouldn't say. It could just have been misplaced."

"If it hasn't turned up in several months you might as well tell me."

Marjorie stepped between us. "Just what does this have to do with our burglary? We didn't call about the last one."

"Exactly. If you withheld information material to the

risk, the company might deny coverage. And I'll tell you, a recent burglary is material."

"You can't prove that we knew there was a theft. Like Joe said, it could have been mislaid."

I sighed. "It looks like we're back to checking with the alarm company again. Could you give me their name or do I need to get up and read it off the box?"

For a moment no one said anything. Then Marjorie spoke. "It was four months ago and about two thousand dollars in cash was taken. Satisfied?"

"Not yet. Tell me about the cash."

"It was in my desk drawer," he said. "Unlocked."

She turned on him again. "I told you it was a temptation leaving it there like that."

"To who?" I asked.

They both looked at me. I looked at Joe and repeated my question.

"Our son," he said.

"He's taken things before?"

"Well," he said. "Things would disappear. It's hard . . ."

"Was he living here?"

"Till the money in the desk business," he said. "Then I threw him out."

"So he hasn't lived here in about four months?"

"That's right."

"Let's get back to the new burglary. Just when did you call the police?"

Marjorie answered. "Uh—that evening, of course." But she wasn't meeting my eyes.

"You got home around midnight?"

"I suppose."

"Well, that's what you said. And if I check the police records what time will they have your call logged in?"

They looked at each other and no one said anything. "I'm willing to bet that if I pick up your phone and call

Bonowitcz I'll find out that some time went by before you called it in." Again, no reaction.

By now I was on a roll. I stood up and started off purposefully, looking for a phone. I didn't know if I was headed in the right direction or not, but I never had to find out.

"Wait, Mr. Goldman!" It was the husband.

I took out the notebook again. "You have something to tell me?"

He looked at his wife, then back to me. "We called it in around one." He let out his breath. "A little over an hour went by."

I came back to where they were standing, close together but each of them alone. "I think you'd better tell me why, don't you?"

"We thought it might be our son," he said. "He's come in and taken things before, but never anything like this."

"Where is he now?"

"I don't know. After he moved out he stayed with friends for a while, then he moved out of town."

"So what were you doing that night between midnight and one?"

"Calling his old friends, trying to reach him."

"Any success?"

"We reached one friend who swore that he knew that he was out of town, that he couldn't be involved. That was as far as we got."

"What do you think?"

He started to say something, but his wife interrupted. "Joe, stop it! You've said way too much already."

"Did you tell the police your suspicions?"

Marjorie stood up and put her hands on her hips. "Mr. Goldman, I'm going to ask you to leave right now, without saying another word. Now get out right now or I call the police."

When I pulled out of the driveway I could see her watching for my license number.

Chapter Six

Wednesday 10:00 A.M.

I retraced my route back down the hill, toward the airport. As I descended, the green spaces gradually disappeared and the houses turned cheap and ugly again. The drive suited my mood. Eleven hours of ceaseless work and nothing to show for it.

I dropped off the car at the rental agency and bought a seat for the next shuttle back to Philadelphia. Then I changed five dollars into quarters and hunted up a pay phone.

My first call was Bonowitcz, the detective handling the burglary investigation. He wasn't in. The way my day was going, I wasn't surprised. I left my home phone number, which had an answering machine.

Next I tried Kate's number.

"Hello?" It was a woman's voice, and for an instant I thought it might be Kate. Then I realized it was her daughter. "Annie?"

"Mr. Garrett?" she asked.

"Yes."

"How are you?" she said brightly. Then I realized, before I could blurt out any bad news, that her father might not have told her anything yet. "Uh, fine . . . how are you doing?"

"Okay. You know, it's funny talking to you like this. I mean, Mom's done nothing but talk about you for two months, especially the last few days, but I've never even said hello to you before."

Obviously she was in the dark. I started to form a resentment toward McMahan for not telling her—until I remembered that *he* hadn't had an affair with *my* wife. "I'm glad to finally get a chance to talk. What's your dad told you about your mom's trip up here?"

"Well, that he and mom are getting a divorce and she's coming to stay with you."

"How does that make you feel?"

"They separated a couple of times before when we were younger, once for almost a year."

I felt myself smiling. "You're like your mother, you know. You don't always answer the question."

"Mom and Dad were never Ozzie and Harriet." There was a catch in her voice. "Even if I wanted them to be. But I knew from way back that this was going to happen, sooner or later."

"I hope you don't dislike me when we get to meet, whenever that's going to be."

"If half of what Mom says about you is true I'm going to like you just fine. It's not your fault."

It made me feel good to hear that. "Did your dad tell you anything else about her flight up here?"

"Is there something else to tell?"

"I don't know yet. Is he there?"

"Is this about her suitcase? Because it's all right, I've got it."

"What?" I barely kept myself from shouting.

"Well, they delivered it from the airport half an hour ago. They said it was unclaimed. They said to come out and get it and I said, no way, you deliver it out here. And they did. They said they don't normally do that, but they had to come out this way anyway for somebody else."

"You have your mother's suitcase?"

"Sure. Right in the front hall. What's she doing for clothes? She only had the one bag."

"How did it get back down there?"

"I wrote all the information down for you. I figured Mom would be pissed." Her voice faded for a moment and came back on. "They said it was checked as her luggage on American flight 133 in Philadelphia, which left at 1:10 this morning, arrived here 3:40. They called here about eight. Awful early, if you ask me, huh?"

"Are you sure it's her bag?"

"Sure I'm sure. I helped her pack."

"Do me a favor, Annie. Open it up and take a quick look. See if there's anything unusual or unfamiliar."

That stopped her. "Like—what?"

"Like, I don't know."

"Okay. Hold on."

As I waited I tried to make sense of the latest development. Why would Kate fly right back to Miami? And then not pick up her bag or tell anyone she was back?

"No, there's nothing that isn't hers. Why'd you ask?"

I closed my eyes and shook my head. Things were happening too fast. "Can I speak to your dad a minute, please?"

"He's not here. He left about eight, just before the airport called about the bag."

"What's his work number, then?"

"No, I mean he took a plane. To Harrisburg, Pennsylvania." Her tone was changing. When she was upset, she sounded more like her mother. "You'd better tell me what's going on. This is all sounding weird."

"What did he say about his trip?"

"Just that it was business and that he'd only be gone a day or two."

"Anything else?"

"I'm not saying another word until you tell me what this is all about." Her voice was cracking.

"Your father and I . . . aren't sure where your mother is. She didn't get off the plane in Philadelphia."

"That's crazy."

"But it's true—"

"She went to see you. Why shouldn't she be there? This is some kind of joke, isn't it?"

"I don't know what it is, but it's not a joke."

"What have you done with her?"

"Nothing at all. I haven't even seen her in two months."

"That's what you say!"

I tried to keep the anger out of my voice. "If I was responsible, why would I call?"

"To cover yourself," she snapped back.

It was my turn to snap. "If I was guilty I'd do a hell of a lot better job than this." Then I caught myself and took a breath. "No, Annie, I'm just as upset about this as you are. And you can either believe that, and help me, or you can hang up."

"You know I'm not going to do that."

"I'm sorry; I didn't mean to make this any harder. It's just that I'm really tired. I haven't slept yet. Until a few minutes ago I thought I had a lead, but it turned out not to go anywhere."

"What are you going to do now?"

"Turn in a missing person's report, if you can tell me what else there is to know."

"I can't think of anything else. Except that Dad's trip might have to do with Mom. He doesn't do much traveling outside the state, and he's never been to Pennsylvania at all, that I know of."

"Do you know what flight he took?"

"He didn't have a reservation. He said he was just going

to go out to the airport and get on the first plane he could."

"Did he make any phone calls to anyone, or get any calls, that you know of? Since you got up this morning, I mean."

"He mentioned you had called, but not more than that. Anyway, I was asleep till right before he left. He woke me up to tell me he was going, and before I could get back to sleep the airport called. Is there anything I can do?"

"Yes. Two things. First of all, stay home. I may need to be in touch and I want to be able to reach you. Okay?"

"And the second thing?"

I was so tired I didn't realize I hadn't given her two instructions. "Right. Call the travel agent you work for. See if anyone called in, asking for information on your mom. We need to talk to everyone who would have known what flight she was going to take."

"This doesn't sound real good, does it?"

"I don't know *what* it is, yet. All I know is that she didn't get off the plane, as far as I can tell."

"Our family doesn't seem very lucky this way. First Aunt Anne up in Lancaster and now this."

"What I need down there most is a clear head. I hope I can count on you. Wait, one more thing." I wasn't thinking clearly and I knew it. Time for some more coffee. "You have any way of getting in touch with your dad?"

"Not exactly, but when he travels he usually calls in."

"If he does, give him my numbers and tell him I want to see him." I gave her my home and office numbers and had her repeat them back to me.

"I'll tell him."

"Good-bye, then."

"Mr. Garrett?"

"Yes?"

"Please be careful."

"Sure I will." I wanted to say that being careful might

not be the best way to find her mother, but I think she knew that already.

By the time I was done it was the final boarding call. I collapsed into my seat and watched the countryside unroll underneath. In the forty-minute flight back to Philadelphia, I saw both spring and winter going on at the same time—snow in the foothills, and lush green grass in the valleys. The trees were in every stage from bare to leafy. If I'd been in a better mood it would have been a fascinating preview of the spring that was just around the corner. But today it just looked like chaos, and I had plenty of that already.

As soon as I landed in Philadelphia I went to the airport security office. Half a dozen cops in black leather jackets were sitting around, watching the video monitors and drinking coffee. The local soft rock oldies station, WMGK, was playing in the background. It wasn't a room in which anything urgent ever happened.

"Excuse me."

The officer nearest me, a sergeant with a bushy mustache, took a sip of coffee and looked up. "Yes, sir?"

It was a bad omen. So far, the people who'd been polite had all been unhelpful. "I want to report a missing person."

"How long have they been missing?"

That was a good question. "Since eleven last evening."

"We normally don't take reports till the person has been missing twenty-four hours, unless a child is involved."

"This is an adult, but it's very suspicious."

"Oh? How do you mean?"

"She was coming up to see me. She boarded a plane in Miami, with a stopover in Harrisburg. She wasn't on the plane when it landed here. And a cabdriver in Harrisburg saw a woman answering her general description get into the back of a van and drive away."

He started taking notes. "Did you check the plane when it arrived?"

"They wouldn't let me on, but they told me she wasn't aboard."

He nodded. "Was she on the manifest out of Miami?"

"Her ticket was used, all the way to Philadelphia." And then she apparently went right back again, or at least her luggage did, but I wasn't going to complicate things before I had to.

"Is the missing person your wife?"

"No. It's kind of complicated." I summarized our personal situation as quickly as I could. By the time I was finished he'd stopped taking notes.

"Is it possible she changed her mind? Got cold feet?"

I was glad I hadn't mentioned the return flight. "What about the cabdriver?" I asked.

"Can he make a positive ID?"

"I don't know."

"Can he say she was being forced?"

"Not really. But she doesn't know anyone in Harrisburg—"

"How do you know *that,* for sure?"

I sighed. "Well, I don't."

"Did she have any baggage? We'd need to see it."

"Well, it's not around."

"Where is it?"

It was all going to have to come out, after all. "Her suitcase was here and went to unclaimed baggage. Then someone picked it up and flew back to Miami with it."

He leaned back in his chair. "That someone have the ticket and claim check?"

"Yes."

"Answer her description?"

"In a general way, but—"

"Sir . . . it doesn't seem like a police matter to me."

I was on a fool's errand and I knew it. "Do me one favor? Take the information, and file the report if she doesn't turn up."

"Okay. But you got to call me. I don't want to gum up the works unless I have to."

It was as much of a victory as I could have expected. I filled out the forms, took his name, and gave him one of my cards—a genuine one, this time.

My Civic started on the first try, although it seemed to be making a new noise until it warmed up, a high squeal coming from the front that sounded like it was going to cost at least a hundred bucks.

Home was a shabby apartment in a large garden apartment complex near Rosemont, just off the Main Line in the suburbs west of Philadelphia. I'd let my ex-wife keep most of the furniture, and it was furnished with hand-me-downs from old friends, to the extent it was furnished at all. Most of the time I paid no attention to the interior, but today I had to face the fresh flowers on the kitchen table and the big Welcome banner I'd hung across the front hall. I threw myself down on the sofa and felt sorry for myself for about ten minutes. Sitting down was a mistake. The room seemed to recede. I was going to crash, and this time it wouldn't just be for half an hour. If Kate had really just changed her mind I might as well sleep for a week. But unless I was sure she wasn't in danger . . . I forced myself to my feet and shuffled into the bathroom. In the medicine cabinet, behind a bottle of coagulated cough syrup, I found what I was looking for. A bottle of blue-and-yellow pills. Fastin. My ex-wife had tried them once, years ago, when she was trying to diet. She took two and didn't sleep for twenty-four hours.

I'd just finished swallowing two when the phone rang.

"Dave Garrett."

"Mr. Garrett, this is Lieutenant Bonowitcz, Whitehall Township."

"Thanks for calling, Lieutenant."

"I ought to be calling to arrange for you to come in to be arrested, you turkey."

"Oh?"

"If you're going to impersonate somebody, next time don't pick Goldman. He's the biggest jerkoff I've met in months. Had me on the phone for half an hour about how he wanted our department to stop everything until you'd been caught."

"I always thought that I was helping his public image."

"Very funny. And it happens to be true. Want to know how I found you so fast?"

"You decided to return my call."

"That, I would have done tomorrow. But the Kuwalchacks were all over me about this suspicious claims investigator. I checked it out and it was bogus. I figured maybe you were in on things and you were casing the place for another run. Anyway, the Kuwalchacks gave me the plate number, and I got your name from the car rental agency. Your record's clean, and I checked you out. I got a buddy on the force down there, says you're a straight guy."

"Thanks."

"So give. And make it fast before I change my mind. What were you doing up here?"

"Actually, I was hoping for some information from you—"

"You tell me what you got, then I decide."

I told him the story. He grunted periodically, and once or twice he asked me to repeat something, which I took to mean he was taking notes, or at least paying close attention.

"You have any idea who the woman with the rental car is?" he asked.

"I don't even have a really reliable description. I don't even know for sure if it ties in with my girlfriend. She could have pulled the ticket and the claim check out of the trash."

"Even if she didn't, that's what she'll say," he said. "You left the car at the rental agency?"

"Right." Then I realized why he was asking. "Sorry. I didn't think about giving you guys a crack at it. The agency's probably cleaned it up by now."

"It would probably have been a waste of time. Could be prints from everyone who'd ever rented or cleaned the car. And we can't tie it in with a crime in the township anyway. But you never know. Might have been worth a try. You think your girl's up here?"

"I can't see how. And I can't figure how Allentown figures into this. Lieutenant, I've been up front on this, and I want to know if there's anything you can give me."

"Mmm. Maybe."

"Please."

"I can't say it's going to do you any good," he said.

"I've been hearing that a lot lately."

"This is off the record and I'm not going to go into any more detail than I give you right now. I'm not going to jeopardize any ongoing investigations."

"Anything you can give me. I'm at the end of my rope."

"The Kuwalchack case isn't unique. We've had a string of burglaries in the township. All the same MO. Very professional. Always use stolen cars. The victims are away for the evening, or the weekend, no sign of forcible entry, security system's disarmed, and only the best stuff is taken, things that can be fenced easy. Always real expensive homes. Nothing ever turns up local. We ran a sting operation, phony fence—got plenty of other guys but not them."

"So what is there that might help?"

"Well, if it's any use to you, we have some stolen gas credit cards from some other burglaries that show purchases near Philadelphia, in Marcus Hook. And some cars stolen in Allentown have been dumped there. From the timing of the thefts, they may have been used in the burglaries."

"So whoever took Kate's bag has a connection to the Allentown burglaries."

"It may be nothing." I could almost see him shrugging. "Could be that the girl who rented the car just bought the ID hot and she may not know anything. But if you don't have anywhere else to look, you might try it."

I was back in business. Maybe.

Chapter Seven

Wednesday Noon

I called the Marcus Hook Police Department and reached Joe Ianucci on my first call. Not only was he glad to hear from me, he was willing to meet me for lunch in forty minutes. We agreed on the place right next to the station, the Marcus Hook Diner.

I hadn't seen Joe in about three years. The last time we'd worked together I'd been an attorney, he had a string of burglaries he wanted to clear, and I had a client facing a Receiving charge who just happened to have some information. The arrangement had worked nicely, except for a couple of fellows who'd pulled long stretches at Graterford.

Marcus Hook is about five miles southwest of Philadelphia, just on the Pennsylvania side of the Delaware line. It's a small borough, consisting of disconnected residential areas sandwiched between large tracts of factories, warehouses, and piers. It's a pleasant place, with friendly people and a pretty riverside park along the Delaware. Except for one unfortunate circumstance it was just like the other half dozen old industrial towns around Philadelphia that dated from the heyday of American industry. In the sixties, when the drugs hit, the Pagans had established their Pennsylvania headquarters in Marcus Hook, and within a short time they had a virtual monopoly on drug sales in the county. Later they branched out into firearms, hijackings, prostitution, and protection rackets, and for years the money just rolled in. Besides drugs, the town exported muscle all over the eastern seaboard, and bodies to most of the marshes within fifty miles. In Marcus Hook itself they were as close to model citizens as they could manage—they were too smart to foul their own nest. Not counting the innumerable instances of disorderly conduct and public drunkenness, they played it straight within the borough.

Fortunately, after a few years the tide began to recede. The ranks of the Pagans were thinned by wars with rival gangs like the Warlocks and the Flying Cross Motorcycle Club, by accidents, and, with increasing frequency, by convictions. The key local players went to jail. Federal informants ate their way through the club structure, aided by new antiracketeering and forfeiture laws. The survivors finally pulled up stakes and decentralized their operations. The crime left but the reputation stuck, especially among Philadelphians. None of my friends from the city would have gone there on a bet.

I crossed into the borough, made a right on Post Road, the main street, and parked in the lot near the municipal building. It was an old, windowless, boxy structure, a cross between a WPA version of a Grecian temple and a pillbox, and it didn't exactly blend in with the gas station on one side or the diner on the other.

I passed by the building and saw Ianucci on the steps of the diner, waiting for me. He was a thin, dark man with a pencil mustache. He wore a black suit with a narrow black tie. Despite the pleasant weather, he was also wearing a black hat.

I made a show of looking him up and down. "Joe? What you doing? Gone into the family business?"

Ianucci's Funeral Home was a few blocks up the street.

Of the three sons, he was the only one who wasn't in the business. He gave a half smile and that slow, exaggerated shrug that can mean anything. "Good to see you, Dave."

We shook hands, and he looked at my hair. "You're looking distinguished, Counselor."

I touched my temples; I'd forgotten about the talcum powder. "Just a disguise," I said. "Underneath I'm as undistinguished as ever."

"Working on a case?"

"That's what I need to see you about."

We took seats at the counter and ordered the sandwich platter special. For four bucks you got a good sandwich, a cup of soup, coffee, cole slaw, and some of the best fries outside of South Philadelphia. The only drawback was that the diner seemed to be built on Jell-O; every time someone walked by, the place quivered. It didn't rattle the silverware, but there was enough motion to jostle your stomach.

"So how are they treating you, Counselor?" he asked when our coffee arrived.

"Guess you didn't hear. It's not 'counselor' anymore."

His eyes widened. "They make you a judge? Great! I always—"

"It went the other way. I was disbarred."

"You're kidding. You were the only honest Philadelphia lawyer I ever knew."

"Well, however many there are, there's one less. Remember my wife, Terri?"

"I remember you mentioning her."

"She went to law school after me. Took the bar over and over, couldn't pass. A mental block thing. She was smart enough. She even made sort of a suicide attempt after one time. Anyway, she talked me into taking it for her."

"And you did it?"

"Sure it was dumb, but when it's your own wife . . . Sickness and health and all that." I repeated Ianucci's shrug back at him. "Anyway, I got caught."

"Come on, how can you take the bar exam for somebody else?"

"It's not as hard as you think. Not then it wasn't. Now they check ID, but back then nobody thought about it. There's thousands of people taking it—nobody knows anybody by sight. You just sit down and sign Terri Garrett, and away you go."

"Yeah, away you go." He drained his cup. "Must have been hard on the two of you."

"Not at all. The minute it all came down she moved out and filed for divorce."

"I don't believe it."

"She said I was mired in my own problems and wasn't paying enough attention to her."

"No."

"Joe, I couldn't make up something like this."

He shook his head. "I'm sorry."

"It's a done thing," I said.

"So, what are you doing now?"

"I took out a private detective's license. Actually, they cut me a little bit of a break there. Normally you have to have investigative experience in law enforcement, like a detective or at least an officer who spends most of his time doing investigations. They allowed me to count my time as a lawyer."

"You got a better attitude than I would have."

I smiled. "What else are you going to do?"

"Losing your career and your wife in one shot. Guys eat their pieces over less."

I looked at my cup. "It crossed my mind, Joe, it really did. Back in the war, there was a new guy in my squad who killed himself rather than go out on his first patrol. Pulled the pin on a grenade and held it to his belly. But he didn't lie down on it, and a lot of the explosion was dissipated in the air. I found him myself. The doctors worked on him like crazy, pouring blood into him like there was no tomorrow. Took him a day and a half to die. And what could have happened to him on that patrol that was any worse than what he did to himself?"

"So you keep going."

"Uh-huh. And now I need your help."

"What can I do?"

For maybe the tenth time in as many hours, I told the story. With each retelling it was becoming less immediate and more abstract. Kate was less of a real person and more just part of the puzzle. I realized how crime victims, or their survivors, must feel when they tell their story in court. The victim isn't someone who works every day and tries to do the right thing for his kids and maybe gambles a little more than he should—he's simply the entity who was walking north at the time in question. . . .

When I was finished Joe thought for a moment. "I don't think I can help you. You're in the wrong place."

"The cars turn up here. At least, most of them do."

He worked a toothpick into a spot between a couple of his lower teeth. "I know about the abandoned cars. Don't mean nothing. This Allentown business, these guys are either first-class professionals or they're addicts who are smart. If these guys are real pros, and if I've never heard of them operating out of my borough, there's no way in hell you're going to turn them up on your own, at least not in time to help find your girl."

"Is it that bad?"

"The clearance rate on burglaries stinks. Unless one of his confederates flips over, or he gets unlucky and gets caught in the act, somebody who knows alarm systems and plans his jobs right can go for years without getting caught."

"What if it's addicts?"

"They're not in Marcus Hook. This is still a small town where everybody knows everybody. We know who deals and who uses, and every once in a while we go round them up. The kind of money and planning that goes into doing burglaries the better part of a hundred miles away, there's nobody in town who's in deep enough and organized enough to do it."

"So you can't help?"

"I can tell you you're looking in the wrong place. Lots of stolen cars from other places get dumped here. I don't know why exactly. Maybe they don't want to take them across state lines, maybe it's just that the roads make it convenient. We're right off 95, and the main street is a U.S. highway. But if I were you, I'd try Chester."

"Why?"

"I think you may be looking for Chester people who just wanted to dump their cars down here to cover their tracks."

"But why Chester?"

He smiled. "You ever been there?"

"A long time ago, I went to some games at Widener University."

"Well, you weren't exactly in Chester. Take a drive up there now and you'll see what I mean. Are you carrying?"

"In the car."

"Keep it handy. They have as many homicides in a month as we have in ten years."

"Where exactly should I start looking?"

"If you want to meet druggies, start with the hookers. You find a girl on crack, she'll roll over on her own mother for ten bucks and sell you her baby for a hundred. Try Sproul Street, between Seventh and Ninth."

"Thanks."

"Dave? Good luck. You're going to need it."

It didn't take long to find what Joe meant. Chester was just north of Marcus Hook, but it might as well have been in the South Bronx. Driving up Seventh Street was a self-guided tour of hell. If Chester wasn't a dead city, it was at least half dead. No people on the streets, and no cars in front of most of the houses. Blocks of abandoned houses alternated with blocks that were only partially abandoned. At one point I counted five consecutive blocks where every single house was boarded up. The few people I saw on the street were doing nothing at all. Not walking, not talking, just standing and staring at nothing in particular. About half the people I saw were black, and the rest were about evenly divided between Hispanic and white. But it was hardly a scientific survey—I drove through most of the city and saw less than thirty people.

I passed by a low-rise housing project, a three-block-long series of brick row houses with flat roofs and four windows each. The houses were new and none of the windows was broken, but they reminded me of prison cells. Evidently the occupants felt the same way, because some of them were already covered with graffiti. The only slogan I could read was Housing Now—New York '89. I wondered what it meant.

From my map, it looked like the best way to get to Sproul was to cut down Avenue of the States, which turned out to be the main north-south business street. As bad as the residential areas were, the central business district was worse. Or rather, what *had* been the central business district. Almost every business was closed, and the few open ones were thrift shops and used-goods operations. At two in the afternoon there was no pedestrian traffic. The plywood on the boarded-up businesses was gray with age, making me wonder how long it had been up. The street was grimy and dark, especially at the southern end, at Sixth, where a railroad embankment cut off the light. On the other hand, I wasn't so sure I wanted to see the street in the full light of day.

I made a right onto Sixth and went one block to Sproul, which turned out to be a one-way street running north. The intersection consisted of four vacant lots, all of them overshadowed by the embankment. Not a soul was in sight. I made a right onto Sproul and headed north. Except for a sign advertising Sister Anne—Spiritual Reader, there was not a single operating business between Sixth and Seventh. If Sister Anne had any good advice to give, it would be to get the hell out.

Between Seventh and Eighth I saw a bus stop shelter, more vacant lots, and more closed businesses. On the left was the red brick bulk of the local armory, three stories high with a wide stone staircase. At one time it must have been a handsome building, but now nearly all of its windows were broken, the front lawn had turned to weeds, and a white surf of trash lapped up against the building on all sides. Across the street was the parking lot at the end of the world. A huge weather-beaten sign proclaimed that the lot was the private property of the YMCA and that trespassing was prohibited. The lot was completely empty. Evidently the good citizens of Chester took the warning seriously—or, more likely, no one in his right mind stopped in downtown Chester.

I pulled in and parked.

After a few minutes I saw a woman walking up Sproul toward me. She stopped by the bus stop and stood with her legs wide apart and her hands on her hips, watching the traffic with practiced eyes. There was, I estimated, about a hundred and seventy pounds of her, solid as a rock, squeezed into a too-short pink skirt and a screaming green scoop-neck blouse that did nothing to hide her beefy arms or broad shoulders. She had a chest that matched the rest of her equipment. Judging from the one strap that was visible, it was supported by a bra of industrial strength. No other women were in sight—I couldn't imagine anyone trying to run her off her corner without a tank.

I pulled out onto Sproul, made a right, and went around again on Avenue of the States. The district hadn't made much of a recovery in my absence. I got back onto Sproul, pulled up to the bus stop, and rolled down the passenger's side window. Miss Fuck-Me-If-You're-Man-

Enough wobbled over unsteadily on high heels and leaned her forearms on the sill. I caught a glimpse of some tattoos. "How's it hanging, friend?" she asked. The smell of some ghastly perfume filled the interior.

"Could be better."

She looked around the inside of the car, saw the mismatched door, and made a face. "You get in an accident or something?"

"You might say that. You working?"

She snapped her gum. I tried to guess her age, but the makeup was so thick I couldn't even get a good look at her features. "I could find time for a party."

"What kind of prices we talking?"

She shook her head. "I don't mention prices. First, that is."

She was right. I recalled from my days as a small-time criminal lawyer that if the officer mentioned price first, a solicitation charge would be dismissed on the grounds of entrapment. "Okay, what's your name?"

"Suzie-Q." She snapped her gum again.

I didn't bother asking what the Q stood for. "I've got forty bucks. How much time I get for that?"

Again she shook her head. Her eyes wandered around the car again. "You offer, and I'll tell you if I'm interested." We might as well have been discussing the price of an oil change.

"French in a room for the forty?"

"Nope. French in the car's only twenty, but the room's thirty."

An interesting commentary on the value of labor in a capitalist society, I thought. "What if we just went to the room to talk? I won't lay a finger on you."

"I don't do any weird stuff, buddy. You want the regular stuff, you come to the right place, but nothing funny, you know."

"No, I mean, just talk."

For the first time I had her complete attention. "About what?"

"I'm looking for somebody."

She snapped her gum and looked me over again. "Cop?"

"Private."

"What for?"

"A friend of mine disappeared. The person I'm looking for may know something about it."

"What's the name of the one you're looking for?"

I decided not to let her know I didn't have a name. "She's real thin, average to tall, short red hair, white, pale complexion."

Something passed across her face. "Shove off, buddy."

"What's the problem?"

"Problem is, you're the problem." She spun on her heel and walked away. For a big woman in high heels, she moved fast. Before I could make a decision whether to go after her, she was gone.

I interviewed two more working girls, neither of whom was any more cooperative than the first. By the time I was finished the pills were starting to wear off.

Up ahead was a thin black girl with blond hair, probably not out of her teens, in a black pantsuit with a chain around her waist. She was watching the traffic like a New Yorker trying to hail a cab. As I got closer I saw garish jewelry and heavy makeup. Her eyes locked on to my Honda as I cut to her side of the street and pulled to the curb.

She was at my window before I could finish rolling it down. She was trembling; I wondered if it was DTs or drug withdrawal or illness—or all three. "Howyadoin', mister. Wanna party?"

"You don't waste any time."

"I need to make some money fast. Whatdoyouwant?" She hugged herself, although it wasn't cold.

"I got forty bucks, but all I want is information."

"Huh?" Her look was totally blank. It occurred to me that, short of murder, there was no act so painful or degrading that she wouldn't let a total stranger perform on her for forty bucks. The world was full of men who found the thought exciting, but I wasn't one of them.

"I want to know if you can help me find somebody."

She looked up and down the block. "What you want to know?"

"Get in and we'll talk."

Up close was more strong perfume, a different scent from Suzie-Q's but just as cloying. It wasn't powerful enough to mask an odor of urine and vomit and sweat. "What's your name?"

"Oh . . . Ashley."

"Ashley, I'm looking for someone who may live around here."

"Yeah, like, what's his name?" She was bouncing back and forth in the seat. If it was DTs, it was a bad case.

"A woman." I repeated my description and saw her nod. She knew something.

Her tongue moved across her lips. "You got the money?"

"You know who it is?"

"First the money."

"Nope." In her condition, she would have promised to lead me to the Seven Cities of Gold if I just paid in advance. "You take me to her first."

She made a face, but the concentration necessary to conduct an argument wasn't there. "Go up to Ninth and make a left."

Ninth was a busy two-way street, but we weren't on it long. Her directions took me to a sorry bar with a cracked formstone facade and an open door that led to a dark interior. In the front window were neon signs advertising several brands of beer.

Her trembling was worse, and I could see sweat breaking through the makeup on her forehead. "There's where she works. Now, give me my money."

"Not so fast. Who is she?"

"Name's Maggie. Maggie Mason. That's her street name, anyways."

"What do you know about her?"

"She runs with some of the guys, you know."

"What does she do for a living?"

"A little of this and that." She shrugged. "Like me."

"How well do you know her?"

"We shot up a few times, hung out, you know. Now come on."

"You know the names of any of her friends? What they do?"

"Damn it, give it to me!" She grabbed my arm and lunged for my jacket pocket, although she had no way of knowing if the money was there. I shoved her away roughly against the door and she curled into a ball, her face hidden by her knees.

I counted out four tens and handed them over, feeling every bit the accomplice in a self-murder. If the injection she bought with the money didn't give her an overdose, or AIDS, or a fatal case of hepatitis, then the next one would, or the one after, and I was helping her get it. I thought about Kate, but it didn't make me like myself any better.

She was out of the car so fast she didn't bother to shut the door. I reached over and pulled it shut, and put on my phony bifocals again. Then I walked across the street to the bar.

It was dim inside, but it wasn't hard to tell the history of the place. Like Chester itself, it had started high and was on a long slide down. Although the ceiling was pierced with plumbing and painted a hideous shade of green, it was an original pressed tin ceiling, with an intricate design that even a dozen coats of paint couldn't obliterate. The bar was scarred and darkened, but it was inlaid with brass fixtures, including a foot rail. I suspected that under the cracked linoleum was a hardwood floor.

The mirror behind the bartender was cracked, producing two images of the moose head that hung on the opposite wall. It looked like the moose head doubled as a dartboard. The bartender was a young man with wavy long hair, parted in the middle. He looked me over and put both hands on the bar, wide apart. His expression made me glance down at his hands to confirm that they were empty.

"Afternoon," I said.

"You want something?"

"I'm looking for somebody. A girl named Maggie."

He looked down, and one of the fingers of his right hand described a couple of lazy circles on the bar top before he answered. "What about her?"

"She hangs out here, I'm told."

"What you want with her?"

"Talk."

He looked up, his eyes narrow. "You LCB?"

"I don't even know what you're talking about."

He smirked. "Liquor Control Board, as if you didn't know."

"I'm not the law. I just need to talk to her."

He didn't like my answers any more than I liked his questions. "Don't know anything about it, buddy."

I sighed. "Then just give me a beer." I saw a hot dog machine behind the bar, but I decided to keep it simple. I put a dollar on the bar and found a table in the back. My corner was so dark I had trouble seeing my glass two feet in front of me.

I didn't have long to wait. I wasn't more than half finished nursing the beer when the door opened and a man and a woman came in. He was in his early twenties, big, but awkward, as if he hadn't quite grown into his body. He had longish hair and a small beard, but it was the woman that caught my attention. Tall, very thin, short hair. A shapeless dress with a short hem but long sleeves. She was a brunette now, and she was clearly younger than Kate, but with some makeup and a red wig . . . I felt my pulse speed up, the same feeling I'd had when I had the Allentown lead. Whatever was going on, I was getting closer to it.

The man stayed at the bar and the woman headed in my direction. For a moment I thought she was coming to see me; then I realized the rest rooms were behind me.

"Maggie?"

She turned and I got a close look. If she wasn't the woman from the airport she sure looked like her. I leaned back in my chair into the darkness, hoping that she didn't take too close a look at me. My disguise wasn't exactly impenetrable. I struggled to keep my voice casual. "How you doing?"

"Okay." Our eyes met over the top of my bifocals. There was no sign of recognition in her face.

I pushed a chair away from the table in her direction. I figured it was more gallantry as she was used to. "Have a seat."

She came up to the chair but didn't sit down. She looked at the man at the bar, then back to me. "We got something to talk about?" she wanted to know.

"You look tired. Take a load off your feet."

She sat down. "You're right about that. I ain't been to bed yet."

"How about a drink?"

She smiled, just a little, and played with the ends of her hair. "Why not? Double peach schnapps, on the rocks."

I called over the bartender and put in her order, plus another beer for myself. The bartender looked suspiciously at my half-full glass, but brought our drinks without comment.

She knocked back half her drink in one swallow. "Good shit. Now, how you know my name?"

"Oh, ran into a friend of yours, Ashley. She told me where to find you." She giggled. "Did I say something funny?" I asked.

"That's not her name, it's a nickname she got. 'Cause she likes to get it in the ass."

"So how does Maggie like it?"

The question didn't surprise her, and she didn't try to pretend that it did. She looked at the man at the bar, who was starting to pay attention to us, and shook her head at him, a little more than she needed to. "I'm out of that life now. I'm moving up. I could maybe give you some names." She lit a cigarette.

"I don't know. I heard you were really special. But what's this about moving up?"

"What's it to you?"

I shrugged. "Hey, it's always good to hear when somebody's getting ahead, right? Want another drink?"

She nodded, and the bartender brought another round. This time he stared openly at my untouched beer.

Maggie belted down half the second one and wiped her mouth on the back of her hand. "Who are you, mister?"

"Just a guy looking for some action."

She looked at the man at the bar again. If he gave her a signal I missed it. "Well, you came to the wrong place."

"Because you're moving up?"

She nodded. "Things been hard, you know? But I got friends now, they're into business, you know? There's ways to get a good score without doing any bad shit."

"I know. I used to make a living that way myself."

"You? Come on."

I took a pull at my beer. "I used to have a situation, up in Philly. No outdoor work, no muscle, completely legit, steady, and good money."

"Really?" She blew out a cloud of smoke. "So what happened?"

"I got disbarred."

She laughed so hard she started to cough. She drained her second schnapps to stop the coughing. "Come on, honey, don't bullshit me."

"I'm not kidding. I used to be a lawyer."

"Well, you look like one. That, or a cop."

"I'm not a cop."

"Hell, I know that. I know all the cops in town. Plus, even if you were, I wouldn't be worried."

"Oh?"

"The people I work for got things covered, you know?"

"I know. Another drink?"

"One more and I'm gonna want to sleep."

"Sure. Let's call it a nightcap, then." I signaled the bartender. "You live around here?"

"Just a block up. Why?"

"I figured I'll make sure you get home okay."

"Joe can do that."

I looked over at the bar. "Joe left."

She saw it was true. "Well, shit."

"Hey, it's only a block away, isn't it? And I'm here."

"No, it's, he owes me money. I got expenses."

"From your work?" I asked.

"I dropped 'bout eight large yesterday and today."

I whistled. Our drinks arrived, and I raised my glass. "To getting your eight hundred dollars back."

She clinked glasses, but this time she only took a sip. The alcohol was starting to get to her. "So tell me, Maggie, what kind of job makes the employee shell out serious money like that? Seems like it should be going the other way."

"Lot of traveling. Airplane tickets and rental cars."

"Gee, seems to me they should have fronted the money. It's a shame to have to use your own."

"Yeah, and I didn't have enough of my own by the time I was through. Had to put some of it on the credit card."

"Doesn't matter if you use a credit card," I ventured. "You've still got to pay for it in the end."

She stubbed out her cigarette and gave me a knowing smile. "Mmm. Not always."

"You ready to go?" I asked.

She drained her glass and stood up. "I got to lay down before I fall down."

I threw a twenty on the table. "Lead the way."

We went outside and I put my arm around her waist as we walked. She didn't resist, and it helped steady her. "You sure you don't need some extra money?" I asked.

"Well . . . if that son of a bitch Joe had come through I wouldn't have to."

"But he didn't." I patted her ass.

"No, he didn't." She returned the pat. "Can you do it quick?"

"Slow is better."

"More expensive."

"I got what it takes."

She giggled again. "Well, so do I."

We were standing in front of a brick row house with a two-step concrete porch. Or rather, I was standing and she was leaning against me. Either she was really fatigued or she had been drinking on an empty stomach. "Well," I said. "Can I come up?"

She smiled lazily. "If you got a hundred bucks you can come sideways, honey." She pulled out her key.

I stepped back a bit to let her work the lock. It was slow going; twice she missed the keyhole, and the third time she tried to fit the key upside down. Finally I saw it slide inside and turn. I was so close to finding out what she knew. . . .

I never got that far. Just as she started to push the door open I heard shouting behind us. I remember opening my mouth and starting to speak, and then a burning pain in the back of my head. I remember going down on my knees, and the way Maggie looked down on me with a mixture of shock and incomprehension.

I felt a second pain in my head, on the top this time. I didn't remember anything after that.

Chapter Eight

Wednesday 7:00 P.M.

The first thing was the pain in my head, like a brand across the back of my skull. I don't know how long I lay that way, with no other awareness except for the pain, but gradually I became aware of other things. That I was lying on something hard, that I was warm, and that something salty was in my mouth. I spit it out and felt better.

I opened my eyes. At first the scene didn't make sense. Then I realized I was inside Maggie's apartment, lying on the living room floor. I could see the legs of a coffee table directly in front of me, and the bottom pleats of a sofa beyond. I was lying on a cheap nylon rug that was criss-crossed with cigarette burns.

Very slowly, I lifted my head and looked around. Two windows faced the street. No curtains, but the shades were pulled all the way down. Beyond the living room was a tiny kitchen. The sink and counters were crowded with dirty glasses—just glasses and no dishes. The place smelled of cigarettes and sweat and poverty.

I tried to sit up. My head felt like it was going to explode, and I put my hand back reflexively. It came away bloody. Slowly I worked my way to my feet and made it to the refrigerator. I wrapped some ice cubes in a dish towel and put it against the back of my head. After a couple of minutes my head started to settle down. It still hurt like hell, but at least I could move around without wanting to scream.

Maggie's purse was on the coffee table. I dumped it out and then, one by one, put things back. No credit cards or purchase slips to tell me where she'd been, and only a few dollars in cash. I found a current Pennsylvania driver's license with her picture and the name "Alberta Witmer." According to her date of birth she was only twenty-nine. I also found a medical card from the Department of Public Welfare in the same name. A small can of Mace. The only other item of obvious interest was a creased photograph of her and Joe. It looked like a summer picture, maybe from the Jersey shore. She was wearing a bathing suit and a big hat, and was waving at the camera with one hand while the other was around Joe. He stood with his arms crossed and his eyes hidden by sunglasses, just watching. It was a small photograph, and it was impossible to tell what he was thinking. I had a feeling, though, that a better photograph wouldn't help much.

I looked through the rest of the purse with care. Inside her wallet, behind a flap, was twenty dollars. Not much of a financial cushion. I was working my way through the usual collection of lipstick, mascara, scissors, and eyeliner when I felt something sharp against my fingertip. My first thought was that I'd found her works, and I began adding AIDS to my list of troubles. Then I saw it was only a nail file. That was odd, I thought; the tips were usually blunt. But not on this one, I saw. It was ordinary in shape and size, but someone had ground on both an edge and a point. The handle looked unremarkable, but when I picked it up there was something different about it. Not how it looked—how it felt. Someone had dipped the last three or four inches of the base in some kind of clear epoxy, giving it a bit of heft. Not enough of a grip to be of use to a person like me, but for someone with small hands it represented a real handle. One of these slid between your ribs could cause a lot of damage. Was this standard issue for hookers, or was this how she was able to get a weapon past airport security?

I checked the kitchen, but found nothing except the usual pots and pans. Somewhere there was probably a stash of drugs but I didn't care about that. I tried the bathroom, with negative results.

Then I tried the bedroom.

I'd seen my share of bodies, some of them torn up pretty badly. But even the tidiest corpse in the world is a shocker when you're not expecting one.

Maggie was face up, lying crossways on the bed. She was nude except for her panty hose, which were wrapped tightly around her throat. Her fingers were still clawing at the noose in death. I saw that her fingernails were almost all broken—I tried to remember if they'd been intact when I saw her in the bar.

Drunk as she was, she'd put up a hell of a fight. The bedside lamp was smashed, and a chair was overturned. The bed itself was at an angle from the wall, and the covers were scattered around the room.

I moved closer to the body. She had been an attractive woman, but undertakers earn their money the hard way making corpses look presentable. The face was discolored, her normal muscle tone was gone, and she'd evacuated her bowels and bladder. Not much resemblance to the girl I'd been talking to a couple of hours before. I studied her arms as carefully as I could without disturbing anything, and sure enough, I saw track marks. She'd been wearing a long-sleeved dress for a good reason.

I surveyed the wreckage. The clothes she'd been wearing were thrown over a chair. The dresser drawers were still shut, and so was the drawer to the bedside table. The closet door was hanging open, but the clothes were still on the hangers and nothing was obviously missing.

I looked around the closet. It seemed to be used more for junk than clothes. Some winter things. And some kid's toys. So Maggie was more than a drug user and a small-time crook and a hooker. She was a mother, too. The toys looked like they were for little kids—building blocks and dolls. I wondered if the father had custody, or Children and Youth.

I found a rag and carefully went through the dresser drawers, being as careful as I could not to leave any prints. The first drawer was lingerie. And panty hose, just like the pair around her neck. It bothered me to think of someone being killed with one of her own possessions. The next two drawers were sweaters and blouses. More of the same in the bottom drawer, except that my hand felt something hairy. For a crazy moment my nerves got to me and I thought I'd found a severed head. But then I realized it was soft. I pulled it out.

It was a wig. With short red hair.

I had no way of knowing if she'd really worn it or if the killer had planted it. Or whether it had anything to do with the case. But I held it in my hands like it was the Holy Grail for a long time before it went back in the drawer. The feeling of being close to something was back.

I searched the rest of the apartment as best I could without leaving obvious traces, but nothing more turned up. No airline tickets, no credit card slips, no phone numbers. The rest of the place was a blank.

I sat down on the sofa. My fatigue was gaining on me again. Wherever Kate was, I was no closer to finding her. As a matter of fact I was further away. Maggie was my only lead, and now she was gone. I hadn't been given much to work with, but I'd managed to waste what little I had. I should have . . .

I put down the iced towel and tried to think. If I went through the place any more thoroughly it would screw up the crime scene for the police. I'd done enough damage already, handling things and leaving fingerprints in the other rooms. I could sit here and wait, but what would that accomplish? Obviously she lived alone, and the killer knew she was dead, so why would anybody be coming by? I could call in the body from here, but I'd just have to spend precious time explaining myself to the Chester police. Or I could do what I do best in these situations—beat it out of there and phone it in anonymously.

I'd just decided to do exactly that when there was a knock at the door. "Police. Open up in there."

Chapter Nine

Wednesday 8:00 P.M.

The detective held a grimy card well away from her face and hunted for the right distance to bring it into focus. "You have the right to remain silent," she began. Her words stumbled out one at a time, as if she had never read them before and was having trouble with English. I realized it was force of habit, from too many interviews with suspects who spoke only a little English, or pretended to. In addition to speaking slowly, she used a relentless monotone. The Supreme Court hadn't given her any deathless prose to work with, and she wasn't wasting any energy with her delivery. "You have the right to consult with an attorney before answering any questions. If you cannot afford the services of an attorney one will be appointed for you free of charge. If you decide to speak to us you may stop at any time. Do you understand each and every one of the rights I have just read to you?"

"Yeah."

She pushed a slip of paper across the coffee table to me and said in the same formal voice, "Please sign this acknowledgment that I've read your rights to you."

I signed it and passed it back. She folded it carefully and placed it in her briefcase. At last we were ready to begin.

Her name was Brill, and she was in charge of the homicide investigation. Her polyester suit was ten years out of date and her skin was pale from too little sun. Her blond hair was neatly combed, but the dye job was spotty and the muddy brown roots were showing. A lumpy figure and a frayed blouse that bulged at the wrong buttons from too many hoagies. Fingernails bitten down to the quick. Nicotine stains on the forefinger of her right hand, though she wasn't smoking now. Her appearance gave me some hope—if she was on the take she'd probably look more prosperous.

Her fingers drummed on the coffee table. "I'd rather be doing this at the station, Mr. Garrett. We have better facilities there."

"I've already told you what I know off the record. Do we even need to go through this?"

She rolled her eyes. "You're found in an apartment with a fresh corpse and you ask me questions like that?"

"Like I said, if we talk on the record at all, we talk here. Now would you rather have the statement here, or not at all?"

She flipped open her notebook by way of an answer. "We already have the ID stuff, so I'm going to go right to what I want to know. For the record, do I have your permission to record this?"

"Yes, you do."

She picked up a battered pocket-size tape recorder held together with a piece of strapping tape. "This is Detective Shirley Brill of the Chester City Department of Police. Present here with me is Mr. David Garrett, of Radnor Township." She rattled off the date, time, and location of the interview. "Mr. Garrett, have you been advised of your rights?" She held out the recorder toward me.

"Yes, I have."

"I now show you the waiver card you've signed. Is that your signature?"

"Yes, it is."

"And does it indicate today's date?"

"I'm going to die of old age before we get to the point."

"Please answer my question."

"Yes, it does."

"Are you ready to begin?"

"Go right ahead."

She put the recorder down on the table between us. "When did you meet the deceased?"

"About two this afternoon. In a bar about a block from here."

"Name of the bar?"

"I didn't catch it. But it's right around the corner."

"Ever see her before that?"

I shook my head.

"Please make your responses verbal."

"Sorry. No, I never saw her before."

"How did you meet?"

"I picked her up."

She frowned. "She wasn't into that no more."

"She was for me."

She rubbed her chin. "You know, Mr. Garrett, it's small stuff, and I don't have to do this, but soliciting a prostitute is an offense, too. I should warn you about that."

My God, I thought, there's a dead woman in the next room and she thinks I'm worried about conspiracy to solicit. Well, at least she's thorough. "I'm prepared to take the consequences for my actions," I said.

She gave me a puzzled look, not certain if I was being sarcastic. "Now then, what was the offer and the deal?"

"A hundred bucks for anything I wanted."

She raised her eyebrows, but didn't comment on Maggie's fee schedule.

"Whose idea was it to come back here?" Brill asked.

"Hers. She didn't say anything about going anywhere else."

"Ever been here before?"

"Never even been in Chester before."

"See anybody you knew on the walk over, or when you got here?"

The literal answer to her question was no, but it didn't take a rocket scientist to figure out that Joe was the one who knocked me out and killed Maggie. Now it was time to decide whether to trust Brill. While we'd been talking I was studying her face. It was an open face, with large eyes and the beginnings of jowls, the face of a family person, the kind who went to all the PTA meetings and tried to get her kids to better themselves, to get ahead in the world. I looked at her hand for a wedding ring, and there it was. And right next to it, on her wrist, a Rolex watch. In a town like this, a detective probably earned thirty-five, forty, maybe a little more with overtime. But even if she made fifty, if she had kids there wasn't enough left over for a Rolex. I couldn't tell if the watch was genuine, but I wasn't ready to bet that it wasn't.

"No, Detective, I never saw anyone else."

"So what happened?"

"I got rolled, like I told you. We were at the door. She was putting in her key and I was standing next to her, watching her. Then there was a pain in the back of my head and I went down. I woke up in here and she was dead."

"What'd you do when you woke up?"

"Got some ice in a towel for the back of my head, then walked around to the bedroom and found her. The next thing I knew, the patrol car was here."

She nodded. The bloody towel had already been carted off by the evidence people.

"And what else did you do in here?"

The trouble with lying is that so often you wind up having to play dumb. It was time to make her think she was earning her pay. "Nothing, Officer."

"Are you sure about that?"

I hung my head. "Well, nothing, really."

"Come on, Mr. Garrett."

"Well, I did go through her purse," I admitted. That one was a throwaway; she must have already figured that from the way everything was messed up.

"Why?"

I did my best to look embarrassed. "Well, when I woke up I had no idea she was here. I mean, all I knew was that I'd been rolled. I was mad, and I thought I might be able to get some of my money back, or at least find out who she was."

"If your possessions had been there, or some money, what would you have done?"

"I would have taken it and kept my mouth shut."

"You didn't think it was funny that they'd leave you in her apartment and leave her purse?"

"Not at the time." For once, at least, I could tell the truth. "I didn't think about it."

"You say you were rolled. What's missing?"

I thought fast. "They left me my cards and some money, but the hundred I flashed, it's gone." I held up the wallet to demonstrate how the hundred was gone. As I did so, I wondered whose picture was on a hundred-dollar bill. "Oh," I added. "Looks like they took my wedding ring, too."

"You a married man?"

"Not as married as I should be, I guess." I tried for a chagrined look.

Brill was about to say something when one of the uniformed officers came in and whispered something in her ear. She picked up the recorder. "Do I have your permission to turn this off?"

"Sure, if you want."

"This interview is now being terminated, at twenty forty-four hours." She put it down. "Mr. Garrett, would you mind taking off your shirt?"

"Why?"

"Just humor us a minute, will you?"

I took off my tie, shirt, and undershirt. While I was undressing, a couple of burly orderlies showed up with a body bag and a litter. From their knees to their shoes they were covered with blood. I wondered what kind of call they'd been on. They moved past me without a word and disappeared into the bedroom.

"Could you stand up and turn around, please?" I complied. When I turned back around, the uniformed officer took my picture several times.

"Hey, what's going on?"

"Sorry, sir," Brill said. "You can get dressed now. This is for your own protection. The victim has skin under her fingernails, and not just a trace, either. We figure it's from the murderer, and that he's got some pretty deep scratches. We're establishing that you're clean."

"Appreciate that. Anyway, doesn't the bartender back up my story?"

She made a face. "For what a bartender's word is worth, yeah. He remembers seeing you and her drinking and the two of you leaving together. From the way he tells it she did most of the drinking."

"That's right."

She sighed and shut her notebook. "Bottom line is, you don't make much of a suspect, unless we're looking at a conspiracy, and there's nothing now to suggest that it was. The medical examiner says the cuts on the back of your head couldn't be self-inflicted. I figure the guy we're looking for is her pimp." Her eyes narrowed. "One last time. You *sure* you met only her?"

"Sure I'm sure."

"Well, that's what the bartender says, too."

"So I'm free to go?"

"I didn't say that."

"Oh."

"Your ID says you're a private eye. From Philadelphia. What the hell are you doing in my town?"

"Well, I told you."

She snorted. "That'll be the day, when they run all the working girls out of Philadelphia. Come on, what are you doing here?"

I thought about her Rolex and avoided giving her a direct answer. "If I was working on a case this would be a pretty stupid way to go about it, wouldn't it?"

"What do you mean?"

"Let's say this girl was a lead and I wanted information from her. You don't interrogate someone by strangling them. If it got physical you might throw them around the walls or do something else, but you want them to be able to talk. Whoever went after her didn't want to learn anything; they just wanted her dead."

"Maybe there was something physical you wanted. Some object, I mean."

"I never got out of the apartment and you didn't find anything on me, did you? And the place hasn't been tossed."

"Maybe you were still looking when we got here. And you were real careful how you looked around."

"And then left a body in plain sight? Whoever did this didn't give a damn about covering their tracks."

She shrugged and rummaged in her purse for a cigarette. She wasn't serious about me as a suspect anymore, and we both knew it. "If you can just tell us where to reach you, then you're free to go."

We exchanged business cards and said our good-byes.

Outside it was dark, and a chill wind was blowing off the river. The street was deserted except for the police cars parked haphazardly out front. I thought that the street looked bad enough by daylight, but it was worse in the dark. The shades on all the houses were drawn down tight, and I was the only person on the street. As I walked my feet crackled on broken glass and, occasionally, on empty crack vials.

I had only gone a few feet when I heard a door open behind me and saw the orderlies coming down the steps with the body bag on the litter. They had zipped it shut but hadn't thrown a sheet over it. There was nothing for me to do, but I stood there, waiting, till she was inside the ambulance. I wondered how old her child was, and whether he would understand about death. And I tried hard not to think about Kate.

Chapter Ten

Wednesday 11:00 P.M.

I found my car and went looking for a gas station with a phone. I watched my mirrors and did a few evasive maneuvers, but I seemed to be alone. I finally turned up a Texaco on 291, almost under the towering bulk of Commodore Barry Bridge, a fragment of a long-forgotten transportation plan that arched gracefully across the Delaware, connecting nothing. I parked near the booth and waited in my car for the caller ahead of me to finish his drug deal. His friends didn't exactly welcome me, but they didn't try to run me off, either.

Eventually the phone was free. I couldn't remember the number, but I got her mother's listing through Philadelphia information.

She answered the phone herself. "Hello?"

"Lisa, it's Dave."

"Oh. Uh—hi." She sounded flustered and uncertain, which made two of us.

"How are you doing?" I asked. Snappy repartee has always been one of my strong points.

"Fine, fine. I—just didn't expect to be hearing from you."

"I was going to call you anyway, when things had cooled down a little more." It was a dumb thing to say, and I realized it just as soon as I'd said it. "I feel a little awkward, calling you like this."

"It's good to hear from you," she said. "I want you to know that I'm sorry about how things turned out."

"You don't owe me any apologies," I said.

"I sure do. What happened in Mexico was every bit my fault." The line was quiet for a couple of heartbeats and then she went on. "Hey, I wanted to tell you, the rest of the money came through from my case. Thanks again for all your help."

"I was glad I could do it." Another awkward pause. "I wish I'd done as well for myself. The government seized my share. They said they thought it was the proceeds of criminal activity. I've got a tax lawyer and an accountant trying to straighten things out." Then I realized she might be thinking I was trying to hit her up for a loan. "But I wasn't calling about that," I added quickly. "I need a favor, if you're interested."

"What's that?"

"I'm calling to offer you a job."

She laughed. "What kind of a job? My typing isn't anything to write home about, and if I remember your office right, there's nothing to file."

"I'd like you to work with me as an investigator."

"You've got to be kidding."

"Not permanent, I mean, just for a few days. I need your help on a case. I know this is sudden, but it's breaking fast."

"Why me? You must know lots of people."

"Because you've already saved my life twice, and because I trust your judgment."

"Saving your life was just luck."

"No, it wasn't. It took a lot of nerve. And anyway, I need your luck. I haven't had much of my own lately."

"And you don't want to push it trying to get help from anyone else at this time of night."

"That, too. But there's no one else I'd rather have."

"I'm flattered. But I'm not qualified."

"This case is serious," I said. "Life and death. One person's dead already."

I heard an intake of breath. "That's all the more reason you should get someone who really knows what they're doing."

"For old time's sake, will you hear me out at least?"

"I can promise you that much. Go ahead."

"It's more than I can get into over the phone. I don't even understand it all myself. Can you meet me at my place in an hour?"

"All right."

"How does a hundred dollars a day sound? That's the going rate for assistants."

"I haven't even said I'm comfortable with this. Frankly, I don't think I am."

"You did a hell of a job back in January."

"And it still scares me."

"But if you want the job, would the pay be all right?" I asked.

"*If* I want it, and if you'll pick up my expenses, and pay me under the table, you'd have a deal."

"You drive a hard bargain."

"I expect I'll be earning it. Life has a way of getting real interesting when you're around."

"See you soon," I said, and hung up.

I closed my eyes and leaned against the dirty glass of the phone booth. Yes, life had been interesting when we'd been together—in the first three days I knew her I had to kill a man and several times we nearly got killed ourselves. For a woman who'd spent the last seven years in the coal regions, it must have been a hell of a weekend. But if Lisa was hesitating because she didn't think she could handle the job, she was doing what she did best—underestimating herself. She was raised in a rough Philadelphia neighborhood that usually produced only dropouts, but she won enough scholarships along the way so that she had just as much education as I did. For the last seven years she'd lived entirely on her own in a tiny worked-out coal town, making as good a living as could be made there. My most vivid memory of Lisa? Not from our ten days in Mexico, though those were clear enough. It was the half hour I'd spent digging out the glass that was buried deep in the back of her hand. I must have taken out a couple of dozen shards, without any anesthetic, and there was blood all over the tiny bathroom. Her hand never moved and her face never changed expression. I wondered if I was that tough. I didn't think so.

The bar was a lot more crowded this time, and a lot more dangerous. A volatile mixture of druggies, unemployed blue-collar workers, pimps, hustlers, and prostitutes filled the room. Most of them were smoking, and it was hard to see more than a few feet. No one took any notice of me, for which I was thankful. The crowd was subdivided into groups of three to a dozen, most of the groups arguing heatedly, obscenely, and loudly. As I drifted through on the way to the bar I caught bits of conversation—if that was the right word—about how Muhammad Ali was really a pussy; the best way to cold-cock someone; the merits of the supercharged 486 hemi; and how the Japs were ruining our schools. My personal favorite was the group nearest the bar, who were arguing about whose wife or girlfriend gave the best head. Every speaker was shouting a few inches from the faces of his listeners, who shouted right back the minute someone paused for breath. Surprisingly, none of the groups came to blows—not even the ones near the bar, where the level of dispute had reached a dangerous intensity.

I was in luck. One of the bartenders on duty was the

same one I'd seen that afternoon. I waited for him to come by. When he did, it was clear he wasn't glad to see me.

"What'll it be, buddy?"

"I'm looking for Joe."

"Fuck you, asshole."

"Just what do you mean by that?"

"Huh?"

"It's important I see him."

"Dream on."

"I'm not kidding. I've got to see him tonight or the deal's off."

"What deal?"

"The deal that keeps his ass out of jail."

"What the hell are you talking about?"

"That part is none of your business. Can you get a message to him?"

"Why would I want to, asshole?"

"You want Joe after you?"

"Me? Hell, no."

"Because if my message doesn't get to him he's going to jail. But before he goes in, he'll find out it was because you didn't pass it along."

"Come on, shithead. I don't buy that."

"Then buy this. You told the cops Joe wasn't here. Fine for you. Well, I told them I don't know who hit me, that I was just a john getting rolled. It's a bet that whoever hit me killed Maggie. Joe meets with me tonight or I give him to the cops."

He followed my logic, but he wasn't impressed. "Your word against his."

"Not for the next week or two. Seen him in the last couple hours?"

"No."

"Before she died she scratched him up. If the police get him before he heals, he's in trouble."

He thought about it. "Well, maybe I can get a message to him."

I put a twenty on the bar. "Three this morning."

"Where?"

That was a good question. I could barely navigate my way around the city. Then I remembered a place that would suit. "At the armory, on Sproul at Eighth. Tell him to come alone and not to bring a piece."

"He ain't going to meet with someone he don't know."

I slapped one of my business cards on top of the twenty. "So now he knows."

The bartender studied my card. "I figured something like this. What's he supposed to know, anyway?"

"That's a good question. Maybe nothing I'm interested in at all."

"Then why you want to meet?"

" 'Cause I don't have anywhere else to look."

He gave me a puzzled look but he took the twenty and the card.

Chapter Eleven

Wednesday Midnight

Light from a pair of headlights brushed my kitchen window and I looked out over the parking lot. Lisa, in blue jeans and a windbreaker, was getting out of a car I'd never seen before. I looked at it and whistled. Even in the dark, I could recognize a brand-new Legend when I saw one. I remembered her old rattletrap with the mismatched doors, and I was sorry to think that it was gone. That car had saved our lives, and its backseat was the first place we'd made love. No, come to think of it, the second. Or the third, depending on how you count.

She was tall and athletically built, with flowing dark brown hair that fell down below her shoulders. She came up the walk with a loose, rangy stride, her arms swinging, that made her upper body seem out of synch with the rest of her. The windbreaker swished loosely around her slim hips.

I got a good look as she came up the walk. Her eyes were down but she wasn't watching the ground. For a moment I wondered what she was thinking about.

I opened the door before she had a chance to knock and we stood there, inches apart. It was the first time we'd seen each other since January, and for a moment we both just looked. Her face was pale, which made her dark eyes even larger. They were staring at me now, moving slowly over my face. She shifted her weight and tried to brush her hair back behind her ear.

"Lisa, thanks for coming." Not very original, but it would have to do.

"I'm still surprised you asked."

"You're smart, you keep your head, you shoot straight, and you can drive like hell. What more could I need?"

She put her head down, blushing, and then looked up again. She brushed her hair back again, nervously. The scars on the back of her hand were jagged and nearly as raw as they'd looked in Mexico. "You said life and death. How could I turn you down?"

Then she stepped closer and gave me a brief hug, and for a moment her breasts pressed against me. To my embarrassment, my body responded immediately. I hoped she didn't notice. "Want some coffee?" I said. "We're going to be up late."

"Sure. Are you okay?"

"How do you mean?"

She studied my face again while she hunted for the right word. "Strung out."

I turned away to pour coffee from my ancient stainless steel percolator. If I looked this bad to a friend, how impressive would I appear to Joe? A beat-up old guy he didn't need to worry about? "I was up all night, and I've been taking diet pills to keep going. And I got myself hit over the head this afternoon. Other than that, life's just a bowl of cherries."

She sat down on the sofa and held her mug with both hands. "Tell me the whole thing, starting from the top."

"It all starts in February, after you and I broke up."

"Go on."

I did. I told her about Kate, her husband, and everything that had happened in the last twenty-six hours. A few times she interrupted with questions. Mostly she just listened.

"You're sure it was Joe that killed Maggie?" she asked when I was done. "I mean, you never saw him."

"It's a safe bet that whoever knocked me out killed her. He was her pimp and he probably thought she was seeing a customer without him."

"Do you think this Joe will show up?"

"I don't know. I don't even know who he is, really."

"What happens if he doesn't?"

"I give him up to the police and hope they can get something else out of him. With a murder charge on the table he may be willing to deal."

"Why not give him up now?"

"If he hears the police are after him he'll go to ground and no one will find him for weeks. And even if they bring him in, I probably won't be able to see him. Besides, why should he deal with me then? Now I've still got something to trade."

"And what will you do if he shows?"

I let out my breath. "Talk sweetly and try to persuade him to help?"

"Nice. What's your second plan?"

"Sandbag the son of a bitch and get it out of him any way I have to."

"Better."

"The trouble is, I don't know if he knows anything."

She held out her mug for a refill. "If he's just a pimp, he may not know anything about Maggie going to Miami even assuming that she went at all."

"You're full of good news tonight."

"Maggie said she'd traveled. She never said Miami or Harrisburg or Allentown, did she?" Lisa asked.

"But I *recognized* her."

"From the glimpse in the airport? Dave, you used to be

a criminal defense lawyer. If you were in court think how they'd rip into you. Fifty feet away, she was just one head among many bobbing up and down. You first thought she was Kate, who's—how much—fifteen years older. You stopped paying any attention to her the minute you realized it wasn't her, and went back to looking for your girlfriend. Right?"

"What about the wig? And do you want some more coffee while I'm up?"

"Please. The woman was a prostitute," she pointed out. "She probably had all sorts of costumes for different customers."

I poured out coffee and put the percolator back in the kitchen. "Brill said she was out of the life."

"And how would she know that? Did Maggie fail to renew her hooker's license the last time it expired?"

"Maybe there's more truth in that than you realize. Remember Brill's Rolex?" I said. "She may be closing her eyes to a lot of things."

"The watch could be a fifty-dollar knockoff or a present from her husband. You're reading a lot into the situation. Just because the city's crummy doesn't mean the cops are—" We were interrupted by a knock at the door. A loud, insistent knocking that sounded like trouble.

I opened the door and found myself face to face with a man I'd hoped never to see again. He was a big man, with the kind of barrel-chested physique that never looks right in a suit no matter how well it's tailored.

"Sergeant Risser, isn't it?"

He stepped closer and leveled a finger at my chest. "I want to talk to you, Garrett."

"Got a warrant?"

I could see the cords of the muscles on the side of his neck standing out. "I can get one inside of an hour."

"Then get it." I started to shut the door. He blocked it with his foot. "Don't mess with me, Garrett."

I made a point of looking down at his shoe. "There seems to be something stuck—"

That was as far as I got. He threw his weight against the door, hard and fast, and sent me flying back down my hallway. I went backward until my back hit the opposite wall, eight feet behind. Before I could react he was nearly up against me, his fists up, waiting for the slightest excuse.

I didn't move, not even to turn my head toward the living room. "Lisa, I'd like you to meet Sergeant Risser, Tinnicum Township. Sergeant, this is Lisa Wilson."

He looked at her and a sour expression crossed his face. "What's she doing here?"

I looked at her, too. She was standing by the sofa with a slightly startled, pleasant expression, looking as demure as any woman can who stands five foot nine in her stocking feet. Her right hand was holding the coffeepot. For a moment I wondered why—I'd just poured for us both. Then I saw how she was holding it, not down at her waist the way you pour, but up at the level of her chest. The biggest, hottest set of brass knuckles I could imagine, and the whiteness of her knuckles around the handle told me she was fully prepared to use it.

"What she's doing here is none of your business," I said. "This is private property and I can have any visitors I want. And you're not even in your jurisdiction. Now either start punching me in front of a witness, or back off." It was a dangerous thing to say, but my blood was up, too. If he made a move he'd never know what hit him. The trouble was, when he woke up, he would.

Fortunately for all three of us, he backed off and let me move away from the wall. "Now, what makes you think I'd want to punch you?"

I made a show of straightening my clothing. "It's what you did the last time we met, in west Philadelphia," I said. "Or have you forgotten?"

"You, I don't forget." But he allowed me to pass by, and the three of us stood in an uneasy circle in the living room.

I turned to Lisa. "Sergeant Risser and I met last month. He tried to use me as a pogo stick." She blinked and looked from one of us to the other, but kept quiet. The coffeepot stayed at chest level.

"Garrett, I'm going to read you your rights."

"It's that bad?"

"Yeah."

"What's going on?"

"First, I give you your rights." He fished a card out of his shirt pocket.

I saw the clock on the wall behind his head. It was already one-thirty. An hour and a half till my meeting at the armory, and it was a good forty-minute drive. "Just tell me what's going on and I'll talk to you off the record."

For a moment he couldn't think of anything to say. "You're kidding."

"No, I'm not. Tell me what you want and I'll spill, right now. If you think my answers are incriminating you can give me my rights and I'll make a statement later."

He looked at me with suspicion. "Why are you being so cooperative?"

"Because I don't have anything to lose."

"Everybody does," he said.

"I don't have a lot of time to fool around tonight, and if we do this by the numbers you won't have what you want till dawn."

He put the card away and took out a notebook. Lisa and I sat on the sofa and he pulled up a kitchen chair and sat down on it backward. She leaned back and crossed her legs, but kept the coffeepot right in front of her on the table.

"What time did you get home this evening?" he asked.

"A little before midnight."

"Any witnesses to that?"

I tried to slide around it. "Ms. Wilson here. She arrived just after twelve."

He wasn't having any. "Does she know what time you got here?"

"No."

"Does anybody?"

"Not really."

He smiled a little. He was liking my answers. "Where were you between eight and nine this evening?"

"With Detective Brill, over in Chester. I've got one of her cards here."

"I know her." He waved it off. "What about at seven?"

"Same answer."

"What were you doing with her?"

"I was making a report. I got rolled in Chester. Hit on the back of the head."

"Who?"

"That was what Brill was working on." It was at least a half-truth.

He frowned. "You own a black Cougar?"

"White Honda Civic. I can show you the registration if you want, and anyway, it's parked right outside."

"I saw it," he said impatiently. "Were you alone this evening? After you left Brill?"

"Yes."

"Sure you weren't in the company of a white female, about fifty?"

"I'm sure."

"Ever been to a bar named Joey's in Lester?"

"Never in my life. Want to try for the really big prize, or take your winnings and go?"

"Know a hooker with the street name of Ashley?"

I stopped thinking it was all so funny. "Yeah, I do."

"When did you see her last?"

"Chester, early this afternoon." I started to sweat. The Tinnicum police wouldn't be at my door at one in the morning on a missing persons case, at least not for a street person like her.

He looked at Lisa, then back to me, before he asked the next one. "You know this Ashley girl very well?"

I hesitated, not sure how to play it. Then Lisa bought me some time. "Don't worry about asking personal questions in front of me," she said. "I'm just a business associate."

She didn't look much like a business associate, at least not in jeans and a sweater in the middle of the night on my sofa, and that got Risser's attention. "Would you mind showing me some ID, ma'am?"

"No problem at all, Officer." She took her time fishing it out of her handbag. He looked over her driver's license, made some notes, and handed it back.

"Now back to you, Garrett. What about this Ashley?"

In the interval I'd decided how to play it. "Never saw her before today. She gave me information on a case I'm working on."

"She won't be giving you anything more."

"What happened?"

"OD. Found her in an alley behind the bar."

"Suspicious?"

"The toxicology people'll take a look, but with junkies you never know."

"How'd you get to me?"

"Anonymous tip that you'd been seen with her that day. You know any of her friends or associates?"

"I don't even know where she lived." It wasn't a direct answer, but this time the slider went on through.

"She didn't live anywhere, really, as far as we can tell so far. When you were with her, did you see a black Cougar?"

"No, no one else."

"Where'd you last see her?"

"She got out of my car in front of a bar in Chester. It

must have been between two and three. She just walked away."

"See her get in another car? Get a customer?"

"She didn't need one. I gave her forty bucks and she was on her way to shoot up."

"Huh."

"I know what you're thinking. I was thinking the same thing myself when I gave her the money."

Risser surprised me. "Hey, it ain't your fault."

"There's what you feel and then there's what you know."

"Tell me about it. What did you get for your money?" He colored. "The information, I mean."

I was bumping right into the story I'd told Brill. It was time for a tough choice and I didn't feel up to making it. "I was looking for someone. Didn't find them, though."

"Let's hear it."

I shrugged. "It's a missing persons case, maybe. Not from here—it's a Miami matter, anyway."

"What made you think she would know anything about it?"

"I didn't. She was just one person I talked to. I was cruising the hookers, hoping one of them could help me find someone who knew something. Nothing."

"You have any idea who would want to kill her?"

"I didn't know her."

"Cut the shit, Garrett."

I thought about giving him Joe and decided against it. I had a fair idea Joe had killed Maggie, but what had happened to Ashley was anybody's guess, and I didn't feel like going over mug shots the rest of the night. "Nope, no idea."

He asked me some more questions, but I couldn't be any more help. When he finally left, with a gruff warning to stay out of trouble in his township, it was after two o'clock.

I shut the door after him and leaned against it. "Now you know why I need you along."

She looked at the door and shook her head. "When he came in he was really on the edge of going after you. His hands were shaking."

"That was quick thinking."

"Come on," she said. "Let's get out of here."

"Does that mean you'll help?"

She brushed the hair back from her face again. "It's the middle of the night. What else is there to do?"

Chapter Twelve

Thursday 3:00 A.M.

We took Lisa's car. It was in better shape, and after a day of cruising the streets, mine was sure to be spotted.

The plan was simple. It had to be—we didn't have time for anything complicated. Lisa would park on Sproul a block south of the armory and I would wait in the shadow of the steps. Since the street was one-way for northbound traffic, Joe would have to pass between her and me, and we'd have him boxed in.

A cold wind was blowing off the Delaware, and I wished I'd brought a warmer coat. Sproul Street was absolutely quiet. And dark, too. None of the streetlights was functioning. I hadn't counted on that, and I cursed Risser for keeping me from having a chance to scout out the area first. Of course, there wasn't anything to be done about it, but this was Joe's town, and I felt that darkness gave him an edge. At least the moon was near full.

The wind blew bits of paper around my ankles—old newspapers, candy wrappers, and less identifiable trash. Three came, then 3:10, and no cars came by. Up north, where Sproul ran into Ninth, I could see traffic moving on

Ninth. Not much, maybe one car a minute, and it was moving quickly. No one wanted to linger in downtown Chester in the middle of the night. Except us two idiots.

It was a little past 3:15 when a car turned off Ninth toward us and cut its lights. It came the wrong way down Sproul and stopped just north of the armory, a good seventy-five yards from where Lisa was parked. There was just enough moonlight to see that it was a dark-colored Cougar, and that a big man was getting out of the passenger's side.

We'd been caught out of position, but there was nothing to do but press on. I stepped out onto the sidewalk, away from the safety of the masonry stair rail. He circled around the back of the Cougar and stood next to the driver's door. "You Joe?" I yelled.

"Yeah, and who the fuck are you, man?"

"I want to talk to you."

"You want to burn me, asshole, for something I don't know nothing about."

"Come a little closer. I'm tired of shouting."

A pause. He seemed to be getting his instructions from the driver. "You packing?"

"No."

"You're full of shit."

"The only way you're going to know is to come closer."

Another pause. "Okay, but put your hands up."

"If you will. I don't trust you, either."

It was an odd sight, two men inching closer, both of them with their hands up high. We ended up about twenty feet apart, in the middle of the street. We were a lot closer to the Cougar than to Lisa's car, but there were so many things about the situation I didn't like that one more didn't seem too important.

"Take off the coat and let me see," he said.

"If you do, too."

We went through a slow dance of removing our coats

and turning around, first him and then me. In another context it could have been funny. I felt certain he had something stashed somewhere and that he'd use it the second he thought he was being crossed. I'd come unarmed for exactly that reason, so he'd have no excuse to start blasting away. My only protection was the bulletproof vest under my shirt.

"Can we put our hands down now?" I asked. We were close enough now to talk at a conversational level.

"Yeah, I guess. Now what do you want?"

"I want to keep you out of jail, my friend, but you're not making it easy."

"Nobody *ever* made it easy for me, man. Not a fucking thing in my whole life."

"Hey, cool it." Either he was on something or he was naturally strung as tight as a violin. "I just want to talk."

"Why?"

"I'm looking for somebody."

"Who are you?"

"I'm not a cop," I said.

"Bullshit you're not."

I looked around at the shadows of the buildings pressing in on both sides. "Is this the way cops operate? I'm private."

"Big difference, if you're not lying anyway."

"I'll show you my ID if you want."

"I've had a bellyful of you guys."

That stopped me cold. "Private detectives?"

"And always the same thing, too. Wanting to take me home. Well, I ain't having none of it. I know my rights and I don't have to go."

"Hey, easy, buddy. I'm not here for you."

His voice turned scornful. "You lying sack of shit. First thing you said was, you were looking for somebody—"

"Who said it was you?"

Now it was his turn to be caught off balance. "You mean, you're not looking for me?"

"No." He was so startled he took a couple of steps closer. It was my first good look at him, and there was something familiar about him. Something besides seeing him at the bar, and outside Maggie's. Something that tied in with the fact that private detectives were looking for him. "Why should I be?" I asked.

He ignored my question. "What did you want with Maggie?"

"Same thing as with Ashley, and Suzie-Q. I'm looking for a woman. I think she's in danger. And you're the only one left to talk to."

"Talk never did nobody no good."

"You never talked to me before. About how you can stay out of jail."

"Why would I go to jail?"

"Maggie's murder, Ashley's murder, burglarizing Maggie's apartment, and an aggravated assault on me. That enough of a start?"

"Hey, you can't pin any of that shit on me."

"Can't I?"

"Man, you're just like the rest, a pile of threats and nothing to back it up."

"I don't want to be threatening you, Joe. I just want to find my friend. Her name's Kate McMahan."

He folded his arms across his chest. "And you don't think that ain't a threat?"

"I'm just telling you why I'm here. And I want to know what you know about her."

"I don't know nothing, man. Go back and tell them that."

"Them?"

"Don't try to shit me."

If Lisa had been with me she would have known, right away. She knew all about pain and lies and hiding out. But she was in the backfield and it was my play. "You say you don't know anything. But you didn't seem surprised when I said Ashley was dead."

"Chicks like her turn up dead all the time."

"Murdered?"

"Sometimes. It's the way it is, man."

"Was Maggie in Miami Tuesday?"

He laughed. "Go ask her."

"I'm asking you. It's important."

"Like, how important?"

"Like the difference between you going to jail, or leaving here tonight with something for your trouble."

He started to look back at the Cougar and caught himself. He stepped a little closer and dropped his voice. He was almost within reach. I looked at his face. Something registered, but it stopped short of a full thought. "How much?" he wanted to know.

"A fellow can always use a couple extra bucks, can't he?"

"This is heavy shit you want, man." He was trying to sound tough, but it came out halfway to a whine.

"So you say. What have you got?"

"I know somebody who knows who's got her, maybe."

"Kate McMahan?"

He nodded.

My pulse speeded up and I felt my face flushing. I struggled to keep my voice under control. "You know where she is?"

"Not exactly, but I got a pretty good idea."

"Is she okay?"

"I make it my business not to know that shit."

"Come on, you have to have some idea." Now I was the one whining.

"Yeah, I figure she is. But I don't know, you understand. So how much is it worth to you?"

I cursed Kate's husband for his unavailability and totaled up the entire amount I thought I could beg, borrow, or steal. "One offer, because it's all I've got. Five thousand in cash by noon."

He made a face and then laughed. "Five thousand? This kind of information, it ought to be worth ten times that."

"It ought to be. But it's only worth what somebody can afford to pay. I might be able to get lots more from her husband, but that's all I can afford to do for now."

"You're shitting me."

I held up my car keys. "I'll throw in my '80 Civic. It's got body rust and it needs new tires. And that's all I've got in the world, pal."

He jerked his chin in the direction of Lisa's car. "What about that?"

"It's not mine."

He rubbed the side of his face. "Be right back." He went to the driver's door of the Cougar. I saw the driver's window go down, but without changing position I couldn't see anything more.

After a couple of minutes he started back. His walk was more relaxed now, a walk that was familiar. This time I made the connection.

I started to open my mouth, but at that moment I heard the roar of a car starting. At first I thought it was Lisa, but then I realized it was coming from in front, not from behind. The Cougar jerked away from the curb and headed straight for us, squealing its tires. Joe turned, and as he did the high-beam headlights came on, blinding him. He threw up his hands to protect his eyes, and at the next instant the car caught him square at the hips, knocking him flat and rolling right over him. I heard a sickening thud as his ribs collapsed under the weight and the breath went out of him.

The Cougar came after me, too, but it had farther to go and I was prepared. I made a dash for the armory steps and got behind them just as it climbed the sidewalk toward me. I felt the rush of the air as it swept by like an angel of death. The driver never slowed, just cut back onto the street and headed south. When it reached the corner its lights went out and I lost it.

Lisa pulled up to where Joe was lying and turned on her headlights. He was a sorry sight, his body covered with blood and road dirt from his chest to his knees. I knelt down but I could have saved myself the trouble. His eyes were wide open and there was no pulse.

Lisa knelt down beside me. "So this is Joe?"

"At least it was quick. Poor bastard never knew what hit him."

"You're being pretty generous to someone who killed at least one person and probably two."

I shook my head. "I don't think Joe killed anybody."

"What?"

"Look at his face. And his arms. No scratches. He didn't kill Maggie. He probably didn't even hit me over the head. He was an accomplice, I suppose, but that's all. A poor schmuck who was in over his head. He doesn't even come from all that bad a background. In some ways, that is."

"You seem to know a lot about him for not knowing his last name."

"Oh, I know it all right. And his address, too. Look at his driver's license. Five bucks says his name is Joseph Kuwalchack, Jr., and he's from Allentown."

She reached underneath him and pulled out his wallet. She held up his license in front of the headlights. "I suppose Joseph the third counts. You know the family?"

"Very wealthy. A self-absorbed mother. The kind that give ruthless bitches a bad name. The father—I don't know. The two of them fought like cats and dogs. Joe was into drugs. Probably was for a long time."

"Do you know what he was using?"

"Whatever it was, he was feeding an expensive habit. By

stealing from his parents' friends and even his own parents."

She nodded. "It'd be easy for him. He'd know which houses had nice things and when people would be out of town."

"Right. Now let's get to a phone booth. You need to call this in, anonymously."

"Why me?"

"Because nobody knows your voice, except Risser, and he's up in Tinnicum. All police departments record phone calls and I don't want my voice on tape. I'm listed as an important witness in two homicides already. I can't have somebody deciding that the third means I should be held as a material witness."

As we got into the car, she asked, "What am I going to say?"

"Well, tell them about the body in front of the armory. Detective Brill should be alerted personally. And tell them to watch for a black Cougar being driven by a white female, heavy build, around fifty, who calls herself Suzie-Q. She'll probably have scratches on her face and arms, and she may be in possession of works for injecting drugs."

We headed north. Lisa made a wide detour around Joe's body, wider and slower than necessary. It was her salute to the luckless of the world who do evil they never intended.

Chapter Thirteen

Thursday 5:00 A.M.

After the call, Lisa drove us to an all-night restaurant off 95. It might have been a Denny's or an Elby's or a Bob Evans or God knows what—one of those places where you can't remember what you had twenty minutes after you ate. But we weren't there for the food. We spread out a map of Pennsylvania and tried to plan our next move.

Lisa set down her coffee cup. "We know two things now, for sure, that we didn't know before. That Kate has definitely been kidnapped, and that it has something to do with drugs."

"So how does that help us locate her?"

"It doesn't." She looked at the map again, then leaned back in her seat. "I'm stuck and I admit it."

"We've got enough for some intelligent guessing," I said.

She rubbed her eyes. "I'm not feeling very intelligent right now."

"You get your enemies the same way you get your friends, by regular contact. Kate has lived in Miami more than twenty years. She's only been to Pennsylvania once. So whoever has her are basically Florida people."

"So they make their move in Harrisburg not because they want to but because it's the only place she'll be alone?"

I nodded. "That's the *where* of it. Now let's think about *who*. First of all, we have to assume these people are big. You don't go around kidnapping people for a missing deposit bottle. They have a big presence somewhere. Florida, probably. But they didn't use their own people up here, either because they're too small up here, or because they want to keep a low profile. So they tied in with a small-time gang from Chester—Suzie-Q and Maggie and Joe."

"So what does that tell us?"

"From what Joe said, the Chester people turned her over to somebody else. Presumably to the local organization of the Florida group that hired them in the first place."

"Why do you say that?"

"I have to assume the Florida people want her alive. If they wanted her dead they could have taken care of that at either end of the trip."

"You're reaching."

"It's what I do best. Look, just assume that we're dealing with Florida people who are big enough locally to have an organization, and have a place to hide Kate, but for whatever reason they don't want to do the kidnapping themselves. Okay?"

"Okay."

"So we're looking for a complicated criminal organization, one that's probably been in place for a while."

"No shit."

"I mean, that tells us what to do next. The police should be able to give us some answers."

"I must have missed something here. You've been *avoiding* the police like crazy. And what makes you think they'll help you?"

"The Chester people won't. Or Tinnicum. And my contact in Marcus Hook doesn't know anything specific. But there's somebody who does, and he owes us a favor."

"Who's that?"

"I'll give you a hint. We just cleared up a string of burglaries for him."

"Bonowitcz."

From there we hit a snag, one I should have foreseen. When I called his department from the restaurant pay phone I found he'd left town late Wednesday night. The dispatcher had no authority to give out any information. No, he wouldn't forward a message for me. If I wanted to wait till after lunch, the chief would be in. I looked at my watch—a seven-hour wait, minimum, and maybe much longer. And in the meantime, I couldn't think of a single thing to do.

I went back to our table and explained the problem to Lisa. She listened politely.

"Lisa, I may be too sleepy to notice, but this doesn't seem to be bothering you."

"How badly do we need to reach Bonowitcz?"

"There are no more leads in Chester unless Suzie-Q decides to flip over on herself, and the police aren't going to let me within a hundred miles of her even if they do pick her up."

"What about going to the police about Kate again? You said you'd already submitted a missing persons report. Maybe they'll take it more seriously this time."

"Where do we tell them to look?"

She shrugged and played with the rim of her cup. "Around, I guess."

"If I could have interested the police in this right away—I mean, within a few minutes of when she was abducted—that could have made a difference. But they've got her wherever they want her now, under wraps. She's not driving around anymore. She's not going to turn up in a routine traffic stop."

"You're going to follow up anyway, aren't you?"

"Of course I am. I'm going to call the sergeant I've been working with at the airport and bring him up to date. And I'm sure he'll put it in the computer and even send a special notice to Harrisburg, for all the good it's going to do. But if she's going to be found in time we'd better expect to do it ourselves."

She brushed her hair away from her face. "So, it's pretty important to reach Bonowitcz, huh?"

"If we can't we might as well go home until we can."

She looked down at the table, but she wasn't focused on the map. "I think I can reach him."

"How?"

"Well, I used to live not all that far from Allentown. A long time ago I dated an Allentown city detective. He'd have to know Bonowitcz."

"You're not exactly running for the phone."

"It ended really badly."

"It was a long time ago."

Her voice dropped so far I had to lean closer to catch her words. "I don't mean hurt feelings, I mean being punched out and thrown naked out of his place at two in the morning, with my clothes thrown out after me, and a lot of nasty things being shouted at me."

"Oh."

She looked up and brushed back her hair again. She was flushed and her eyes were wet. "So give me some quarters and let's get this over with."

The pay phone was in the foyer of the restaurant. There was no privacy because even at that hour customers were passing by, but it was close to the cash register, which was more important. In between rounds of listening at her ear I must have made five separate trips for change before it was all over.

Watching her work, I knew I'd done the right thing in bringing her along. She kept her eyes shut and a finger from one hand jammed into the ear she didn't have pressed to the telephone. She concentrated so completely that she never noticed the passersby, the drafts of cold air when the door was opened, or the noise and clatter of the restaurant. With her old boyfriend she was restrained, persistent, and distant. She got Bonowitcz's unlisted home number out of him without any mention of their past. To Mrs. Bonowitcz she was a best friend in trouble. She played on every fear of a policeman's wife—the danger, the tension of not knowing, the indifference of the higher-ups, and, most of all, the innocent lives at stake. Lisa made Kate sound like her own sister, painting a picture of violence and drugs and death meted out casually by strangers. To get off the phone she had to promise to call Mrs. Bonowitcz back and let her know how it all turned out. The desk clerk at Bonowitcz's motel never had a chance. This time she was officious, short and nasty, and brushed aside his excuses like Patton heading for the Rhine. She played Bonowitcz himself like a violin, first businesslike, then more gentle, almost seductive. When he resisted she retreated, then approached by another route. She shifted from wheedling to quiet threats within the same sentence, never losing the thread.

She hung up and slung her purse over her shoulder. "He'll meet with us in his room in half an hour."

"If you've ever done telemarketing, or phone sex for a living, I don't want to know about it." She gave me the kind of mysterious smile that told me that I didn't know as much about her as I thought I did. What the hell; if she'd sold phone sex I could forgive her.

Telemarketing was another story.

The motel was on 291, not far from the airport, the kind of facility they used to call a motor court. The sign out front advertised phones in each room as the big selling point. In the fifties, when 291 was a major thoroughfare for private cars, it must have been a prosperous place. But Interstate 95 had drawn the travelers off 291, and now it subsisted on truck drivers and travelers on a budget, like police officers.

Bonowitcz was in his room, dressed but not shaven, when we arrived. He met us at the door. His remaining fringe of white hair was uncombed. He was a big man with an open manner, a red face, and a belly that would have done credit to a woman in her sixth month.

"Good to finally meet you, Lieutenant," I said.

He shook my hand and looked me up and down, taking his time about it. I had the feeling that if he was asked to describe me ten years from now, he'd do a good job. "Remind me someday to sic Goldman on you."

"I dealt with him once. That was plenty."

Lisa introduced herself. They shook hands, too, but this time his eyes moved even slower. I couldn't blame him.

We entered a grimy room that reeked of cigarette smoke and garlic. "I wouldn't normally do something like this," he said, "but like I told Miss Wilson, I owe you guys something."

"We're glad to be of service," I lied.

"More than you know. The Chester police went to Kuwalchack's apartment to notify whoever might be there. They found a woman who calls herself Suzie-Q. She was in the middle of destroying stuff, stolen IDs and lists of who would buy hot goods without asking questions. Some got burned but it looks like there's going to be enough evidence to clear a bunch of my burglaries."

"Are they holding her for those?"

"Hell no. They don't have jurisdiction, for one thing, and they haven't had time, for another. That's why I'm down here, to do the paperwork."

"This must have a pretty high priority, getting a lieutenant up in the middle of the night."

He shrugged. "The victims are some of the biggest political contributors in the county, and this is an election year."

"This woman's not on the street is she?"

"No way. Chester is getting ready to take her to a preliminary arraignment on a homicide right now. Victim was a girl named Maggie Mason. The suspect has scratches on her face and forearms. Chester tells me they think there's enough epidermis under the victim's fingernails for DNA matching, now that they have a suspect."

"Good for Maggie. I was hoping for that."

"Chester thinks they might be able to get her for two more, but that's not my problem. Ready to do some business?"

We sat around a tiny circular table and spread out our road map, now ringed with brown circles from coffee cups. Lisa had updated him over the phone, of course, but he had a few more questions before he was ready to talk.

"First of all," he said. "The most important thing. This conversation *never happened.* In drug work you spend years building up a network of informants, and if they think word is getting out to civilians, they either dry up on you or start giving you bullshit. Okay?"

We both nodded.

"One more thing," Lisa said. "We'd like to have your recommendation on whether we should be doing this ourselves."

He rubbed his face while he thought about it. "Yeah, and I'll tell you why. You've got a hell of a lot of suspicious circumstances, but not a lot of a case. This ain't Nazi Germany—we can't go busting down the doors of everyone in Pennsylvania who's got a muddy van. You get some more information, you can get help."

She nodded. "Thanks, go ahead."

"What you guys have already thought through, that this is probably some local arm of a Florida group, I think you may be right. Not saying you are, but your thinking sounds right to me. Let's start with the idea that she's probably not in the Harrisburg area. I have pretty good connections over there and this doesn't sound like anything the Harrisburg people would get into. There's a lot of drugs there, but it's almost all black, and it's a local scene. And if they wanted to take somebody at the airport themselves, why drag in Chester?"

"So if she's not there, then where?" I asked.

He poked at the map with a stubby finger. "Look here. There's four ways away from Harrisburg. You go east, you get to Philadelphia. South, Baltimore. Either way, there are plenty of strong local drug organizations. Competition. Hard for a small operation to survive, even if there's a big parent somewhere else."

"But what about west and north?" I said.

"Ah, now you're getting somewhere. West, you've got the turnpike. Rural. Not much of a drug scene till you get all the way to Pittsburgh, and then you run into the same problems as Philadelphia or Baltimore. I'm not saying she might not be somewhere to the west, like Johnstown or Altoona, but we got to play the percentages. It's a big state and you don't have much time."

"Go on."

He traced his finger north from Harrisburg, snaking up the middle of the state toward the New York line. "Here's my bet, folks. U.S. routes 11 and 15. Same road's got two numbers. Don't ask me why. If I knew stuff like that I wouldn't be stuck in crappy motels. Runs along the west bank of the Susquehanna from Maryland to the middle of the state, then they split around Sunbury. Fifteen keeps going north all the way to New York and 11 goes northeast and connects up with Interstate 81 near Scranton. So 11 and 15's a major highway, with good connections at both ends, running through the middle of nowhere. It's got drugs coming up from Florida from guys who don't want to use 95, and from Chicago by dealers who take the turnpike to Harrisburg and then head north. And it goes the other way, too. Drugs coming out of New York and New

England get distributed all over central Pennsylvania through this road."

"But it's three hundred miles long," I said. "Where do we start?"

"We're looking for somebody who's close to 11 and 15, but secluded enough to stay out of sight. Especially if he's holding a kidnap victim. So that excludes the major towns themselves, like Williamsport, Sunbury, Lewisburg, Wellsboro, Selinsgrove. My bet would be somewhere off 15, between Middleburg and Williamsport."

I looked at the map, and then the scale. "That still covers seventy miles of road, and who knows how much country off to the side."

"They may have made it easier for you."

"Oh?"

"If the victim is being held by a dealer who is working out of a distribution site for just a few days, you'll never find it. You have to assume they have a permanent location or you might as well go back to bed."

"That's not very encouraging."

"Encouragement ain't my business."

"What should I be looking for? I mean, when I see the place, what will I be looking at?"

He leaned back and put his hands behind his head. "That's one I don't have to think about much. Something fairly isolated, like a farmhouse or cabin, set well back from the road, but with a good road nearby."

"Can I expect guards or fences?"

"No fences, definitely not. Maybe a couple of guards if they're in the middle of something, like getting rid of a major shipment. Otherwise they try to keep a real low profile."

"Can you give us an introduction to somebody in law enforcement in the area?"

He looked at the map. "I'm on a regional drug task force. I work with Lewisburg sometimes, and Williamsport, but—hey, wait a minute. There's a detective on the Selinsgrove force. Vic Peters." An unpleasant expression crossed his face, and he looked at his watch. "I'll give him a call once it gets a little later."

"Thanks," I said.

He stood up and showed us to the door. I shook his hand. "I appreciate your help. Thanks again for everything."

"Hope I turn out to be some help."

At that moment the phone rang and he picked it up. After a moment he turned to us with his hand over the speaker. "It's my wife. Am I getting a raft. She's worried about me. Thinks I'm on a dangerous assignment."

"Imagine that," said Lisa.

Chapter Fourteen

Thursday 10:00 A.M.

We stopped at my place long enough to shower and change. The water turned pink when I washed my hair. Until I saw the blood I had forgotten the cuts on my head. The hot water was relaxing, so much so that I needed two more Fastins afterward just to keep moving. I put on a fresh suit—it was shiny at the knees and the lining was ripped, but it was the best I had left. Then I called my office and left word that if Frank McMahan called, we would be at the Harrisburg airport around noon.

I was warming some of last night's coffee in the microwave when Lisa came into the kitchen, drying her hair on one of my bath towels. She was dressed for a day at the office; a white blouse buttoned to the neck, dark skirt, and flat shoes. No jewelry or makeup; Lisa didn't need any. And no nylons, I noticed. She didn't need those, either, except to stay warm in the winter. She sat at the kitchen table, still rubbing her hair, and I set down a mug of coffee for her.

"Do we need to take anything special?" she asked. "Anything from your office?"

"The only thing we need is lots of money for bribes, and I don't have any."

Something about being teamed with Lisa—for the second time in eight hours I'd delivered myself of a stupidity. She gave her hair one final shake and put down her towel. "I'd be happy to help," she said, "if that's what it takes."

"We're not talking about fifty bucks to fix a speeding ticket. We're talking thousands, maybe tens of thousands, and you might not ever get it back, at least not anytime soon."

"So?"

I tried to avoid answering her. "You're pretty casual about money."

"I survived before I had it and I'll survive without it if I need to."

"You'd do that for her? You've never even met her."

She shook her head. "You saved my life, too, you know. I'd do it for you."

"You've been more help already than I have the right to ask for."

"It's not just that you helped me, David. That part was your job." She avoided my eyes and ran one of her fingernails around the rim of her mug. "It's that you know who I am and it doesn't bother you."

"There are lots of people who wouldn't be bothered. There's nothing special about me."

She gave a little snort of disbelief. "You sell yourself *way* short, David. Way short."

"I think you're the one who sells herself short."

She looked at me, startled, without saying anything. Then she set down her cup and left the room without meeting my eyes. A moment later I heard the whirr of the hair dryer.

We had a minor argument about transportation arrangements that was resolved with Lisa's car being left behind and her driving my Civic. Like most compromises, it made both of us about equally unhappy.

We had just reached the turnpike when she decided she wanted to talk. "It's going to be a good two hours up there. Why don't you get some sleep?"

"Thanks. I'd just as soon stay awake."

"David, you haven't slept since Tuesday night, and you're going to need your wits about you."

"I don't feel right, sleeping."

"Oh." She was quiet for a while. "You mean, you don't want to sleep till this is all over."

I looked out the window. "I've got this funny feeling that staying awake keeps her alive. It's something I'm doing for her."

"And if you go to sleep?"

"That I don't deserve her."

"Huh."

"I was talking to a bartender at the airport. It's got my mind going in some funny directions."

"Sounds more like you're remembering your mythology. Orpheus and Eurydice."

"I'm not remembering it *that* well. Tell me the story and help me stay awake."

"Orpheus played an instrument, a flute or a lyre or something. He played the most beautiful music in the world. He was madly in love with Eurydice. I can't remember if they were married or not. She was bitten by a snake and died. Orpheus was crazy with grief. He went down after her to the underworld. There was a three-headed dog, Cerberus, who guarded the entrance, but it let him pass when he played his music. Then he played before the god of the underworld himself, Hades. He played so beautifully that Hades felt pity and cried. He let Eurydice go."

"But that's not the point of the story, is it?"

"You want the rest?"

"Yeah."

"There was a condition. Orpheus wasn't to look at her till they reached the surface. He climbed and climbed. He heard her footsteps behind him the whole way. He was almost to the surface when he turned and looked back. In that instant she was snatched away—all he got was a glimpse of her fading back into the shadows. He tried to go back again but they wouldn't let him pass a second time. He wandered the earth alone and died of a broken heart."

I looked out the window again. "Nothing like a cheery story."

"You said you wanted it all." Then her voice became sharper. "David, look at me."

"Why?"

"Just do it." I turned my face toward her. "David, you're crying."

I wiped my eyes on the sleeve of my raincoat. "It's just that the story reminds me of something Kate said once."

"She must really be something."

"Why do you say that?"

"I've never had a man cry for *me*. That's a pretty flattering thing, you know."

"Let's hope she gets a chance to appreciate it."

"So, tell me about her."

"As long as you're not going to be jealous."

She laughed. "Dave, as far as being involved, you and I are strictly history. I'm dating somebody and I'm very happy that you've found Kate. You're a friend in trouble who helped me when I needed it, and that's all. So go ahead. It's not going to hurt my feelings."

I wasn't surprised, but somehow I felt better with that out of the way. "What do you want to know?"

"Anything you want to tell me."

"She's a very striking woman. Not cute or pretty, but you notice her. She has a real Irish redhead complexion, that kind of creamy skin, and big, bright green eyes. Really clear, emerald green, not that muddy brown color. Flaming red hair. It's quite a contrast with her skin. She has no chest or hips at all. Lean and wiry, and very strong for her size. Works out with weights a lot. She's an English teacher. What got to me just now was that she thinks in terms of Greek myths, too. For a second it was like having her here in the car."

"Just how well do you know her?"

"As well as two people can, under the circumstances, I guess. She understands things about me that I don't. Like the dream about Vietnam I used to have?"

"You scared the heck out of me. I thought you were going nuts."

"I talked it out with her and I haven't had it since."

"I'm impressed. So what's she like as a person?"

It was the kind of question women always ask and men never answer very well. "I don't know what to say. She's smart, very smart. And very independent. She loved teaching but every time we talked she complained about regulations and red tape." I fell silent when I realized I was talking about her in the past tense.

We watched the scenery roll by. Lisa talked about herself for a while after that, filling me in on some of the loose ends of her own case. Then, almost in midsentence, she was back to Kate. "David, we're going to be at the Harrisburg airport pretty soon, aren't we?"

"Maybe ten more minutes."

"I hadn't thought of that, but yes. I'll go in and ask for McMahan." She brushed her hair behind her ear. "And—uh—I think you ought to look for that cabdriver again."

"He told me he was telling me all that he knew."

"He was lying. If he had nothing to hide he wouldn't have given you such a hard time. He saw something he shouldn't have. Something very specific. Maybe he recognized at least some of the people she was with."

I thought about it every way I could. She was right. "Okay, so I screwed up. Let's see if I can make it up."

We stopped at the Harrisburg airport and Lisa went inside to look for Frank, or any messages. I looked for the cabbie but he was nowhere to be found. I asked the other drivers. The man I was looking for was a temporary driver who only worked once or twice a week. No one knew where he lived or when he'd be working again. The cab company refused to even confirm that he worked for them.

I waited for Lisa near my car. She'd done a little better, but not much. Frank McMahan, or at least someone using his name, had arrived the day before at 1:15 P.M. on a flight from Atlanta that had left Miami at 9:30 that morning. No return reservation. He'd rented a car from National and hadn't been seen since. The car hadn't been returned to any National office.

I looked out at the parking lot, wondering where the van had been parked. And where the cabdriver was. And why I'd made a mess of interrogating him. Sloppy. Then I closed my eyes and rubbed my hand across my face. When I opened them Lisa was looking at me.

"Dave, take a few minutes and get some coffee."

"You're right about the cabdriver," I said. "If he hadn't known who it was, he wouldn't have been scared."

"There's nothing to do about it now."

"I had an *eyewitness* and I let him get away," I said.

"So we go on from here."

"So I can screw up somewhere else?"

She put her hand on my arm. "We don't have time for this," she said quietly. "Go get some coffee and let's keep going. You're too tired to think clearly."

She was right about that. I asked her if she wanted to come along but she said no. I think she wanted me to have a few minutes by myself. I went back into the terminal and sat down in the snack shop with a large coffee and something yellow and stale they claimed was a Danish. After a few sips of coffee things started coming back into focus. I chewed the Danish methodically—the only way it could be eaten—and started thinking about the search.

A shadow fell across the table and I looked up. A big, swarthy man in a tropical pattern shirt was staring down at me. A bulging pair of hairy forearms were folded across his chest. The neck of his shirt was open, and I could see a few links of gold chain nested among the chest hairs that started just below his neck. Except for a hint of gray at the temples, his close-cropped hair was black. His face showed the signs of the premature aging caused by too much time in the tropical sun.

I felt my face flush red and my palms go moist, part of the hidden wiring that kept my ancestors alive when they were still swinging in the trees. I'd been caught off base with someone else's mate, and all my instincts were telling me to run. No matter what kind of a husband he'd been, I'd taken his wife and I was in the wrong. "I guess you're Frank McMahan."

"I was wondering what you would look like." I sensed a hint of alcohol in the air after he spoke.

"I'm sorry we had to meet like this," I said. "Have a seat."

He didn't move. "I'd appreciate it if you stayed away from other men's wives."

I looked him in the eye. "Let's talk about things we can change, okay?"

"Who's that with you? I seen you in the parking lot after they paged me."

"Her name's Lisa. I brought her along as my assistant."

"You sure you can trust her?"

"Absolutely. She's been a lot of help already."

"A lot of help? So where's Kate?"

I sighed. "I didn't say we've found her, just that we're making progress. Sit down and I'll tell you."

He sat down and leaned back in his chair, his arms still folded. "I want you to know—"

"Do you want Kate to get out of this safely or not? If you just want to take cheap shots at me, fine. It's just that I don't have time for that right now."

"All I see you doing is sitting around drinking coffee," he grumbled. But at least he'd uncrossed his arms.

I didn't feel like confessing to him how tired I was. "What made you decide to come up?" I asked.

"What kind of a question is that?"

"I mean, what's your plan?" I asked.

"If she's not in Miami and she's not in Philly, she's here, or somewhere around here. What are you doing to find her?"

I ignored him. "What does Kate have to do with drugs?"

"Nothing, nothing at all," he said quickly.

"You're lying, Frank."

"You have the nerve to call me—"

"Cut it out, once and for all. We don't have time for this."

He shoved his chair back and stood up. I didn't know if he was going to take a swing or if he was just threatening to leave.

"Sit down," I said. "Either that, or stop wasting my time. I've already talked to the police. I can always go talk to them again."

He looked at me for a long moment, then sat down again. It was a while before he spoke again, and when he did, the belligerence was gone. "Nobody likes the government sticking its nose into your business, especially if you're self-employed."

"Depends what you're self-employed at."

"Think you're pretty funny, don't you?" But he kept his voice low, and he sounded more frightened than angry.

"Tell me just what the police are going to find if they come around."

He looked down at the plastic tabletop and drummed his fingers for a minute before he raised his eyes. "It's not easy being a small businessman in South Florida. There's—"

"Give me the one-minute version. I'm not from the Small Business Administration."

He took a deep breath and looked around to make sure no one was listening. Then he leaned closer. "I gotta know that I can trust you not to let this go any further. I would be in real deep shit if it did."

There was no privilege of confidentiality in Pennsylvania between a private detective and his client, let alone between myself and McMahan, but I didn't feel like telling him that. I just said, "Go on."

"I do work on the mainland, but on some of the islands, too. Private houses, small hotels, stuff like that. A few years back I was finishing a job, a private pier in the Bahamas, when a guy comes up to me and says he wants to buy my heavy equipment, a front-end loader and a small roller. He pays a good price and it saves me the shipping home. But back in Miami, I get this call, my container shipment is in. I think to myself, what container? I go down to the docks and this guy, different one, tells me not to worry, just sign for it and walk away. While I'm thinking about what to do, he hands me an envelope with some serious cash inside. So I did." He shrugged and fell silent.

The details of the story sounded a little embellished, but the broad outline seemed plausible enough. "And how many times did something like this happen?"

"Just the once."

"Come on."

"Okay, maybe a couple more."

"How about, every time you had an offshore job after that?" When he didn't answer I went on. "A smuggling ring wouldn't take the risk and trouble of setting you up as a cover and just use you once."

"Maybe half a dozen times. Offshore's been slow the last couple years."

I figured his memory was still on the foggy side, but I wasn't investigating McMahan Construction, anyway. "Did they know Kate was leaving?"

"I don't know. I think they must have."

"And that made them nervous?"

"I don't know," he said. "I'm thinking that it did. You see, I don't have any way of contacting these guys. They always came to me. No names. Different people most of the time."

"You're sure of that?" I asked. "There's no way to even get a message to them?"

"If there was I wouldn't be here."

I told him what Bonowitcz and Lisa and I had discussed. I went over the geography with the help of a road map from the newsstand. I watched him while I talked. He was a muscular man, probably played a hell of a game of football once, but now he was going to seed the way athletes often do at a certain age. He had the beginnings of a bulge around his middle and another, smaller one around his collar. He looked like he needed a shave already, even though I could smell aftershave along with the alcohol.

"So," he said when I was through, "your cop friend was right about Harrisburg. I've spent twenty-four hours driving around, all I seen is a bunch of junkies trying to get from one fix to the next."

"Talk to the police?"

"Sure. Hospitals, too. Nobody knows nothin'. I asked everybody I could think of. I even bought a scanner at Radio Shack, the kind you can plug into your cigarette lighter."

If he was expecting me to be impressed with his hardware, he was wrong. "I thought you didn't want to deal with the police."

He looked around and then leaned closer. The smell of alcohol was stronger. "I like cops just fine. Just not South Florida drug agents." He started to say something, then stopped.

There was something about his expression that interested me. "What?"

"I guess you think I'm being a jerk," he said.

"Yeah, I do. But you're entitled."

"I don't handle the pressure like I did years ago," he admitted. "My nerves aren't what they used to be."

"All the more reason to stay off the sauce. Kate needs as many clear heads as she can get."

"Don't try to tell me what I know already." Then he grunted and looked down at the map. "This Williamsport a big town?"

"Bigger than Selinsgrove, anyway."

He nodded. "Let's say I start asking questions in Williamsport and you take Selinsgrove."

"Ever done any investigating? Or interviewing?"

"No."

"Why don't you let me do this? If you go about this the wrong way, we might spook the wrong people."

"I didn't come up here to sit on my ass."

"Frank, I'll make you a deal. When I want a house built I won't try to do it myself."

"Uh-uh"—he shook his head—"I want to keep an eye on what you're doing."

The awful possibility crossed my mind that he might want to tag along with Lisa and me every step of the way. "Well," I said, "maybe you're right. Tell you what; we'll divide forces, like you said. You take Williamsport and we'll take Selinsgrove."

He looked at the map again and grunted his approval. I gave him my business card. "When you get a room," I said, "let me know where you're going to be staying. If it's after five you can leave a message on the answering machine. I can take off my calls from here." He shoved it into his shirt pocket.

I made one final effort to keep him in the background. "Look, Frank, what do you really expect to accomplish?"

"What are you going to do?" he countered. "Exactly, I mean?"

"Well, look around and ask questions."

"I can ask questions as good as you."

"I hope you're right about that."

He stood up and walked away without shaking hands. I stood up, too. My coffee was cold, and anyway, Lisa and I had a lot to talk about.

Chapter Fifteen

Thursday 1:00 P.M.

We went around Harrisburg and then north on 22 on the east bank of the Susquehanna. It's a shallow river, dotted with islands even during the spring high water, and wide. The low banks make it look even bigger. A few miles above Harrisburg we crossed the river and continued north on the west bank on 11 and 15. It was only two lanes, but very busy with heavy trucks, buses, and cars. The scenery was beautiful—a series of wooded ridges and valleys, with the river on our right. It was too bad neither of us was paying much attention.

Selinsgrove was a quiet town with a broad main street, its brick and clapboard buildings spread out along the western bank of the river. The streets and yards were dotted with old shade trees, most of which were already in leaf. To the right, through gaps in the trees, the river sparkled blue and gray in the sunlight. Some early spring boaters were out, some fishing and some just enjoying the morning. Out of nowhere, I had a sudden, chill vision of Kate at the bottom of the river and I felt like crying again. I blamed it on the caffeine and the pills and kept it to myself.

On our left was a two-story blue stucco house with a wraparound front porch and big white pillars. A sign identified it as the Blue Lion Inn, and Lisa wondered out loud if they had rooms. It was the first lodging I'd seen and I didn't want to waste time. "Looks like it would be okay."

Inside, it was more than okay. It was the kind of place you'd only seen a couple of times before, when you were a kid. It was where a friend of your grandmother's lived, the one whose husband made his money back in railroads at the turn of the century and who'd been collecting furniture and art ever since. Most of the downstairs was an enormous sitting room, with salmon walls and white trim. The room was packed with carpets, sofas, Queen Anne chairs, and bookcases, and it gave off a warm, pleasant, slightly musty smell. Just looking around made me want to take off my shoes and stretch out for a rest.

Lisa was bending over the fireplace, checking to see if it was real, when I heard footsteps behind me. I turned and saw a pleasant-faced woman in jeans and a sweatshirt, with short gray hair. She held a wet rag in one hand and an adjustable wrench in the other. "Hi, I'm Marilyn. Can I help you?"

We were in luck. The place was solidly booked for the weekend, and through most of the summer, but if we only needed rooms through Thursday night she could accommodate us. She ditched the wrench and the rag and showed us upstairs.

If anything, the place was more richly furnished on the second floor, with small statues in stairway niches, chandeliers in the hallways, and oriental runners throughout. Marilyn showed us our rooms, explained the routine, and then went back downstairs, presumably to deal with the plumbing. My room had a double bed with a golden Chinese fan above the headboard and an oriental decor.

I crossed the hall. Lisa had a corner room that faced toward the river. Her queensize bed was dwarfed by an elaborately carved headboard in dark wood with brass trim.

"David, what are you thinking?"

"Unhelpful thoughts."

"Tell me."

"How much I'd like it if Kate and I were here just by ourselves, and this whole thing wasn't happening." I looked around the room. "Ready to get to work?"

"That's what we're here for."

I called my office and let the receptionist know where I was staying. Then we drove two blocks up the road, into the center of town.

Downtown Selinsgrove was an informal, comfortable place that, except for the cars, hadn't changed much in ninety years. The buildings were two-and three-story, mainly brick and mainly Victorian, with a few Queen Annes and Greek Revivals thrown in. Bot's Café. BJ's—A Place for Ribs. Wenzel's Hardware. A sign for Susquehanna University, and another for something called the Isle of Que. George Kinny Antiques. DJ Ernest Books (Used and Rare). About a block past the bookstore the town began to peter out, so I turned around and started to hunt for the police station. "Doesn't look like a lot of drugs get done around here," I said.

"I was thinking the same thing myself."

"Bonowitcz didn't say it would be right in town."

"No." Whatever else she was thinking, she kept it to herself.

The municipal building turned out to be a modern rectangle of brick and glass just outside of the center of town that still managed to blend in with the older buildings nearby. The upper floor was the borough library and council chambers. The police station was in the basement.

We announced ourselves to the dispatcher and asked to see Detective Peters. I would have preferred the chief—I'd dealt with him in a case years before, and I knew him to be a man of good sense. But if Peters was our contact, there was nothing to do but follow through. I sat on a wooden bench in the waiting room while Lisa read the wanted and missing persons notices on the bulletin board.

"Look at this one," she said. "Fifteen-year-old girl named Tara Leigh Calico in New Mexico is riding her bicycle along a state highway. She's last seen a little before noon September 20, 1988."

"Sounds like a runaway, at that age."

"And then June 15, 1989, somebody in a convenience store in a place called Port St. Joe, Florida, finds a picture in the parking lot."

"Of what?"

"It's right here, look. It's a Polaroid, she's tied up inside a car, bound and gagged, and there's a little boy in the background who's tied up, too."

I got up and looked. A slender girl with long blond hair and a T-shirt. It was a clear picture, and I could see her eyes. The girl was terrified. I wondered what had happened to her in those nine months. I wondered what was happening to her now. "This has got to be real," I said.

"Looks like the FBI thinks so, and the parents. There's a reward and an 800 number. The police think the picture was taken in a white late-model Toyota cargo van."

Every time I thought my cup was the most bitter I had a peek at someone else's. "The poor parents," I said. "What kind of thoughts must—" I was interrupted by the appearance of Detective Peters. He was a small man in his early thirties, with a thin face, short dark hair, and a ragged dark mustache. His blazer was buttoned, and cut tight to show off his trim waist. Cut a little too tight for my taste—the bulge of his shoulder holster was obvious if you knew where to look.

"Afternoon, Detective," I said, extending my hand. "We appreciate you seeing us on short notice."

He shook once and dropped my hand. He looked past me. "And who's 'we'?"

"This is Lisa Wilson, my assistant. Lisa, Detective Peters."

Lisa offered her hand, which he accepted without comment. "Back this way, please."

He led us to his tiny windowless office with painted concrete block walls and a table. As we walked in I noticed that he was shorter than Lisa. Somehow it gave me a bad feeling. The walls were covered with newspaper clippings of his cases and photographs of himself in front of the courthouse or shaking hands with what looked like local politicians. My bad feeling became worse.

We sat down and he folded his hands in front of himself on the table. "I received a call about you from Detective Bonowitcz."

I tried to smile. "I hope he said good things about us."

"He said he didn't know you well."

"I asked him to call and introduce us."

"He did that."

"Well, I suppose he told you what we're working on. Can you help us?"

"Did he tell you we had a drug problem in Snyder County? Or in the borough?"

It was Lisa who answered. "He said . . . that 11 and 15 brought in a bad element and that you work hard at controlling it."

He favored us with a tiny smile that disappeared almost as fast as it arrived. "I'm glad he made that clear. Now, what exactly do you want?"

"Well," I said, "we've got a very suspicious disappearance on our hands, and we think it may be linked to drug activity in the county. Not local people, just a local branch of a much larger organization, from Florida maybe."

"I want to show you something," he said. He pointed at a map taped to the wall. "As you can see, the county is basically a square, narrowing as you go west. The western half is largely mountains—there's a couple of big state parks over there, and some state game lands. It's rugged country with bad roads. Except for the valleys, the most use it gets is during deer season—it's dotted with hunting camps. The eastern half, where most of the people live, is more or less tillable. We've got 11 and 15 in the east, along the river, bringing in their trash, and they have all these mountains to hide in. If this woman is in those mountains you'll never find her. Maybe a hunter will, someday, but I wouldn't bet on it."

I restrained my urge to tell him that I didn't need his help to read a map. "We were hoping for some specific help from you. Information."

"You know how drug enforcement works? We put the pinch on users who turn in low-level dealers and work our way up the line. The further you go the harder it gets. And the whole chain can unravel if there's a breakdown in—expectations, shall we say."

"What he's telling us," I said to Lisa, "is no, he won't help."

"No, that's not true," he said. "I'm prepared to give you a list of known dealers in the county, on the condition that you don't tell them how you learned their names."

I was impressed. "Well, that would be great. We appreciate that."

"Do I have your word? Both of you?"

"Yes."

He handed over a typewritten sheet of paper with six names and addresses. I looked at the list and then at the map. "These are all bars and stores in Selinsgrove and Shamokin Dam and Middleburg."

"That's right."

I swallowed hard and worked on keeping my voice businesslike. "Detective, we're not looking to score a joint. We're looking for a major criminal organization. I don't think we're going to find it at"—I consulted the list—"the Dew Drop By in Middleburg."

"Well, we don't know that yet, do we?" His lips made a prim, narrow line.

"If you're not going to help why don't you just say so?"

"I *am* helping." He pointed his finger at the list in my hand. "If you don't like the food, don't eat it."

"The person I'm looking for needs all the help you can give."

"And this is it."

"Like hell."

We faced each other angrily across the table till Lisa put a hand on my arm and gave a squeeze. She was right. Time was short, and we might as well get to work with what we had. We thanked Peters curtly and left. On the way out, Lisa reminded me that we ought to tell Peters where to find us. I wrote my name on a Blue Lion business card and handed it to the receptionist without comment.

We went back to the bed-and-breakfast, carried our bags inside, and unpacked. I tried running some cold water over my face, but it didn't help. I was losing my way, slowing down, and I knew it. Soon I was going to run into an obstacle I wouldn't have the drive to overcome and that would be it. I would peter out, go to sleep, and whatever was going to happen would happen without me. . . .

I saw that Lisa was sitting on my bed. "What's on your mind?" she asked.

"Why are you asking?"

"Because you're standing there like you're in a fog. You're tired."

"Yeah," I admitted.

"And something else is on your mind."

"I've got this bad feeling. That somehow we're going about this all wrong." I rubbed my hand across my face, feeling the stubble I'd missed.

"What should we be doing?"

"I don't know. Just that this doesn't feel right."

"You want to try Harrisburg? Or farther west?"

I shook my head. "No. This is as good a place as any. Bonowitcz made sense to me. There's just something wrong with this whole thing and I can't decide what it is."

"You've got to get some rest."

"I can rest when this is over," I said.

"You've been lucky so far. The next chance you take could get you killed."

"Then there'll be plenty of time to rest."

"What makes you so sure we have to be in such a hurry?"

"Are you prepared to bet her life that we can afford business as usual?"

"Do you trust Frank McMahan?" she asked.

"He knows more than he's telling."

"Could he be working with the people who kidnapped her?"

"No," I said. "If he is, he's going about it in a pretty funny way. He's into them deeper than he wants to admit to us, or maybe even to himself, but I think he really wants to see that she's safe."

"Then why isn't he being more helpful to us?"

"Because he doesn't trust us any more than we trust him. Anyway, he may not know anything useful. It's one thing for him to admit the exact number of drug shipments he was involved with, but that doesn't mean he knows where she is."

She sighed. "So what next?"

"It's time to split up," I told her. "At least for a little while. Two of the places on the list are right here in Selinsgrove. I'm going to run them down, for what good they are. You're going to need to stay by the phone in case Frank or Annie calls. As a matter of fact, call Annie and make sure she knows where we are. And find yourself a good map of the county and see if you come up with any ideas of where else to look."

"I think we'd be better off staying together."

"You're just saying that because you like going to dives."

She gave me a shrug that reminded me of Ianucci.

My first stop was the Corbett Hotel, on the northern edge of town, only a few blocks away. The afternoon was warming up so I decided to walk. I was glad I did; the exercise got my blood moving, at least a little, and by the time I reached the hotel I was probably up to nearly 60 percent of my normal level of alertness.

I'd never been in the Corbett Hotel before, but I might as well have. It was the kind of small-town bar you might find around almost any bend in the road. An old brick building, two stories, with a sagging tin roof and an addition on the back made out of unpainted cinder block. The name was displayed on a small neon sign in the filthy front window.

Inside it was a little more pleasant. The barroom was wallpapered with a mural of a hunting scene, done in delicate greens and yellows, that had to be fifty years old. A couple of old-timers were sitting at the bar, still wearing their red checked jackets and baseball caps. A plump woman in the rear, by the cooler, was sitting at a table, going over a ledger book. She didn't look too happy with the figures. When she saw me she put down her pencil and waddled over.

"Afternoon, sir. What can I get you?"

"I'll start with a beer. What do you have on tap?"

"Bud and Rolling Rock."

"Rolling Rock."

"Bar or table?"

"Table, please."

She wiped off the table before she set down the glass, which wasn't just a polite gesture. "You the owner?" I asked.

"My husband and I."

"Have a seat a second. I need to talk to you."

She pulled up a chair and put down her towel. "What's this about?"

I took a sip of my beer. Keeping my voice low, I leaned toward her. "I hear a fellow can get more than beer here."

She looked over her shoulder at the regulars, but they were paying no attention. "Where'd you hear that?"

"Mmm. Around."

"I don't think I've ever seen you before."

"My name's Dave Garrett. I live down near Philadelphia."

"You're not with the LCB, are you?"

"Hell, no."

"Good. Those creeps gave me a thirty-day suspension last summer for serving minors, lost the last part of July and near the whole month of August. Just about run us out of business."

"I don't care about any of that. I'm not even that much of a drinker."

"So you need something a little different, huh?"

I smiled. "You've got that one right."

She dropped her voice so far I could barely hear. "I could meet you somewhere off the property and sell you some marijuana cigarettes."

"Oh?"

She licked her lips nervously. "Dollar apiece."

"I was thinking in terms of something a little larger. Maybe a couple of lids."

"How much is that?" she asked.

"Well, how many cigarettes you got?"

She thought about it. "About four, if he ain't smoked them yet."

"You have any of it loose?"

"No, just them cigarettes."

I asked about every drug I could think of and received

a steady stream of negative answers. "Tell me," I finally asked. "If I was interested in something else, got anybody I should go see?"

She thought about it. "I don't know. Maybe if you drove up to Williamsport you might run into somebody. It's a big town."

"You know about anybody local? I've heard that somebody who drives a van has some good stuff. I'm not sure, but I've heard that he's Hispanic."

"You mean a Mex?"

So much for political correctness in Selinsgrove. "Or maybe Puerto Rican."

She considered: "We got some Mexes working a mushroom operation over near Milton. But none of thems got no van. They're all illegals. Don't even have driver's licenses, I suspect."

"Could they have drugs?"

She laughed. "Mister, they don't have no pots to piss in and no windows to throw it out of. They ain't selling nothing."

"Well, thanks for your time." I stood up and put a dollar on the table.

"You still want the cigarettes?"

"I'll think about it."

"I could go dollar-fifty for two."

"Thanks, I'll let you know."

In ten minutes I was back at the bed-and-breakfast. Lisa was sitting at a table in the downstairs sitting room, a telephone book in her lap and a county map spread out on the table. "How'd it go?" she asked.

I sat across from her and leaned close. "I could have had more action in any Philadelphia schoolyard on a Sunday morning. The Corbett Hotel people aren't exactly desperadoes. They probably pay sales tax on the dope they sell."

"The rest of the list looked like more of the same," she said.

I unfolded it. "One of them is a bait shop. A damned *bait shop.*" I threw it down on the table. "This isn't getting us anywhere."

"So we need a lead of our own," she said. "Someplace not so squeaky clean."

"And how are we going to do that?"

"There's a cocktail lounge just down the street."

"So?"

She pursed her lips. "Give me a chance."

She took a piece of red ribbon from around a flower arrangement, stood in front of one of the big floor-to-ceiling mirrors, and tied up her hair. As many times as I'd seen her without clothes, I'd never really noticed she had such a long and beautiful neck. She left a single dark tendril of hair curling down toward one ear. She put on some perfume, and started opening buttons till the lace of her bra was showing.

She looked at herself critically in the mirror and turned her head slowly from side to side. "I'm looking to create a certain effect."

"If you want to know if you look like a wet dream, you do."

She played with the curl by her ear, studying her reflection, and frowned. "No. Not yet, anyway. I don't look desperate enough."

"What?"

She unzipped her skirt and let it fall to the floor. She wasn't wearing a slip, and the bottom of her blouse reached about a third of the way down her thighs. I wondered what she was going to put on instead, but she just took the belt out of her skirt and cinched it tight around her waist. The hem of her blouse rode up even further.

"Jesus Christ," was all I could say.

She continued watching her reflection. "Yeah, that's more like it."

"You can't go out like that."

"Sure I can. People will think it's just a short dress. Now I'm going over to the lounge, tell them I'm dee-vorced and lookin' for a place where a girl can have some *real* fun."

"Aren't you going to need your purse?"

She shook her head. "I won't be paying for anything."

"You can't go out like that," I insisted. "I mean, your underwear is going to be showing."

She shook her head definitely. "No, it won't."

She was out the door before I figured it out.

I poured myself a couple of cups of the complimentary coffee while I studied the map. She'd found a large-scale map of Snyder County, showing every little hamlet, creek, and secondary road. It was depressing to think how big the county really was, and how easy it would be to hide one van and a woman. The job had seemed more manageable when I was working off a smaller map. And who was to say she was here at all?

Lisa was back in a little more than an hour, smelling of cigarettes and scotch. But if she'd been doing any drinking herself, it didn't show. "Know where Richfield is?"

"With the map I bet we can find it."

"We're looking for the Low Down Pub."

"Sounds dirty and dangerous."

"Yeah." She smiled. "That's what I hear, too."

Chapter Sixteen

Thursday 4:00 P.M.

The Low Down Pub wasn't in Richfield, exactly, or on the road to Richfield. In fact, it wasn't on a road at all. If we hadn't stopped for directions at the only gas station in Richfield we'd never have found it. Our route took us out of town on a secondary road, then onto a dirt road that led into a patch of woods. After that we saw a scrapyard, which on closer examination turned out to be a trailer park. The front yards were littered with old cars, washing machines, bedding, and broken furniture. I even saw a lawn mower, though I couldn't imagine where there was any grass to mow. The trailers themselves were in only marginally better condition than the junk out front.

"It's like the third world," Lisa said.

"I can turn up the heat. You look like you're cold."

"That's not why I'm shivering. These poor people . . . What a way to live."

I continued up the dirt road through the middle of the park and out the other end. We entered another patch of woods and then came into a large clearing, with the pub in the middle. I couldn't say if I was looking at half a dozen buildings that had grown together or one building that had sprouted lots of dissimilar additions. The largest part was a weather-beaten wood frame building with a high roof that looked like it might have started out as a farmhouse. Built onto one side was a big brick square with no windows. The other side was a gas station built of unpainted block. Peeking out from behind the gas station was the top of a storage shed that must have stood twenty feet high. About a dozen vehicles were parked out front, mostly pickup trucks. Not the fancy ones with two-tone paint jobs and plastic liners in the beds—these were working trucks, with dents, body rust, and NRA stickers on the bumpers. Most were loaded with hay or firewood.

"There isn't a sign," I said.

"Any doubt we're in the right place?"

"None at all."

"Let me go in first," she suggested. "I'll be able to make friends a lot easier if I'm alone."

"I'll give you five minutes and get a seat at the bar," I said. "Be careful."

She thought that was funny. "We're not here for careful."

"You know what I mean. Don't take any unnecessary chances and don't get out of my sight."

"Okay, boss."

I got out of the car and walked slowly around the building while she went inside. A mobile home was built into the rear of the building, and what looked like a loading dock of pressure-treated lumber was attached to the rear. I guessed that the mobile home was used for storage. Three tow trucks were parked to the rear, all new. None of them had any writing on the doors. Or yellow caution lights on the roofs. Whatever the trucks were used for, they were obviously kept busy. The mud was crisscrossed with dozens of sets of tire tracks and the trucks themselves were dirty. I could hear noises coming from the big storage shed, but the overhead doors were shut and I couldn't see what was going on. It sounded like car repair noises. Or maybe car disassembly noises. As I circled back around toward the front I came upon the unpainted block gas station. A pickup truck with no wheels was on the lift but no one was in sight. I walked back around to the front and went inside.

The place was dark, and for a moment I couldn't see anything at all. Then my eyes started to get adjusted. At first it didn't look like a bar at all. For one thing, there was no bar. The place was crowded with small tables, all bearing green glass ashtrays so large that there was no room for dishes, only glasses. Toward the back I saw the inevitable pool table with a bunch of men in baseball caps and cue sticks clustered around. The bartender was working off of an ordinary kitchen table with the bottles, glasses, and mixers spread out on top. No mirror behind him, rows of bottles, or taps. No neon beer signs. The tables were all set with silverware, though I couldn't see how there was any table room for food. I remembered there was no sign out front, and smiled. This was an unlicensed bar, ready to turn into a simple country café on a few minutes' notice if the LCB inspectors should happen by. I had a feeling that just maybe I'd come to the right place.

The bartender, who looked a lot like my image of Paul Bunyan, came out from around the table and headed me off before I could see anything more. "I don't think I know you," he said. Knowing him was obviously a prerequisite to admission.

"I'm just here for a drink."

"Somebody send you?"

"I heard about the place in town. In Selinsgrove."

He looked me up and down. "You know anybody here?"

"My sister's here."

"Where?"

I looked around and pointed to a table nearby, where Lisa

was sitting with a fat man in a baseball cap. He was hunched over, leaning on the table with his elbows. She was leaning back, her legs stretched out and crossed at the ankles. If she wasn't enjoying herself she was a hell of an actress.

"Over there."

"Sister, huh?"

"Yeah."

He came closer and for a moment I thought he was going to throw me out, but he just wanted a little more privacy for our conversation. "Call her what you want," he said in a low voice, "but if she gets any action here the house takes a third."

"Action?"

"Come on, you know what I mean."

I nodded and stroked my chin. "Does that include a room?"

He shook his head. "That's extra. Twenty bucks for twenty minutes."

"Mmm. That's steep."

"Hey, it's got a water bed. And a mirror on the ceiling."

"Your third's your third," I assured him. "But she doesn't need the room. She can work out of one of the trailers for five, or use the car for nothing. That girl can take the chrome off a trailer hitch."

"So you say."

"On a bad day," I said truthfully, "she can make you sit up and howl at the moon."

He looked at her wistfully. "What do you care about how much the room costs? You just pass it along."

The bar was about half full, but Lisa was the only woman. A couple of men at other tables were watching her. "You're the one who should care," I said. "If she doesn't use it, it doesn't get used at all."

He sighed. "The boss ain't gonna like this."

"He'll like it if you bring in something instead of nothing."

"Okay. Ten bucks for twenty minutes till eight. Regular rate after that."

I shook my head sadly. "No, eight's too early. Make it ten o'clock."

"Nine, or the hell with it."

"You got a deal. Now how about a beer?"

"Two bucks. Miller or Yingling."

"Yingling."

I took my beer to a table between Lisa and the door, just out of earshot but close enough to keep an eye on things. I poured it out and reflected that if I ever lost my PI license at least I had a natural aptitude for pimping. If I had five girls and they each worked . . .

I started checking out the room. It was a middle-aged crowd, farmers and blue-collar workers, with a couple of younger men who didn't fit clearly into either category. Most everyone seemed to know one another. Except for the jukebox, which was playing an uninterrupted series of country and western songs, the room was quieter than I would have expected. Then I realized that about a third of the men were trying to eavesdrop on the man who was talking to Lisa. I couldn't tell whether they were urging him on, speculating on whether she was a pro, or just participating vicariously. I kept watch and listened to the music. For a Philadelphia boy I'd always had a soft spot for country music. Rock and roll is fine for teenagers—it's about getting laid, which is all most of them ever think about. But C & W is grown-ups' music. It's about being stuck with who you are—about working at a job you hate, your dreams of getting ahead, trying to get along with your stepkids, and feeling guilty about your bad habits but not being able to stop.

After a while I noticed a skinny young man in a black T-shirt with greasy black hair and a wisp of a mustache. He didn't have a drink in front of him and he was watching me. I nodded slightly to him and he came over without a second urging.

"Mind if I sit down?" he asked.

"Go right ahead." When he put his arms on the table I was amazed at how thin they were. He wasn't wearing any rings or even a wristwatch, but he had two gold earrings in one ear. I guess I'm old-fashioned, but personally I needed a watch a hell of a lot more than I needed even one earring.

"You—ah—with her?" He jerked his head in Lisa's direction.

"Oh, her. Well, yeah, I guess so."

He leaned even closer. "Are you the guy I gotta talk to?"

I took a sip of my beer. It tasted like hell and I spit it back into the glass. I'd had Yinglings before and they never tasted anything like this. I wondered if they were mislabeling, or whether they just didn't take care to keep their beer cold. "You talk to the bartender?"

"He told me to see you."

"Then it's all right. You like her?"

"Sure."

"What did you have in mind?"

He lowered his face and blushed. "You know."

"So nothing special, right?"

He looked puzzled but finally shook his head no.

"You got money?"

"Well, some."

"You know, that's not really a problem."

"That's good."

"Because I'm not really interested in money. I'm interested in finding something out."

" 'Bout what?" He didn't say anything more, but the look on his face told me I'd finally found someone with something to hide. I felt my pulse beating a little faster.

"Hey, relax, I'm not a cop. I just want to know something."

"Yeah?"

I leaned closer until my mouth was only a few inches from his ear. "I'm looking to score some stuff. Big. Not just a joint or a few lids or some coke. I hear there's a major operation around here, guys with connections to Florida. The way I hear it, at least some of them are Spanish. They have cars and a van and they're pretty well hidden. I'm looking to make contact with these guys."

He shook his head. "Jeez, man, I don't know."

"But you know where they are?"

"I know who you mean. But you can't cross these guys, man. They'll come after you and then *me*."

"They don't need to know about you."

"What are you going to tell them? That you saw their ad in the yellow pages?"

"Just let me worry about that one."

"Hey, man, that's not the way it works. I turn you on to them, I'm responsible for you, and I don't know you from shit."

"That's too bad." Pointedly, I looked over at Lisa. Her dress had ridden up a little more. "I was hoping we could do some business."

"What do you want with these guys?"

"I can distribute for them, back where I'm from."

"Where's that?"

"Philadelphia. Look, I'll be happy to pay you a finder's fee once I put a deal together."

"And what about her?"

"When the deal goes down you get one on the house."

He looked around nervously. "Let's go outside and talk."

Then I did one of the stupidest things I'd ever done.

I let him go out the door first.

When I reached the door and started through, I blinked at the bright light. As I stood on the porch and my eyes tried to make the shift from dark to daylight I sensed motion in front of me. Something small, moving fast. It didn't take long to realize he had a baseball bat and was swinging it at my midsection as hard as he could, but it was already too late. My vision cleared just in time to see his determined face, his teeth clenched, as the bat buried itself deep in my gut.

The impact caught me flat footed. I slammed back into the wooden wall like I'd been flattened by a truck, and the breath went out of me. I opened my mouth but no sound came out and no air would go in. Slowly I slid down the wall until I was lying in a heap of discarded beer cans and cigarette butts. Again I tried to breathe and again nothing happened. He stood over me, the bat in both hands over his shoulder, measuring me for his next swing. Neither my arms nor my legs were working in any useful way. When he took the swing I doubted that I'd even be able to roll onto my side. I was just a lump, waiting for the next blow.

I watched him wind up for his swing, and then pause as the door flew open. From the sound of the heels on the concrete it had to be Lisa. He looked up, annoyed. "Get back, cunt, or the next one has your name on it."

He returned his attention to me and started his downswing. I don't know if he just wanted to break my collarbone or if he was trying to split open my head like a melon. We never found out. Because at that moment I saw a silvery flash and something exploded against the side of his head. I heard a crash and saw glass fragments flying in every direction. He went backward off the porch, dropping the bat, and wound up in the mud of the parking lot on his back. Blood was running freely down one side of his face.

He got to his feet and started back toward us, but Lisa had already picked up his bat and was blocking his path.

He thought about making a rush and then thought better. "They know who you are, bitch!"

She blinked. "Who does?"

He glared at her, then at me. Then he wiped his temple

with a rag he pulled from his back pocket and scrambled out of sight around the end of the building. She took a couple steps after him, then looked at me, questioning. I shook my head no. As much as I wanted him, it was far too dangerous. We had no idea how many friends he had back there.

She helped me to my feet and into the car. By the time she got the seat adjusted and started up, I could speak a few words at a time if I was careful to talk as I exhaled. "Selinsgrove," I whispered.

"Okay." She threw the Civic into gear and we bounced back down the track and into the trailer park.

It was forty minutes back to Selinsgrove, ample opportunity to reflect on how we had been so close and seen it slip through our fingers. At least that was what I was thinking about—neither of us said a word. We parked in front of the inn. Lisa helped me out of the car and followed me up the stairs to my room. I lay down on my bed and Lisa carefully pressed her fingers against my abdomen. "Does that hurt?"

"Not any worse than anywhere else."

"How about here?"

"No. Ouch, that one does."

"Sharp or dull?"

"Dull."

"How's the breathing?"

"It's better when I can sit up."

"So go ahead. I'm done. If you hurt your liver there's nothing I can do about it, but you don't seem to have any broken ribs."

"For a marine I was pretty stupid," I said. "The first liberty after boot camp you learn the trick he pulled on me."

"He looked harmless to me, too." I wasn't sure if she was being honest or was just trying to make me feel better. She got off the bed and took a seat in the wing chair near the fireplace. I lay on my back and looked at the ceiling.

"How did they know about us?" I wondered.

"Who says they did? It could have been just talk."

"I don't think so," I said. "All this is making me like Peters less and less. Where would a Snyder County gang be most likely to have an informer?"

She frowned. "Whatever else he is, he's not crooked."

I palpated my abdomen, searching for the spots that hurt the most. "I'm finding it harder to trust people lately."

"You think he gave us up," Lisa said.

"He may have done it to see if it would provoke a reaction."

"David, I know you don't like him, but you don't believe that, do you?"

"Why not? If we're as big a pair of fools as he thinks we are, there's no harm done."

"If Peters doesn't think that the people we're looking for exist, how does he tell them about us?"

"He doesn't, at least not directly. He just lets the word be known among a few people, who can be counted on to tell a few people. . . ."

"I wish you'd let me go after the guy with the bat," Lisa said.

"For all we know there were five guys with shotguns and a van waiting right around the corner. If they were smart enough to set us up they were smart enough for that."

"You'll have to explain the 'us' part to me."

There was a knock on the door and Frank stuck his head inside. "Okay to come in?"

"Sure." I smiled, wondering what else could go wrong. Lisa sat up straight and pulled down her shirt as far as it would go.

McMahan stopped just inside the door, his hands on his hips, looking a lot fresher than he had at the airport. He was wearing a sports jacket and shirt that were more or less suited to a Pennsylvania April, and he'd washed his hair. He didn't exactly need a shave, but his face looked like it could have benefited from a closer acquaintance with his razor.

"I'd like you to meet my assistant, Lisa Wilson." They nodded politely at each other from across the room. I think that she was afraid of how much leg she would show if she let go of the hem and tried to stand up.

He looked around the room. "Nice place you have here."

"This is my room," I explained. "Lisa's is down the hall."

He looked Lisa up and down and then looked at me. "Yeah." There was no point in arguing with him.

He moved a little closer and sat down on the bed. "How we doing?" he wanted to know.

"We thought we had something this afternoon," said Lisa, "but it didn't pan out."

His face began to darken. "This case keeps slipping away from you—"

"Frank, we're making progress. Really, we are." I tried to sound more certain than I felt. The trouble was that McMahan was right.

"So what's this progress?"

I told him the story as briefly as I could, trying not to make myself look like too big an idiot. It wasn't easy. "So," he said when I was done. "Think we ought to go back there? The three of us?"

I shook my head. "We've spooked the game. Anyway, there's no way to know if they knew anything or if this was just some kind of shakedown. It wouldn't have been too hard to hear about us and decide to play us for suckers. Anyway, you get anywhere?"

"I drove around Williamsport half the day. Showed Kate's picture at hotels, restaurants, gas stations, even checked with the police and the hospital. Nada."

"It's like that a lot of the time."

"You really don't know what you're doing, do you? You're just hanging around, asking questions, hoping that something will fall out of the sky."

"Investigations are like that sometimes, especially if

you're not sure you're in the right area. Talk to any cop—it's needles and haystacks."

He wasn't listening. "If she's around here, she's not in a town. We need to check the boonies tomorrow."

I had a vision of Frank in the backseat. "Fine, but let's keep split up. We'll cover more ground that way."

"I've been looking at the map. I'll take the backwoods around Williamsport and you work down here."

I considered. "I don't know. I've driven over most of this county already. Maybe we should try somewhere else tomorrow. Maybe closer to Harrisburg, or farther west."

He hesitated, then shrugged. "Okay. Just be sure I know how to reach you."

"You can check with my office. I'll be sure they know."

He gave me the number of his hotel and let himself out without saying good-bye to either of us. Unless, of course, you count the grunt.

"Hell of a guy," Lisa said.

"You should have seen him this morning. He's better now."

"He's right, though, about where to look. We're not going to find her in any downtown anywhere."

I was too tired to think of an answer. After a while she got up and padded down the hall toward her bathroom. I sat on the bed and pored over the county map.

The phone rang. "Hello?" I said.

"Is this David Garrett?" A male voice, slightly accented.

"Sure is. Go ahead."

The line was quiet for a moment, and I wondered if I'd been cut off. Then a new voice came on, a woman this time.

"David?"

"Yes."

"It's Kate."

Chapter Seventeen

Thursday 6:00 P.M.

"Kate! Are you all right?" I sat down heavily on the bed. "Please tell me you're all right."

"I am, David. I'm fine."

"Where are you? You know I've been looking for you for two days? Where are you? I'll come get you."

"You can't do that, at least not yet."

My brain started to work. "They won't let you say where you are, will they? And we don't have much time before they cut off the call so it can't be traced, right?"

"That's right."

"So you haven't been hurt at all?"

"No, everything's fine. David, I can't say much, but I can tell you this. It's important you understand this. I'm not in any danger. You don't need to look for me anymore. Go back to Philadelphia and wait. Maybe I'll be able to contact you later."

"And maybe not."

"That's all I can say. I have to go now."

"Will you be calling again, at least tell me that."

"Ah—yes, but not here. I'll reach you at your home some time."

"When?"

"I don't—" The connection was broken and I got a dial tone.

Lisa came in, wrapped in a bathrobe and her hair in a towel. "David, I'm sorry—" She looked at my face and stopped. "What's wrong?"

I realized I was still holding the phone. When I set it down I missed the cradle on my first attempt. "She called. Just now. Kate."

"No!"

"It was her, I'm sure of it."

"It couldn't have been a recording?"

"No, I'm sure it wasn't."

"Was there—"

"Look, we can talk about this later. Let's get over to Peters right away."

Somehow, by the time I'd put on my shoes and folded up the map, Lisa had pulled on some jeans and a sweater. We drove to the police station and left the car in the no parking zone out front.

Peters wasn't glad to see us, but at least he was in. He met with us in the same sterile office we'd used before.

"Now, then," he said. "What's this interruption all—"

"Kate called me," I said. "About ten minutes ago, at the Blue Lion."

He took a yellow notepad out of the desk and wrote down the time and date. "Go on."

"She said she couldn't see me and that the call couldn't be long because they didn't want it traced. After a while she was cut off in the middle of a sentence."

"What was the quality of the connection?"

"Excellent. She could have been in the lobby."

"Was there any mention of ransom?"

"No, but there was someone else there, a man with an accent of some kind. He got me on the phone and then put her on."

His pen was poised above the paper. "His name?"

"He didn't leave it."

"Are the room phones direct dial?"

"No, but I already checked with the guy at the desk. He doesn't know anything. He just put it through."

"Did she say anything about when she'd call again?"

"No. But she did say, when I asked her, that she couldn't call me again 'here.' "

"Did she say why?"

"No, but the important thing—" I realized I was starting to shout, so I took a breath and started again. "The important thing is that she said 'here.' Not 'out there' or anything else. That means to me that she's nearby."

"Maybe."

"You don't seem very interested."

"I wouldn't say that. I think it's been an important development."

"I'll say. We know she's alive and possibly close by."

"And that there's no kidnapping," he said.

"Come again?" I asked.

"The 'victim' contacts you herself and talks to you directly. The 'kidnappers' arrange the call and don't make any ransom demand. They don't even tell you if there's going to be a ransom demand. There's no threat of harm to her. As a matter of fact, the whole point of the call is to let you know she's *not* at risk."

"I can't believe I'm hearing this."

"I didn't say we wouldn't be interested in any new information you might turn up. But I hardly think that anyone could say that this call makes a kidnapping a more likely explanation for why your girlfriend doesn't want to see you." He gave me a patronizing smile.

"Then can you explain what happened to me earlier today? At the Low Down?"

"What was that?"

"I was asking around and a white male, early twenties,

skinny, dark hair and mustache, jumped me with a baseball bat. Before he ran off he said, 'We know who you are.' And he claimed to have knowledge of a major drug operation in the area."

"The Low Down isn't in my jurisdiction. You'd need to press an assault matter through the state police."

"Forget the assault. How did he know who we were?"

"Had you been to any of the places on my list?"

"Just one, the Corbett Hotel."

"You talk about the case openly anywhere?"

"A little, in the lobby of the Blue Lion."

"Well, there's two possible leaks right there."

I stood up and leaned over him. "I'm not interested in the possibilities. I want to know if you put the word out on us."

"I'm not going to discuss ongoing police business with civilians."

"So you did, huh?"

I stared hard and he stared right back. "I'm not going to deny it or admit it," he said. I leaned a little closer and I saw his hand inch toward his weapon. Lisa saw it, too. She stood up and took me by the arm. "Come on, David. I think we're through with our business here."

"I keep running into people who don't give a shit," I said. "It's starting to make me mad."

He stood up and moved toward the door, never turning away from us. "I think your friend has the right idea, Garrett. Get out. And if you know what's good for you, don't stop till you're back where you came from." He slammed the station door behind us.

"Jesus Christ." I had to restrain the urge to kick the side of the building.

"He's right, you know, about the call."

"Don't you start on me."

"No, I just mean, why let her call? If they wanted to pass along a message they could have done it themselves."

"And run the risk of somebody's voice being recognized later?"

"Well, they didn't have her ask for a ransom."

"Because I'm just a guy she knows. The family gets the ransom demand. They want me to stay out of their play, just the way they'd want the police out."

"That could be," she conceded. "Wait a minute," she said suddenly. "How did Kate know to call here?"

"Nice try, but that doesn't implicate Frank. My office knows about the hotel and so does Annie. So does Peters, for that matter."

"I forgot," she admitted. "So now what?"

"It's nearly five. Get back to the inn and call Annie. She must be getting worried. Just let her know we're doing everything we can. I'm going to hit one or two more places on the list. Then we'll take a break for dinner and do the rest later."

"Are you sure it's worth the trouble?"

"We sure can't go back to the Low Down, and the only other things to do are knock on doors or throw darts at the map."

She checked her watch. "See you around eight, eight-thirty?"

"Okay. And find us a place for dinner while you're at it."

I interviewed Tex at the Buffalo Creek Hotel in Shamokin Dam, Rosie at Trucker's Rest in Hummel's Wharf, and Big Ernie at the American Rod and Gun Club in Middleburg. All three were petty dealers whose idea of a big score was a hundred dollars at one time. By the time I finished in Middleburg, my eyelids felt like they weighed ten pounds apiece. I headed east on 522, toward Selinsgrove, and thought about what to do tomorrow if the last two names on the list didn't pan out.

I was tired and I was taking it easy on the old Honda, so I didn't pay much attention to the traffic that passed from time to time. Until a blue pickup came up behind me and swung out to pass, that is. He moved abreast and I let off on the gas a little. But he matched my speed and cut over into my lane. Sparks flew where we made contact, and my left mirror vanished. I felt a lurch as we made contact and the wheel jumped out of my hands. I was halfway off the road and dead ahead was a bridge abutment. I cut to the left and slowed down but he matched my speed and I just bounced off.

I couldn't get back on the road and there was no time to stop. I did the only thing left, which was to cut to the right and take it into the creek. The wheel went into a drainage ditch at the side of the road and my head bounced off the roof. I jammed on the brakes, but I was on grass and all I did was start a skid. I fought with the wheel and tried to keep from going sideways and going into a roll.

The nose went down and my head hit the roof again. I saw a strip of water ahead of me, brown and flowing fast. It was the last thing I remembered.

Chapter Eighteen

Thursday 10:00 P.M.

I was swimming. Not in the ocean or a river, because there was no current. The water was calm and warm. I didn't seem to be on the surface, but that didn't matter, somehow. It must have been night, because I couldn't see anything. I didn't remember going swimming. I had a lot to do—though I couldn't remember exactly what—so I decided to start swimming toward the top. I couldn't decide which direction that was, but I picked one and started moving. I slid through the water without effort, but nothing happened. Then, very slowly, the darkness began to fade, and then I saw a light up ahead. It was weak and distant at first, but gradually it came nearer, nearer, until I broke the surface.

I wasn't in a pond, or a lake, or a swimming pool. I was on my back, on something soft, but I was inside. Over my head was a green ceiling and an electric light. I realized I was hurting, but not in any one spot. It was all over, but mainly in my head. I tried to ignore it—it was a part of my body that was used to aching, anyway.

"David!" It was Lisa. I turned my head and there she was, sitting in a chair. She was pale and her hair was uncombed. I said the first thing that came to mind. "You look like a mess."

She didn't seem to mind. She looked to one side, at something out of my field of vision, and spoke slowly and distinctly. "David, Detective Peters is here, from Selinsgrove."

"Where am I?"

"Sunbury Community Hospital. It was the closest one."

The pieces began to come together, slowly. The car accident. I had been out. And the police were here to question me. Lisa was warning me. I hadn't been swimming after all.

Before my thoughts could go any further Detective Peters came into my field of vision. "Evening, Mr. Garrett."

"What time is it?"

"You've been out for a while." He said it like it was a crime—although maybe just a minor one that could be overlooked this time, if I was cooperative. Why couldn't the son of a bitch just tell me exactly what time it was?

I said nothing. I was just enough awake to know that I didn't have all my wits about me, and that the best thing to do was simply to shut up.

"Your car's drivable, but it's going to need some body work." The prospect of spending money on a rusted-out ten-year-old rice burner struck me funny, and I started to laugh. Evidently Peters took this as a sign I was still deranged and took a step back. "Feel up to answering a few questions?"

Lisa interrupted. "Can't you see—"

"It's all right," I said, which showed how right she was.

He flipped open a notepad. "Did you get a look at the driver?"

"No."

"The plate?"

"Sorry."

"Was there a passenger?"

That one required a little more thought. "I saw someone, a man with dark hair, but I don't know if he was the driver or a passenger. It happened too quick."

"We have a witness who saw the whole thing so I don't have to go into that with you. The truck pulled up like it was going to pass, but then bumped into you and knocked you into the creek. Sound right to you?"

"From what I can remember."

"Any idea who did this?"

"Yeah. The guys I'm looking for."

He was ready with another question, but the doctor came in and ordered both him and Lisa out of the room. The doctor was elderly, with white hair and steel-rimmed glasses. On his lab coat he wore an ID badge that must have weighed half a pound. The name of the hospital was in half-inch-high letters, then his name in the same type, his occupation, his picture, his signature, and several other pieces of information that were too small for my tired eyes to read. He gave me a standard neurologic examination and started making notes on my chart.

"You're a lucky man, Mr. Garrett. Aside from a mild concussion, a broken nose, some whiplash, and some scrapes and bruises, you're none the worse for your adventure. But that cut in the back of your head—it should have been sutured at the time, and now it's a couple of days old. You're lucky it didn't burst clean open again. Where did that come from?"

"Chester."

"I did my internship at Chester Hospital years ago, before it became part of Crozier-Chester. It was a plenty tough place even then."

"It hasn't gotten any nicer."

"Evidently. Well, we've given you a tetanus shot and we'll start you on some antibiotics just in case. You'll need to stay here overnight for observation. I don't want to alarm you, but even mild concussions can sometimes take a turn for the worse."

"I can't stay in, Doc. I'm doing something very important."

He sighed. "The medical insurance company would want me to put you on the street right now. The medical malpractice company would want me to keep you so if you stroke out, at least you'll do it in a hospital. Of course, if you're going to have a stroke, you're going to have it anyway."

"I'll take my chances. Just give me some pills for the pain and I'll be out of your hair."

He shook his head. "Sorry, no prescription pain medication for a head injury, even if it's outpatient. Get yourself something over the counter if you want."

I tried to sit up, and that was the last thing I did for several seconds. The room started doing barrel rolls, slowly at first, then faster. When I put my head back down they slowed down and finally stopped.

"I think I may take you up on your offer to spend the night."

"That's being smart. I'll check in on you in the morning. Shall I send your friends back in?"

"Sure. And thanks."

"Don't mention it. I'll fill them in on how you're doing so you don't have to. You ought to get some rest."

When Peters and Lisa came in, he didn't waste time. "Garrett, I want you to know I've been doing some checking on you. In the last two days you've been busy. It's none of my business what you do in other jurisdictions, but if you try to pull any funny stuff in the borough, you're going to pay for it."

"What was your question?"

He leaned so close I could smell his breath. "I want to know what you're *really* doing up here."

"Huh?"

"You used to be a lawyer in Philadelphia. Bet you're used to some pretty high living. Now times are lean. I've seen that piece of shit you drive. There's easy money to be made and anybody can be tempted."

"What?"

"This woman you're looking for, I don't think she exists at all. I think you're a real sharp guy and you're using this cock-and-bull story of yours just to find out more about the drug scene up here."

Lisa did my talking for me. "So that's why you gave him such junk leads. Why didn't you just tell us if you didn't want to cooperate?"

"I don't have to answer your questions, Miss—"

Lisa was mad. "Well, you're going to answer at least this one. Who ran him off the road if these kidnappers are imaginary?"

"You did."

She put her hands on her hips and went nose to nose with him. *"What?"*

"To help set it up for him. Think about it, lady. If there really are desperate drug dealers in Snyder County, why didn't they do the job right? He was in his car in the creek, unconscious. They could have stopped and finished him off with no trouble. The whole thing stinks to me, and if the motorist who saw it had been able to ID you, I'd have your ass in jail right now."

"So that's why you had me hanging around the station, so you could parade him past me."

"It was a she, but yes, that's right."

"You could have told me where Dave was an hour before you did, you just wanted to keep me on a string."

"I was just trying to make my case." Defensiveness was creeping into his voice.

She put her hands on her hips and got right in his face. "It's a nonsense case, and if you were any kind of a cop you'd know it! They didn't finish him off because there was a witness, and because for all they knew, he was dead anyway."

He was starting to wilt under her anger. "Well, maybe."

"Don't give me any of your 'well, maybe' line. You didn't figure it right and you're afraid to admit it and there are killers running around right now and you're *not even in the right damn county*! So why don't you get out of here and get back to work?"

He turned red, almost purple. His mouth worked but no sound came out. Then he turned on his heel and stamped out. If he could have slammed the door, he would have.

Lisa leaned against the door, let out her breath, and looked up at the ceiling. Then she sat in the bedside chair as if nothing had happened.

"I thought you were going to kill him," I said.

She laughed. "Oh, that was an act."

"You'd better explain yourself. I must have hit my head harder than the doc thinks."

"All I did was play into his prejudices. He's a typical sexist male, he thinks that women are all emotion and that if you cross one right before she gets her period she'll bite your head off."

"Why'd you do it?"

"To get rid of him. The fact that he's prejudiced doesn't mean he's dumb, and if you're too dizzy to go home you're too dizzy to play twenty questions with him."

"Thanks."

"I checked with the daughter, Annie. I'm glad I did. She hadn't heard from her father and she was starting to worry about him, too. I brought her up to date."

A nurse's aide came in, a skinny girl no more than twenty, burdened down by an ID badge as big as the doctor's, and asked me if I wanted to try walking to the bathroom, or a bedpan. I passed on both. She fluffed my pillows and left.

"Did Annie give you the list of names?" I asked.

"She sure did. Five names in all. Shall I call an agency in Miami and have them checked out?"

"It'll take too much time to do them all. Just have them run the travel agency and Frank's secretary. The others are just social friends, right?"

"As far as Annie knows, yes."

"Okay, I know what you're saying. Maybe Annie doesn't know everything. But start with the travel arrangements and we'll go from there. We'll see what we turn up . . ." My voice trailed off.

"What are you thinking?" Lisa asked.

"About my luck. I'm in the hospital just a little beaten around, and think of all the people I've run into in the last couple of days who are dead."

"I think you're thinking about more than that."

For the second time Lisa had said the kind of thing Kate would have said. For a moment I wasn't quite sure whom I was talking to. It was an eerie, disorienting experience. "I was thinking about the mistakes I've made and all the people that are dead."

"Except for not following up with the cabbie a little further, and getting yourself nailed with the baseball bat, I think you've done everything exactly right."

"That's a convenient thing to say."

"It happens to be true. You've done a great job of avoiding being held as a suspect or as a material witness."

"I've done a great job at getting people killed. I should have figured that Joe was just a front and Suzie was the really dangerous one."

"What difference would that have made?"

"Joe might still be alive. I should never have let him go back to the car to negotiate. Suzie was afraid he might sell out."

"Dave, Kate's the important one, not Joe or the others. And they brought their troubles on themselves."

"Yeah, I guess."

"That's just your fatigue talking. Get some rest. Kate's counting on you."

"She may be dead already."

"You don't think that, do you?"

"No, I don't." I let out my breath. "I'm just starting to think this case is too much for me."

"I know it's not. Get some rest and I'll come by at eight. We'll see what we can do from there."

She left, turning off the overhead light behind her. My eyes had just adjusted to the dark when the door opened and the light came on again. "Night nurse," she said. "Sorry to wake you."

"That's okay. I wasn't sleeping."

She was middle-aged and stout, with the short haircut that obese women seem to favor, although I've never been able to figure out why. She was wearing a white uniform and cap, with a tiny white tag with her name and a small red cross.

"Mr. Garrett, right?"

"That's me." I must have been in more of a stupor than I realized, because I asked a pointless question. "I guess the night staff doesn't need ID."

"What do you mean?"

"You don't have one of those billboards on your chest."

"Well, don't you worry about that." She smiled. "I'll be right back."

"I won't go anywhere, I promise."

She was back within a minute, carrying a hypodermic. I almost asked if that was the tetanus shot the doctor had mentioned, but my headache was back and I wasn't feeling very conversational. Then I realized it couldn't be—the doctor said they'd *already* given me a tetanus shot. She rolled up the sleeve of my hospital gown and rubbed my bicep with an alcohol swab.

She poised the needle above my arm. "Now this won't hurt a bit, and it'll help you sleep."

At that moment I proved that Lisa was correct. I did something exactly right. As the needle entered my right arm, my left shot across my chest and gripped her wrist as hard as I could. She looked at me with shock and surprise. "Mr. Garrett, please! I'll have to call the orderly if you—"

"You're not calling the orderly because you're not a nurse! Or if you are, you don't work here. And you're trying to shoot me with something the doctor said I wasn't supposed to have. So who the hell are you?"

She stepped back and my grip was broken. Then she ran out of the room without a word.

Chapter Nineteen

Thursday 11:00 P.M.

I lay back in the bed and tried to collect my thoughts. In the last couple of days I'd hardly had any sleep, except for the times I'd been knocked unconscious. I was fully prepared to accept the possibility that I'd imagined the whole bizarre episode. If the light hadn't been on I probably would have dismissed the whole thing as a hallucination. But the light *was* on. All right, then. Odd as it was, it really had happened. Now what?

I was becoming more and more doubtful of my own judgment as I went deeper into the case, and my confrontation with the nurse reinforced my opinion of myself. The doctor might have ordered a medication without consulting me. I could have misunderstood his remark about what drugs he could give me. Maybe he'd changed his mind after we'd talked. And the fact that she didn't have a hospital ID? It could be on her other uniform or at the dry cleaners or the dog could have chewed it or she could have forgotten it on the dresser bureau. I was sure that the hospital had some kind of security system of its own and that strangers weren't allowed to roam the halls at night.

I decided that, once again, I'd made a horse's ass of myself. Any second she'd come barging through the door, accompanied by another nurse or an orderly, and this time I'd get my medication in the form of a suppository, sideways. I thought about how I'd apologize for my behavior, whether I should say how much pressure I'd been under, or if I should just blame it on my concussion. But then a remarkable thing happened.

Nothing at all.

I watched the clock by my bed. She didn't come back in a minute, or two minutes, or five. She'd been in a hell of a hurry to get out of my room—why wasn't she in a hurry to get back? She'd left the door ajar, and I tried to listen for sounds in the corridor. No footsteps and no noises of anyone being paged to any medical emergencies. Where could she have gone?

I don't know exactly what made me get out of bed. The episode with the shot was strange, but strange things happen in hospitals every day. I think I was more curious about what was keeping her than anything else. Very slowly, I raised my head. I found that if I moved by inches, the room stayed where it should. I ached all over, but it was no worse sitting up than lying down.

The bed was next to the wall, and I was able to steady myself as I slid my feet to the floor. The linoleum was ice under my bare feet, but it helped bring me awake. Keeping one hand on the wall, I shuffled over to the door and looked out.

My room was midway down a long corridor, darkened except for dim yellowish lights over the doors to each room. At one end was a brilliantly lit nurses' station with no one in attendance. The other end terminated in what looked like a lounge or waiting area. In the dimness I could see sofas and chairs. And something else, too. The nurse was there, talking to two men. One was medium sized and the other was big, but that was about all I could tell. They seemed to be arguing about something, but whatever their disagreement was, they kept it quiet. Then the bigger of the two men took off his coat, picked up something white from the sofa and put it on. It looked like an orderly's coat to me.

The more I thought about it the more puzzled I became. Why was the nurse arguing with the orderly instead of just giving him orders? Why in the patient lounge? And why was he changing there? I figured the hospital must have a place for employees to change, somewhere. And why was he getting dressed now? In my experience, hospitals ran shifts seven to three, three to eleven, and eleven to seven. This guy was either two hours early or six hours late. Why was he doing this?

Because he's not an orderly at all, schmuck. No more than she's a nurse.

I edged back into my room and went hunting for my clothes, which I found in a small closet next to the bed. I shucked the hospital gown and got dressed as quickly as I could. My poor suit was a mess and my tie and watch were both missing, but at least I was decent and I had my shoes.

I peeked out into the corridor again. The discussion in the lounge seemed to be winding down, and I had a bad feeling that two of them, or maybe all three, would be heading my way very shortly. Getting away from the room looked impossible. I was dead meat the minute I stepped away from the door. The corridor was bare, no gurneys or carts in sight, and once I started to move I'd be silhouetted by the light from the nurses' station. I had no idea where to look for the elevators, and the only red Exit sign in sight was near the lounge.

The problem of how to cross the corridor was solved for me. The shorter man suddenly pointed at me and started toward me at full speed, with the other two close behind.

I shut the door behind me and tried to think. The only object in the room of any size was the bed, and I wasn't in any shape to drag it around to block the door. And with two men pushing, it wouldn't buy me more than a couple of seconds anyway. I might as well use the time to just get the hell out of there.

On the wall opposite the bed were three doors. One, I already knew, was the closet. I tried the next one. A bathroom. The last one looked like it might be a communicating door to another room. I never got the chance to find out. It was locked.

Steadying myself against the wall, I moved over to the window and threw back the curtains. It was a big window, with casement windows on either side. Outside was simply blackness. Looking up, I could dimly see dark shapes on the left, right, and in front, towering several stories above me. At irregular intervals the shapes were pierced with windows, all of which were dark. I figured that I was looking at a courtyard. But how far down to the ground? I had no idea, and no time to find out. I didn't figure a small town would build a high-rise hospital. At worst it was three stories to the ground, and my fall might be broken by bushes and plants. If I landed right, in a nice, tight roll, it might be nothing worse than bumps and bruises. Whatever the drop, my chances were better out there than in here.

I cranked open one of the casement windows as far as it would go and popped out the screen. The cold morning air washed over me, chilling my face and hands. Without looking back I climbed out onto the ledge. Looking down, I saw nothing but blackness. I sat on the edge, teetering, trying to work up the nerve to jump. How far down? Twenty feet? Thirty? And what if I landed on concrete, or the roof of a car? My knees began to shake, and I found myself holding tighter to the edge of the window. Then the door burst open and I heard voices behind me. I closed my eyes and threw myself off into the blackness.

I landed in a bush about two and a half feet below the window.

I pulled myself up and felt my way along the wall to my right, crashing through the shrubbery and sometimes tripping over hidden objects. I was making enough noise for ten men and I didn't care. My only thought was to keep next to the building and to keep moving.

They didn't pursue me. They certainly weren't deterred by the leap—they knew very well my room was on the first floor—and I certainly wasn't dazzling them with my sprinting abilities. Maybe I was making so much noise that they assumed I'd be attracting attention before they could get me.

Then I had another piece of luck. The wall came to an end and I found a stairway leading up and to the left. I followed it and came out at the end of the courtyard, near the ambulance entrance.

Staying in the shadows, I took a rest and inspected the street beyond the parked ambulances. It was a typical residential street, with tidy lawns, old shade trees just starting to bloom, and neatly kept bungalow-style houses. And cars, lots of them. I saw new cars and old cars, brand-new ones and beaters, subcompacts and pickup trucks, but I was only interested in one feature. Were the keys inside? I could pick household locks, given enough time, but hotwiring a car was a skill I wasn't anxious to perfect in the dark when I was barely able to stand up.

I worked my way down the block, moving in the shadows, until I found it. The most beautiful rust-streaked Ford I'd ever seen, parked in front of a double house. The radio antenna had been replaced with a coat hanger and there were no hubcaps, but I wasn't fussy. I started her up and eased her down the block without lights until I was opposite the main entrance of the hospital.

I was just in time. The two men came out with the nurse right behind. The bigger man had shed his orderly jacket and, by the look of him, what remained of his manners as well. He was shouting and gesturing as they walked through the parking lot, and I didn't need to hear the words to get the drift.

The three of them stood together in the parking lot, talking more quietly now. They looked around but made no effort to search for me. Then they split up. The two men walked deeper into the lot and the nurse got into a car and started off.

Wait for the men, or follow the nurse? The big man seemed to be in charge, and I considered tailing him. But what would I do when he reached his destination? I was unarmed and in no shape for a fight. No, I needed to understand this thing from the ground up, and that meant the nurse. When she pulled out onto the street I let her get to the end of the block and then started following her.

I didn't know Sunbury at all, but it was still an easy tail. She was driving a '65 Thunderbird, with taillights that went all the way across in a solid red bar. A man would have to be blind or three days dead to miss it, even from two blocks back. She wound through some twisted, narrow streets, then rolled downhill and through the center of town. At that hour it was nearly deserted and I had to fall a long way back. She crossed over the Susquehanna River and headed south, back toward Selinsgrove. I let a tractor-trailer get between us and settled down for the ride. Surprisingly, driving didn't make my head feel worse—so long as I didn't make any violent motions like checking the mirrors.

Just north of Selinsgrove she signaled and made a right. Now I began earning my money. The road was empty except for the two of us. I used every trick I knew. I passed her, got out of sight, and then pulled off the road and waited for her to pass. I varied my speed and distance. I even tried driving without lights—until I sideswiped a barbed-wire fence and just about lost it in a ditch.

Her speed never varied, and after about twenty minutes she signaled again. This time she pulled into the driveway of a modest one-story house with a steeply peaked roof and a chimney that told me she heated with wood. I drove past and parked out of sight around the next bend.

Sitting there in the dark I thought about my options. One, I could march up to the front door and deal with her as best I could. Two, I could drive back to town and get Lisa. But what would that accomplish? The backup would be nice, especially if the nurse wasn't alone, but what if the nurse left the house while I was away? I wasn't even certain I could find the place again in the dark. Three, I could go to the police. It would have to be police from whatever county Sunbury was in, which meant involving even more police. I was having enough trouble dealing with the ones I had already. And what, exactly, would I tell them? Without the syringe I had nothing at all. She could deny even being at the hospital, and I had no proof to the contrary. And in a swearing contest, the word of an out-of-county person with a head injury and a hot car wouldn't go very far.

My vision started to blur as I sat there. I wasn't sure if it was fatigue or the concussion. I fished around in my jacket pockets and found my supply of Fastin, now dwindling rapidly. I popped two more and got out of the car.

Chapter Twenty

Thursday Midnight

As I walked up the darkened road there was time for a good look at the house. It was set well apart from its neighbors—this far out, a little privacy didn't cost much. The house itself was a sad and tired white clapboard cottage, sagging with the weight of its years. The front lawn, or what once had been a lawn, was a ratty mess of weeds and wild garlic. She'd parked her car in the middle of it all, and I can't say that it was hurting anything of value. The roof and the porch both showed signs of decay, and half the shutters were missing. The shutter on the right side in the center window on the second floor swung at an angle, like a loose tooth ready to drop out.

I rang the buzzer but nothing happened. I waited, then knocked on the aluminum storm door. After a time I heard movement inside and the porch light came on. I stepped back to one side of the door.

When she opened the door, I didn't get the reaction I expected. She didn't scream, or struggle, or try to slam the door in my face. She just looked at me with large round brown eyes and said, "Oh, it's you," as calmly as if I'd been expected all evening. "You'll have to forgive me,

I was a little startled when I first saw you." She had changed into slacks and a baggy sweater, and she was wearing reading glasses.

"I bet you were." I looked over her shoulder down the narrow hall but it seemed we were alone.

"Please, come in and sit down. You must have had a busy day."

"Are we alone?"

"Oh, yes." She seemed surprised at the question.

I followed her into a small sitting room. She sat on a sofa that was losing its stuffing, and I took a seat facing her in a threadbare wing chair. Between us was an old rag rug, worn shiny by uncounted shoes. Her hands were in her lap as she waited for me to begin. They were spread out, palms down, and they didn't move.

"I suppose you ought to start by telling me your name," I said.

"Elsie. Elsie Mankovik."

"Mine's Dave Garrett, but I guess you already know that. Are you a nurse?"

"No, not anymore. I work as a nurse's aide at the Mennonite home now."

"But you used to be?"

"Eighteen years I was a registered nurse," she said proudly.

"Then what happened?" I had so many questions, it was as good a place to start as any.

"I did something I shouldn't have."

Something about her manner told me to use a low-key approach. "That gives us something in common. So did I."

"You were a nurse?"

I shook my head. "A lawyer."

She leaned forward, interested. "What you did—did you do it for someone you loved?"

"Yes."

She nodded. "Well, so did I. For Angela." She smiled wanly. "My daughter."

If I'd learned anything since law school, it was that every story has to be told in its own way, even if it meant going the long way round. "Where is she now?"

She looked down at the sofa. "Away."

"Who were those men tonight?"

Her face showed animation. She tossed her head as if trying to drive out her thoughts. "Evil men. Men with no respect for the Lord or His works."

I couldn't have agreed more. "But who, exactly?"

"I don't know their names and I wouldn't want to."

"But you were working for them."

"I'm—not proud of myself."

"What was in that shot?"

"I don't know. They gave it to me. And then they took it back again. I made them."

"Take the syringe back? Why?"

"Because it was a tool of the devil, whatever it was, and there's been trouble enough already. I knew when you grabbed my arm that you weren't in any danger. The Lord was watching out for you."

I hoped he wouldn't be sending a bill for his services. "Do you know who I am?"

"No, they didn't say."

"Weren't you curious?"

She swallowed. "It was easier not knowing."

"Why did you agree to it?"

"For Angela, of course."

"What does she have to do with this?"

She studied my face for a moment before she answered. "You said you'd done something you shouldn't have, for love. Do you think love ever ends?"

It was a question that deserved more thought than I could give it just then, so I just said, "I don't know."

"My love for her never ends. She's my daughter and I'd

love her even if it wasn't God's will. But sometimes I wish I could be free. It's a terrible burden."

"Burden?"

"Love is a joy but it's also a burden. It makes you vulnerable. They know I'll do their bidding. They claim to be friends of Angela's, but I know they're lying." For the first time she gave a smile. Only a little one, but I'm sure it was there. "They think they can fool an old woman so easily. Well, let them think it."

"Have you ever heard the name Kate McMahan?"

She took her time in answering, but she seemed to be making an honest effort to test her recollection. "No."

"Frank McMahan?"

"No, I'm sorry."

"Have you ever been to Chester or Allentown?"

"Well, no. That's a long way, either one. I go to Williamsport sometimes."

"Do you know why they wanted you to give me that shot?"

"They wanted to kill you."

"But why?"

"I don't know."

I leaned forward and stared hard. "Ma'am, do you have any idea how much trouble you're in?"

She held my eyes, but hers were gentle. "There are burdens that must be borne."

I sighed. "When were you told you needed to bear this particular burden?"

"When they took Angela away."

"Then you'd better tell me about Angela."

Instead of answering she made a slow gesture that encompassed the room. For the first time I looked around, and saw that every wall and every horizontal surface was covered with photographs, each one neatly framed. Some showed a little girl, five or six, on a pony with a man I assumed was Mr. Mankovik. She had short brown hair and was waving at the camera. Some were more formal pictures, looking like they came from grade school. She was a pretty child, with clear skin, large eyes, and a bright smile. Some pictures of her as a young teenager, skinny and awkward, had been taken out of doors. Mr. Mankovik wasn't in evidence any longer. There were other people in the pictures, mostly other teenagers, but a few adult men as well. Fathers of some of the other kids, I guessed. On the wall behind Mrs. Mankovik's head were photos taken at the beach as part of a group. Apparently they were all taken at the same time, because she was wearing the same two-piece suit in every one. She'd blossomed into a real beauty, but something bothered me about the pictures. With a face and figure like hers she should have been the center of attention, but she was on the edges of the group, wrapped up in her own thoughts. On one wall, over a small fireplace, was an oil painting, apparently done from her high school graduation picture, in an ornate frame two feet on a side. It showed her wearing a string of pearls and a black dress with a broad V neck. She was nothing short of stunning. It was the most recent picture I could see.

"How old is she?"

"Twenty-nine."

Whatever had happened in the last eleven years, Mrs. Mankovik evidently didn't want to display it. "So where is she?"

"I told you, away."

"You said they had her, or words to that effect?"

"They took her away and she won't be back for another seventeen months."

The woman's confusion was contagious. Now I was lost, too. "She's coming back? I thought you said they had her."

"Oh, they do. But with time off for good behavior, she'll be back then."

Good behavior. The light came on. I made sure I spoke very slowly. "Ma'am, are you telling me that the same people who told you to try to kill me have your daughter in prison?"

"That's right."

"Are you saying the police are trying to kill me?"

"Oh, not the identical people, of course, but it's all the same, don't you see? It's all a big machine and we little people get ground up. They feed our children drugs and get them hooked so they can't decide for themselves anymore, and they spend all their money, and then when they're broke the others put them in jail, out of the way, to make room for new ones."

"If she's doing that much time she must be at Muncy." The state correctional institute for women.

She nodded, glad that I finally understood. "I visit her every other day. She's learning to be a beautician. Before, she was a registered nurse, but she's lost that, of course."

"For taking drugs from hospital stock?"

"Demerol," she said, nodding. "Any opiate she could find."

"That's what happened to you, too, isn't it?" I asked. "You stole drugs yourself, for her."

She searched my face. "You know what it's like to have someone beg you for something, don't you?"

"The people who came to you about me, when was that?"

"About eight this evening. Maybe a little before. They were waiting for me when I got home from work."

"And told you to drive to Sunbury and give me a shot."

She looked down at the sofa.

"What did they threaten?"

"That they had people in—with Angela. That they would do things to her. With razors. Till no man would ever want to look at her again. Can you imagine how terrible that would be for her? She's always been so proud of her beauty and now it's all she has left."

"You owe me, ma'am. I need your help."

She shook her head. "I don't know what I can do. I never saw the two of them before and I don't know their names."

"Have they contacted you before?"

"Not them, but others like them."

"What for?"

"Nothing like this ever before. Carrying a package, asking a patient things they want to know, checking on medical records. Not too often. Maybe once every six months."

"I need you to at least come to the police with me. They don't believe that anyone is out to stop me. You can verify that it's true."

She looked up. "But—if I tell them then they'll lock me up and no one will be around to take care of Angela."

I leaned forward and put my elbows on my knees. Our faces were only a foot apart. "The woman I'm looking for—her name is Kate—is in danger. The people that threatened your daughter—I think they're holding her. The woman is my fiancée. I've been looking for her for the past two days. It hasn't been easy. Three people have already been killed to keep me from finding out where she is. You're my very last hope. If you don't help me she's probably going to die, too."

"Do you know how important Angela is to me?"

"Her life is important," I said slowly. "It's no less and no more important than Kate's."

"But I'm all that Angela has."

"I'm all that Kate has. If the situation were reversed, you'd want me to help, wouldn't you?"

She looked away and then swallowed. For a moment the room was quiet. I could hear a cheap clock ticking in another room. "They said they'd be calling me later, after they had a chance to think about what to do next."

"Is there an extension?"

"In the kitchen."

"When they call, let me listen in."

"I'm frightened."

"We can call the police. If you would back up my story, they'd help us."

She looked at me. Clearly, I didn't understand. "No, the police would only make it more dangerous. I'm frightened for Angela, not me."

"A little instinct for self-preservation is healthy."

"Not if it puts her in danger. You know what these people are like. A girl in prison Angela knew, she told the guards something about one of their people. She thought no one knew she'd told. The very next day they cornered the girl in the shower and cut off her nose."

"You must worry a lot."

"I don't do anything else. Except pray, that is."

We didn't have long to wait. The phone rang and she ushered me into a small kitchen with a wood cooking stove. "I'll pick up on a count of three," I said. "Let's be sure we do it at the same time." She nodded and left me alone.

I counted off and picked up, being careful to keep my hand over the mouthpiece. "Hello?" she said.

"You know who this is," said a man's voice in a Spanish accent. "We got to get together and make a new plan."

"What more do you want of me?"

"Hey," he chuckled. "I said we wanted to meet. Maybe you don't hear real good? Muncy a tough place. We send you one of her ears you think you could hear better?" Her only response was a gasp, and for a moment I thought she had fainted. "You ready to listen?" he demanded.

"Yes, yes, I am." It was just short of a wail.

"Meet me at three. You know where 35 runs into 104?"

"I can find it."

"Go south on 104 till you get to the lumberyard. Wait in the parking lot."

"How far—"

"Be there," he said, and hung up.

I put down the phone and joined her in the living room. She was breathing through her mouth and her eyes were glassy.

"Do you need a drink?" I asked.

"In the cabinet there." Her voice was dull. I poured some vodka into a kitchen glass and handed it to her. She took a polite sip and set it down.

"Was that the kind of call you were expecting?" I asked.

"They never say much on the phone."

"You didn't answer my question."

"I don't . . . *expect* anything anymore. I just bear what I have to."

"I'm more of an eye-for-an-eye man myself."

She looked down at the glass on the counter and looked up at me. "I believe that God puts us here and tells us to love. And love is hard however we express it, by revenge or by sacrifice or persistence or however. But if you want to live in God's love the one thing you can never do is run away. Because you don't just run from your family, you run from His love, too."

I'd never met anyone like Elsie. I didn't know what to say.

She picked up her drink and knocked the rest of it back in one swallow. "It's time to go."

Chapter Twenty-One

Friday 3:00 A.M.

The intersection of 35 and 104 was a country crossroads with an all-night gas station and an ATM machine. Even at that hour, in an intermittent drizzle, the parking lot was half full. Peeking out from my position on the floor of her backseat, I saw a knot of men standing around the rear of one of the pickup trucks, drinking and looking at her car as we drove by. I guess there was nowhere else to go once the bars closed; and that for some men, watching the cars go by in the middle of the night was better than going home. What was that country song? I'd heard it in the Low Down Pub just the day before. The singer's in the bar trying to pick up women because it's too hot to golf, too hot to fish, and too cold at home.

Elsie made a left and headed south on 104. We watched the pine trees go by on either side and kept our thoughts to ourselves. After a few minutes I saw a light up ahead. She saw it, too, and slowed down.

The forest ended, and on the right was a long, low building with white siding and a sign that read Lester E. Stuck, Building Supply. Floodlights around the building showed us a gravel parking lot, deserted except for a small yellow front-end loader.

We parked, and I looked around as carefully as I could from the backseat. The road was straight, giving us a good view of whoever approached from either direction. Across the road was a field, and in the middle distance was a farmhouse with an exterior light. There was no traffic on the road and no other signs of life.

"You'd better keep down," she said. I lay down on the backseat and pulled a blanket over myself. The car was cramped, but lying down at least helped my head.

We listened to the crickets together. After a while she asked, "What do you think they want from me?"

I'd been thinking about that. "You told them exactly what happened in my room, right?"

"Yes."

"Then they can't use you to try to get me again. Have they ever made you do anything like this before?"

"No."

"It could be they want to warn you face to face to keep your mouth shut. Or maybe Kate is hurt or sick and they want you to treat her. There could be something else entirely they want you to do, something that has nothing to do with me." I paused. "But I don't think any of those are the reason."

"Go on."

"They might want to get rid of you. There's nothing to connect them to a murder attempt except you."

"That's what I've been thinking about."

"You seem pretty calm about it."

"I put my faith in the Lord a long time ago. I've had my joys and if He wants to call me home that's all right with me. It's Angela I'm worried about."

"They threaten her because they want you to do things for them," I pointed out. "Why would they hurt her if there wasn't a point in it?"

"You don't know these people, Mr. Garrett. They do evil for the sake of evil."

"Still, they're in business. They do things for a reason, to help make money."

"They're evil," she repeated.

We were both quiet for a while after that. The only sound was the crickets. "You said you're a private detective?" she asked.

"That's right."

"I want you to make me a promise; that if something happens to me you'll try to help her."

"Three hours ago you were trying to kill me."

"You said you understood about love."

"What do you want me to do?"

"She was unjustly accused and her public defender doesn't believe in her case. She needs someone to help her get out the truth."

Boy, someone in prison who doesn't think life was fair. I'd never run into that one before. "She doesn't have any money, I suppose."

"She gets twenty-five dollars a month in her prison account."

"That buys half an hour of my time."

"Is that all you care about? What about her?"

"I have to make a living, ma'am."

"Then you're no better than those men out there."

"I beg your pardon."

"You said it yourself, they do what they do for money. They don't care about the human consequences. You say you don't care about my daughter unless there's money in it for you. Well, what's the difference?"

The woman had an interesting way of looking at the world. The fact that she was a little nuts didn't make it any less interesting. "All right, you've got yourself a deal."

I couldn't see her face but I could hear the relief in her voice. "Thank you, Mr. Garrett."

"You understand, no guarantees. I just promise I'll look into it, if it comes to that."

"Thank you, thank you. I was hoping I could count on you. I think it was the Lord's doing, bringing us together like this."

"I wouldn't know about that."

"Well—I see some lights. Here they come, I think."

"I'm going to stay out of sight. Tell me what's going on."

"Well, there's one car. He's stopping just across the lot, facing us. He's at the far end, in the dark." I could see the lights shining on the underside of the roof. They went out and came back on again several times, then stayed on.

"They're flashing their lights," she said. "They want me over there."

"Don't do it."

"I trust in the Lord."

"This setup stinks. There's no good reason for them to want you to come to their car. Why don't they just get out?"

"It's part of my burden."

"Be burdened but don't be stupid. Don't get out."

"I have to."

Painfully, I shifted around to the right-hand side of the passenger's seat. It was a two-door, and from the backseat I couldn't quite reach the door handle.

"Elsie, listen. Open your door a crack so that the light comes on, then pop the latch on the passenger door. I'll slip out my side at the same time you get out and I'll work my way around. You just take it real slow going over there and get me some time."

"I can't take that risk."

"But you'd walk up to them in the dark?"

"It's the risk to Angela, Mr. Garrett." She reached across and locked the passenger door. I was stuck.

"Good-bye, Mr. Garrett."

Before I could say anything the interior light came on

briefly as she opened her door and got out. I heard her first few footsteps on the gravel, then they faded away.

It wasn't long in coming. A shotgun blast, close by, followed by a second. Then the sound of an engine revving, tires spinning on gravel, then nothing.

I picked up my head. There was nothing but blackness and a few drops of rain. I crawled out of the back over into the front seat, got the driver's door open, and made it to her as quickly as I could.

I might as well have stayed in the car. She was lying on her back, near the other end of the lot. She'd taken one blast full in the belly and a second one in the chest. I took her pulse, for all the good it did.

I looked at her face. It was calm and composed as ever. I reached down and closed her eyes. At least she went quickly, and doing something that was important to her. It was a better end than most of us got.

I went back to the car, started it up, and pulled onto the road. To my left I could see their taillights in the distance, headed north on 104. I doused my lights until the taillights were out of sight over a hill, then turned my lights back on and pushed Elsie's old car for all it was worth. When I reached the crest of the hill they were just rounding a curve. I stayed back as far as I dared. We were the only cars on the road and they were probably watching their rearview mirror.

As we approached Middleburg there was more traffic and I was able to put two cars in between us and still stay fairly close. They made a left at Middleburg and headed west on 522. As I waited in a gas station while they went out of sight, the moon came out and the drizzle stopped. A big pickup pulling a horse trailer went by, and he was in almost as much of a hurry as my friends. I pulled out behind him. The three of us stayed together, three or four car lengths apart, most of the way across Snyder County.

We had just passed a sign announcing that McClure was five miles ahead when they signaled and made a left onto an unmarked gravel road and headed south. I went right on by, then turned around and headed back. I cut my lights when I made the turn—fortunately, because they were only a hundred yards ahead. Whether they just wanted to take it slow or whether they were checking for a tail, I couldn't tell. But they continued south at a steady pace and I did my best to keep up in the dark, praying like crazy that the moon wouldn't go behind a cloud. Trees crowded in on both sides, putting the road more and more in shadow. Once I sideswept a mailbox and I wondered if the impact had thrown off sparks, but they kept going. We had passed by several lanes when their brake lights came on. I speeded up, ready for their next move.

Their lights went out.

My instinct was to slam on my brakes but I caught myself in time. My brake lights just might advertise my presence. So I just let off the gas and glided up the road, wondering whether they'd seen me or if this was just a standard precaution.

I coasted past a dirt road that went off to the right and then around a turn. I could see a long way in the moonlight, and they weren't in sight. I gave it a little gas at first, then speeded up. I went another two miles that way, passing three more turnoffs, before the road came to a dead end at the base of a mountain.

I brought the car to a stop. I considered going to the police right away. The odds were high that they'd turned in at the dirt road where they'd turned off their lights, but I was a long way from certain. No, I needed something more for the police to act, even in a homicide. I turned around and headed up the road, my lights still out, watching the odometer until another two miles had rolled by. I saw the dirt road, then backed up until it was out of sight. Then I pulled off onto the shoulder as far as I could and parked. The berm was only a couple of feet wide, but I'd left enough room to pass—and I didn't expect any traffic at four in the morning anyway.

I popped another couple of Fastins. It was time for another walk.

Chapter Twenty-Two

Friday 4:00 A.M.

I stood in the middle of the road and considered what I was going to do next. In Vietnam I hadn't been anything exotic, like a SEAL or a Ranger, just a line marine, but I'd done my share of patrolling at night. If there was one rule I remembered, it was to do your thinking before you move. Afterward may be too late.

It would have been simpler, and certainly much faster, to go straight up the lane. The going would be easy in the dark, and I was fairly sure that the lane would come out near any buildings or anything else worthy of investigation. But a route that was easy for me was equally easy for them to anticipate. No, it needed to be done the hard way.

I walked back up the road until I was about fifty yards north of the farm lane. At that point the road was below grade level and I had to climb a five-foot bank. The ground was wet, but the underbrush provided the footing I needed. When I reached the top of the bank I checked for the North Star and the moon. My sense of direction often failed me at night, but I'd never known the North Star to move.

I started due west, into the woods. I didn't have a flashlight and I wouldn't have dared show one if I had. It wasn't much in the way of a forest, mostly widely spaced saplings with lots of underbrush, and peppered with rock outcroppings. I hadn't gone far when I tripped and fell flat on my face. The impact wasn't much, but after all the other insults and abuses my body had taken in the past three days, it took something out of me. I lay there, catching my breath and scraping together the resolve to get up again. But when I tried I found my foot was tangled in a vine. Unlike some of the others I'd blundered into, it didn't seem to be loose at one end. I reached down to pull it free. Even working by feel I could tell it had an odd shape. Odd for a natural object, that is. It was perfectly smooth and round, as far as my hands could reach in either direction, and fairly stiff. An electric cable of some kind.

A power cable or a phone line would either be suspended in the trees or buried. Utility companies don't just leave their equipment on the surface of the ground. It might be just a piece of junk cable, but it could also be something installed by the occupant; and if it was, I was interested. I decided to follow it and see.

The cable ran due south, toward the farm lane. At one point it thickened where someone had made a crude splice, but otherwise it just ran straight and true to the northern edge of the lane. I slowed to a crawl as I got closer, wondering what I'd find.

The cable terminated in a metal box about the size and shape of a loaf of bread, mounted with the long end pointing up, on a post. I had a feeling about what I was dealing with, and I began to move very slowly indeed. I crawled till I was just behind the box, then extended myself until I was the tiniest bit in front. It was divided into two parts, an upper part with a mesh grill and a lower part with an electric eye and a tiny red light. I slowly turned my head and looked across the lane and saw another tiny red light facing me. I'd never seen a setup exactly like this, but I recognized it—a motion sensor coupled with an infrared beam. A car or person coming up the lane couldn't fail to be detected. Quite a system for a farmer afraid of someone stealing chickens.

I felt that I was safe enough from the motion sensor on my side of the lane, because it faced away from me. And the electronic beam wasn't a problem if I stayed out of the road. But the motion sensor facing me was another matter. I began to pull back as slowly as I'd come. The light remained steady, indicating that I wasn't moving fast enough to set it off. I inched back in the direction I'd come until the lane was out of sight.

I sat on my haunches and wiped my forehead while I considered my options. I could continue west and hope I ran into something interesting, or I could follow the cable in the opposite direction, north, and see where it led. Going west meant going blind. The cable, on the other hand, had to end *somewhere*. I decided to follow it. The job was less trouble than going cross-country, because whoever laid the cable had chosen the easiest going they could find. It went around the kinds of rock outcroppings I'd been hitting my shins on, and it favored the level ground instead of the hills.

The cable gradually headed off to my left, turning west, and broke free of the woods. As best I could tell in the moonlight, the trees paralleled the main north-south road to a depth of a couple of hundred yards, then stopped. I was looking at a large, flat field with some buildings due south, probably where the lane came out. They were too far away for me to see any detail. I looked around carefully, but there was nothing in my immediate vicinity but the woods behind me and the field in front. Still, it was a good idea to wait five minutes before changing position.

It was then that I heard the cough.

It wasn't loud, but it wasn't far away, either. My first instinct was to throw myself on the ground, but that would have involved movement. Even in less than ideal concealment I was better off still than moving. So I stopped exactly where I was, on one knee on the edge of the forest, and tried to locate the sound.

Anyone in front of me would be clearly visible in the field, and I was fairly sure no one was behind me, so I concentrated on the edges of the forest on either side. Then I heard him. A sound of distinct footfalls in the underbrush, to my right. One man, making his way along the edge of the woods, and heading toward me. I cautiously backtracked deeper into the woods, a few inches at a time. He passed less than five yards in front of me, but with the woods at my back I wasn't worried about being seen. What *did* worry me was the fact that he was here in the first place. What ordinary farmer patrolled his property at four in the morning? A stupid question that didn't require an answer.

The sound of his footsteps gradually faded to the south, and I decided to give up my tracing of the cable and follow him. The ground was flat, and by staying on the edge of the trees I found that I could keep him in sight without fear of being seen. Up ahead, the dark shapes gradually turned into a complex of buildings—a shed, a two-story farmhouse facing away from me, and a garage. Farther away I could see a low wooded hill to the south beyond the farm buildings.

On my left the woods suddenly ended and a narrow dirt path appeared in front of me. So this was where the farm lane came out. At the same time I noticed that the sentry had changed direction. Instead of going down the lane he made a right and was following the lane back to the buildings. After all, there was no need to patrol a lane that was already covered by an alarm.

I waited until he disappeared into the back of the farmhouse, then waited a couple of minutes more to make sure

I was alone. Then I moved in on the nearest building, the garage. It was built in the shape of a miniature barn, and big enough only for one vehicle. The main door was on the north side, uncomfortably close to the farmhouse, and I was sure that opening it would make noise. Besides, a hundred-watt bulb was shining directly over it. But I found an unlighted rear door on the south side that happened to be unlocked. After checking around one more time I slipped inside.

I was in a small, dark room that smelled of old sawdust. The window admitted enough light to see a bench with a row of tools, and additional tools on the walls. A workshop, and evidently not used recently. I found a door that led into the main part of the garage, also unlocked. Inside, it was dark, but I could see a vehicle parked there. I moved closer. It was a van. Maybe, just maybe, the van Kate had ridden in. If I could find anything to take back to the police, a piece of cloth, a bit of jewelry, maybe even a strand of red hair . . .

Before I could make a move I heard noises outside. Voices. I retreated into the toolroom and shut the door just as the garage lights came on. After so much time in the dark I was dazzled. The door made a noise when it shut, but it was masked by the sounds of at least three sets of feet.

I hid in the far corner of the toolroom and hefted a hammer, ready to at least take someone with me if it came to that, but no one came my way. I heard the noise of a car door slam, and then another, and then the metallic rumbling sound of a van's side door sliding open. Voices, talking rapidly and low, but I couldn't make out any of the words. Then the sound of the garage door opening, and the van being started. I smelled the exhaust fumes for a moment before it backed out. I heard the garage door being lowered. This time I detected the sound of a garage door motor, then silence. After about a minute the sliver of light under the door disappeared. The main light in the garage had gone out. Evidently it was on a time delay coupled with the opening and closing of the door.

I reentered the garage but it was empty now. The main door had a panel of glass, and when I looked out I could see the van parked outside, its engine running, with a pickup truck parked alongside. The truck was red, not blue like the one that had run me off the road. And anyway, it had New York license plates. As I watched, two men came out from behind the truck and opened the rear doors of the van.

I began working on a plan. It was going to have to be complicated, but since they had the advantage in numbers and weapons, there was no other way. There were at least three of them, and who knows how many others I hadn't seen. At least two of them were together a few feet away. If I had a gun I might be able to get the drop on them—but what if shooting started? Even if I took out those two, that left at least one and possibly several other people running around loose and alerted to my presence. There would be some confusion once the shooting started, but I didn't know how to take advantage of it. Was Kate in the shed? In the farmhouse? Or maybe in some other building I hadn't seen?

I had to take them out quietly, one at a time. My biggest asset was surprise, and the first shot, by anybody, would be the end of that. The two or three men just outside were either loading or unloading something. Perhaps when they were finished they, or at least one of them, would drive off somewhere. Even one person gone would help the odds. And the others would disperse, or, better yet, go to bed. So if I just sat tight till they were done, I might wind up with everyone asleep in the farmhouse. If I could just get my hands on a weapon I could get the drop on them. . . .

The garage door opener sounded again and the door started up. At the same time the big interior lights came back on. I headed for the toolroom again, but behind me I heard a shout of alarm, and then another, and then the sound of running feet. I went right through the toolroom and out the back of the garage as fast as my legs could carry me, conscious of how they had cars and probably guns. I looked back and saw lights coming on in the farmhouse and in the shed. Lots of lights, both interior and exterior. In a few seconds the area around the buildings was flooded with illumination for fifty yards in every direction. But the moon chose that time to go behind the clouds, and my pursuers lost me as soon as I was out of the light. I heard more shouting, and then two figures appeared from the farmhouse, swinging bright beams of light over the ground.

I headed into the woods, stopping frequently to watch. A flashlight came away from the complex and went down the lane at a walking pace. Two other flashlights were sweeping the ground in my direction. The two of them worked line abreast about twenty yards apart at a walking pace. The easternmost man was working the edge of the woods and he concentrated his light in my direction. I caught my breath and tried to think. If I stayed much longer I'd be caught where I was. Even if I wasn't, my car would be discovered by the man going down the lane. If they found my car and disabled it, I was dead meat. I didn't know the ground, I wasn't in shape to walk out, and I wasn't armed. If I wanted to live to fight another day, it was time to go.

I turned due east and crashed through the woods, not caring how much noise I made. I slipped and fell on some wet leaves, and a branch slashed at my face as I went down. I lay there for a while as the cold and dampness soaked through my clothes. Finally I pulled myself up by the branch and headed west again. I'd only gone a few yards before I ran into a boulder so hard that I thought I'd broken my shin. Pain shot up my leg all the way to my hip and I went down again. I broke into a sweat despite the cold and tried not to cry out. What I would have given to be anywhere else in the world just then. Anywhere where I wouldn't be scared and cold and wet and in pain. I found myself tucking in my head, rolling into the fetal position. As my tired muscles relaxed I felt my heart and breathing slow down. Even the pain in my leg seemed to drift off. *Just curl up and rest, just for a few minutes.*

But I didn't. Instead I forced my eyes open and tried to listen to the noises around me. Some muffled shouting, a long way off, but coming closer. Soon they'd be close enough for me to hear their footsteps, and soon after that it would be too late. I bit down on my tongue, hard, hoping that the pain would squeeze out some last reserve of adrenaline. I clawed my way up the boulder and painfully pulled myself upright. I'm ashamed to say that by then it had nothing to do with Kate or any sense of mission. I wasn't any Elsie Mankovik. It was only that some little corner of my brain was still sounding the Danger alarm, and that I could still realize that stopping would be the end of me. Fear of dying, pure and simple, got me to my feet. The leg hurt as badly as ever, but at least it didn't collapse when I put my weight on it.

I was already most of the way through the woods, and even at my slow pace it wasn't long till I reached the road. My car, I knew, was up the road to the right. So was the lane. When I looked in that direction I saw a single flashlight coming down the road toward me, swinging from side to side as it went. It was the man who'd taken the lane. He was between me and my car—and fortunately for me, he didn't know it, because the car was further up the road, behind him. It was the only fortunate thing about my situation. I was rapidly being surrounded, and I didn't have either a weapon for fighting or a good set of legs for running away.

Get past the man on the road. Okay, so how? I struggled to think. All I wanted to do was sleep. Just for a few minutes . . . Me, road, man, car. Get to the car without going through man. I heard the noises of the two searchers behind me, closing in. New rule—have to use road—no time to go cross-country. Another rule—can't eliminate man in road without a gun.

It didn't require much genius to think of the answer, which was good for me because I was fresh out. All I needed was a little luck, which that night I possessed in abundance.

I picked up half a dozen small rocks, worked my throwing arm a bit, and gave the first one a pitch in an arc that carried it due east, across the road and maybe thirty yards into the brush on the far side. It didn't make a noise but the second one did. The flashlight stopped its methodical sweeping and pointed into the brush. My next rock went to my left, farther to the north, and made a gratifying little *click* as it struck an outcropping. I threw another rock, this one a little farther to my left, and watched as the flashlight came up the road, fast, bobbing but still on the patch of woods I was using as a target. He ran right by me without stopping. As soon as he was past I slid down the bank and went in the opposite direction, up the road back toward my car. My leg hurt like hell, but I made good time on the level ground. I looked back when I reached the car, and no lights were in sight.

I got behind the wheel and started the engine. They would hear the noise, of course, but what else could I do? It wouldn't take them long to realize I'd given them the slip and was south of the lane instead of north of it. All they had to do then was set up a roadblock and wait me out. Better to get it over with, one way or the other.

I pulled onto the road and floored it. Even the oldest T-bird has some guts left, and it jumped forward so hard it snapped my neck back. The tires squealed and the rear wheels fishtailed on the loose gravel. As I came up on the little bend that separated them from me I thought about how to play it. Keep the lights off? No. I had a better idea. I put on the high beams just as I reached the curve. The lights would give them a great aiming point, but the noise gave them that anyway, and if they looked at the lights it would cost them their night vision.

I came around the bend and saw one of them right in front, a flashlight in one hand and a rifle in the other. He froze in the middle of the road and didn't even attempt to get off a shot. I bore down on him, not trying to hit him but not caring if I did, either. At the last moment he dropped the rifle and the flashlight and dove headfirst into the bushes.

I'd only gone a few yards before I saw the other two. One was in the road, to my right, and the other was on the left, up on the bank. They'd seen me come around the curve and they were set. I heard the boom of a shotgun over the engine noise, and then a sound like hail as the pellets slammed into the car. The windshield cracked in a dozen places, but held. I shot past them and doused the lights. The taillights wouldn't blind them and only gave them a target. I heard the shotgun again, and then the crack of a rifle, but if anything connected I didn't feel it. I was too tired to care about being shot at, so long as I wasn't actually hit.

I counted to ten, let up on the gas, and turned the lights back on. It would take a lucky shot to hurt me now, but without my headlights it was only a matter of time before I ran off the road. No one fired.

In a couple of minutes I was back to the paved road. I stopped at the stop sign and held on to the wheel to keep my hands from trembling. From there the ride back to Selinsgrove was uneventful, just a quiet country drive in the middle of the night. Except, of course, for the fact that every police car between Harrisburg and Williamsport passed me one way or the other trying to figure where all the shooting had come from. I pegged the speedometer five miles below the limit, set my teeth, and stared straight ahead.

Chapter Twenty-Three

Friday 6:00 A.M.

I knocked on the door to Lisa's room and went in. She'd left the curtains open, and the first glow of morning, reflected off the river, was starting to fill the room. She sat up in bed slowly, her hair tousled, and tried to figure out where she was. A pale yellowish light fell across her face and body. It was a scene for Vermeer, except he didn't do nudes.

She shook the hair out of her eyes. "Dave, what are you doing here? You're supposed to be in the hospital." She squinted at me. "And you look like hell, by the way."

I was so covered with mud and blood I was afraid to sit down. I considered the room, the soft light, the warm covers, and Lisa. It was a long way from where I'd spent the night. "It's a long story and I don't have time to tell you everything. We need to move fast."

Without a word she slipped out of bed and began looking for her clothes. She was hopelessly nearsighted, and she had to bend over close to the floor to find what she was looking for. "Keep talking while I get dressed."

"I know where Kate is."

She looked up at me. "No!"

"At least, I'm pretty sure."

She put on her bra, saw that it was inside out, and fastened it anyway. "Well, tell me where, for God's sake."

"It's a farm at the western end of the county, thirty or forty minutes from here."

She struggled into her jeans. "How did you find her?"

"It all started with a nurse." I gave her an abbreviated version of events as she hunted up a sweatshirt and ran a comb through her hair.

"David, do you realize how dangerous that was?"

"Not compared to what kind of danger she's in. It was a good thing I didn't have a gun. I think I would have gone in by myself."

Lisa was naturally pale, but now she went white. "Are you crazy? One man, hurt, against God knows what? Don't tell me you even thought about it."

"I had a lesson in courage last night that left an impression."

"You had a lesson in dumb, is what you had. What kind of good is that woman going to be to her daughter now? And what good would you have been to Kate if you were dead?"

"Look, it was a bad idea and I didn't do it, okay? You get along with Peters a heck of a lot better than I do. Call him up and try to get as many local officials together as soon as possible. Like in two hours."

"Why?"

"I want that farm raided."

"Why Peters? It's not in his jurisdiction."

"If he's on a countywide drug task force, it is. And he's our only local contact."

"What makes you think they'll even meet with us that fast, let alone go out there?"

"Because Snyder County is a small place, and they must be going bonkers over the Mankovik murder already.

Mankovik is the bait to get them to take an interest in Kate."

She thought about it. "You haven't lost your touch." She shook her head. "But you still look like hell. Get a shower and a shave and out of those clothes while I make some calls."

"Order up some coffee, if you can get it, please. I took some pills a couple of hours ago and I'm falling asleep again."

"Done."

The shower was a good idea, but shaving involved looking at my face. It was the first time I'd seen a mirror since the car wreck, and I barely recognized myself. My broken nose had given me two black eyes, a couple of superficial lacerations ran across my forehead, and my face was swollen and covered with purplish bruises. I looked like I'd gone a few rounds with Muhammad Ali, and I felt that way, too.

My suit, the only one I'd brought along, was hopelessly torn and bloody. I tossed it into the wastebasket and put on the only other outfit I'd brought, a pair of jeans, tennis shoes, a work shirt, and a denim jacket.

It was the wrong thing to wear to the meeting, and I knew it as soon as Lisa and I walked into the room. Or maybe it didn't matter; the three of them were talking when we came in, and from the looks on their faces they'd been talking about us.

The meeting was in the borough council chambers, which had the advantage of allowing me to sit farther away from Peters than I'd been able to do at the police station. He stood when we came in but not to shake hands, only to make the introductions.

"Mr. Garrett, I'd like you to meet Linda Burns, from the DA's office." He indicated a sallow-faced, pudgy woman in an unflattering business suit on his left. "And this is Trooper Ettinger from the local barracks of the state police." Ettinger stood up, and kept right on standing, till he was half a head taller than me. Without expression, he offered me a hand the size and shape of a bear paw and sat down again.

"Ms. Burns, Trooper, this is my assistant, Lisa Wilson." They regarded her glumly. We took seats across the long council table from them.

Peters spoke up. "We hear that you have information about the Mankovik homicide that you want to disclose voluntarily."

"Well, of course I—" That was as far as I got. Lisa cut me off. "Is Dave a suspect?"

Peters stirred in his chair. "It's too soon to exclude any possibilities at this early stage of the investigation. But we remain willing to accept any *voluntary* statements he chooses to make."

"If he's a suspect why don't you just say so?"

"If he doesn't want to cooperate, why did he call us?"

"He's tired of being talked about like he wasn't here," I said. "I've got information that can help solve your homicide, save a woman who's been kidnapped, and break up a major drug operation, in one shot."

"Then let's cut the crap and hear it," said Burns. She yawned, and didn't bother to cover it. "It's too early in the morning to play games."

I started telling my story. I told the truth about why I was with Maggie, but otherwise I stuck to the lies and half-truths I'd already told the various departments. As I spoke I realized I needed another lie—I needed to explain how I got to the Mankovik house—so I told them that Lisa had left the Honda with me when she left the hospital. Lisa kept her head down and played with a pencil whenever I was telling a lie, which was quite a bit of the time. I concluded my story with my reconnaissance of the farm earlier that morning.

It was Burns who spoke first. "Did you know Mrs. Mankovik before last evening?"

"No."

"What about her daughter?"

"I still don't know her."

Peters broke in. "Are you saying the daughter doesn't exist?"

"I've never seen her, except for pictures. I don't know if she does or not." I wondered where this was going.

"So is there any more evidence that this McMahan woman exists than this daughter?"

"You get paid extra to ask questions like that?" I asked.

"What's that supposed to mean?"

"That you have a chance to save a life and clear a load of felonies and all you're doing is demonstrating your considerable capacity to be an asshole."

Peters flushed and started to say something, but Burns ignored him. "Mr. Garrett, let me see if I've got this right. You didn't see the occupants of the other vehicle shoot Mrs. Mankovik."

"No, but I heard it, and there was no one else around."

"That makes you a guesser, not an eyewitness. Was the vehicle the same vehicle that ran you off the road yesterday?"

"I don't know. All I ever saw were the lights."

"So you couldn't identify the vehicle in any way, or the passengers, for that matter."

"No."

She frowned. "Tell me again, *exactly* what evidence we have that this farm is connected with the Mankovik homicide."

I let my breath out. "I saw it slow down and turn out its lights near the farm lane. No, I didn't see it turn in, I can't say which vehicle it was, and I can't say that it didn't pull out again and go somewhere else after I drove away."

She nodded sympathetically. "Even assuming that the

vehicle turned in there, can you give us anything that shows that it's connected with the farm?"

"No, I can't."

She looked at Peters and then at the trooper. "Can you tell us anything about that area, Joe?"

Ettinger just sat there, and I thought he hadn't heard, but he was just considering his answer. "Well, we don't have much call to go out that way. Mostly hunting camps, abandoned farms, state lands. Ground's real poor out there, got worked out a long time ago. Not many working farms. Parents die off, kids live in Williamsport or such, no one wants it, so the land just sits. People rent whole farms just for the houses to live in."

"Can you give us anything specific on drug operations in the area?" Burns asked.

"Our troop doesn't have the manpower to just prowl around. When we hear about sales, especially in the schools or to young folk, we land on 'em with both feet. But I haven't heard anything about anything like Mr. Garrett here is talking about." He paused for a moment, considering. "Doesn't mean it's not there, though."

I spoke next. "If this is the kind of operation I think it is, you're not going to hear about it. They don't sell single marijuana cigarettes in local pizza parlors—they sell large quantities to outsiders who take it away. This isn't tied in with local street sales."

It was Peters's turn. "You seem to know an awful lot about drugs."

"I'm not going to respond to that."

"Maybe you should."

"I smoked some dope when I was in my twenties. So did everybody else in this room. I've never bought or sold or traded any drugs in my life. And if I were starting now, I'd find a hell of a lot less visible way to do it."

There was an uncomfortable silence, which was broken

by Burns, the assistant DA. "Let's get back to the homicide. Why did you go to her house?"

"It was a choice of either following her or the two men, and I picked her."

"Why?"

"I don't know. If I had it to do all over again, I'd probably do it differently."

"Could it have been because you knew she'd tried to kill you, but you weren't sure about the others?"

"The others were in on it, too."

"Was she remorseful about what she tried to do to you?"

"No. I was a job she had to do to protect her daughter."

"How did that make you feel?"

"Sad. And sorry for her." And a few other, more complex reactions that were none of their business.

"You weren't enraged?"

"She wasn't the kind of person you could be mad at."

"Even for wanting to kill you?"

"She was very brave, and very strong, in her own way. She had some qualities I admired."

Burns made some notes. "I find it hard to believe you're such a generous person."

"She wasn't a threat to me anymore and she was the only lead I had to the people who put her up to it."

"So you were playing her along?"

"I had nothing to play with. I was just trying to get her cooperation."

"And how did you do that?"

"I asked her."

"Oh, come on."

"When you get the coroner's report there won't be any evidence of violence on the body except for the shotgun wounds. And she wasn't scared of me, anyway."

She put down her pencil. "Alone in the house with a big guy, rough looking, who knew that she'd tried to kill him? You expect us to believe she wasn't scared?"

"She wasn't scared of me and she wasn't even scared of those men, at least for herself. She was scared for Angela."

Burns looked down at her notes. "You say you got into the back of her car and hid there while she went over to the other vehicle."

"Right."

"You said this woman would do whatever it took to protect her daughter."

"There was no question of that in my mind."

"And she freely admitted trying to kill you. So why weren't you afraid that she'd turn you over to them?"

"Because I was too dumb to think of the possibility." That brought everything to a dead stop. All of them stared at me, including Lisa. "And even if I'd thought of it, I think I would have done it anyway. Letting her go to the meeting alone would have been letting go of my only lead."

"That was very dangerous."

"Going there at all was dangerous. That's what I told Mrs. Mankovik. And she did what she thought she had to do. So did I."

Lisa spoke up. "I'm sure you'll agree that David did the right thing. If he hadn't been there to follow the killers, you wouldn't know where to look for them now." She emphasized the last sentence, especially the last word.

Burns and Peters exchanged a look I didn't like, and then Peters spoke. "What would you have us do, Mr. Garrett?"

"You've got probable cause to search the property for evidence of the Mankovik murder. Hit the farmhouse with everything you have, right now. Go in from every direction, if you can, without any warning, and be prepared for a hostage rescue."

Ettinger looked down at the table. That was the only response from any of them.

"What's the matter?" I demanded. "Every single thing

I've told you fits in with Kate being there. And they're not going to keep her alive forever. We have to go in there now."

Lisa picked up the thread. "What if you make casts of the tire treads around the farmland and at the scene of the murder? Wouldn't that be enough physical evidence for you?"

Ettinger shook his head. "Doesn't matter what's at the farm lane—the murder scene was gravel. No tracks at all."

Burns looked at Lisa and then down at her notes. "I'm not at all sure what we can do. I mean, there's information that justifies continuing the investigation, but we're a long way from probable cause." She saw the look on my face. "Could you both excuse us for a few minutes, please? There are some things we need to discuss."

"I have another idea," I said. "Why do we have to be talking in terms of a criminal warrant? The important thing is to get in there. What if you went in there on a pretext, like sending in the Department of Environmental Resources to check on their manure management system, something like that?"

Ettinger looked interested, but Burns shook her head. "Too goddamn cute, Mr. Garrett. We're bound by the Fourth Amendment. No unreasonable searches. If we go in there and seize anything I want to be sure it'll stand up in court."

"I'm a private citizen," I pointed out. "The Fourth Amendment doesn't apply to me. What if I go in myself and you happen along later?"

Peters spoke up. "We don't go in for vigilantism, Garrett. Now wait in the hall, please."

We waited in the corridor, or rather, Lisa sat on a bench and I paced like a caged animal. Moving around made me hurt more, but I didn't care. "I should have lied," I said. "I should have told them I saw the van pull in."

"The reason I work for you isn't that you're a good liar."

"I get an attack of honesty and Kate may die because of it."

"Even if you'd said you'd seen them turn in, the DA probably wouldn't think that was enough."

"Then what's your idea?" I asked.

"Wait. We're almost there. We know where to look. Something will turn up that will link the murder with the farmhouse—a neighbor who saw somebody leave, maybe the shotgun will turn up, something will happen. We keep an eye on the place and try to speed up the process. We just have to give it some time."

"How much more time does Kate have?"

"You asked for what I thought we should do, not for what was easiest."

I looked at the wall. Behind me, I heard Lisa again. "And if they've kept her alive this long, why not assume they'll keep her alive a little longer?"

"Are you saying you think she's dead already?"

"You want an answer?"

"Yes," I said.

"I'm saying you'd better assume she's already dead, and that way if she isn't it'll be a pleasant surprise."

"I could use a pleasant surprise for a change."

I paced the corridor until I became dizzy and leaned against the wall opposite Lisa. My leg was starting to throb from where I'd run into the rock. "That myth you told me?" I said.

"Orpheus and Eurydice?"

"What's the moral?" I asked.

"Greek myths don't have morals like Aesop's fables do."

"Well, what does it mean to you?"

She looked away. "That when you try too hard things slip through your fingers."

"I think it means that all the courage and love and skill in the world don't mean anything, sometimes."

"You're thinking about the war again."

"I was thinking about right now. And about the war, too. And how we're both saying the same things in different ways."

"David, I'm a pessimist. Most of my life has been screwed up one way or another, and I take it for granted that things won't work out. I have no reason at all to think that Kate isn't alive and well right now. If I sound like I think she's dead, then that's just me."

"I appreciate your saying that."

"Come on"—she smiled at me—"how much importance can you attach to the opinions of someone who can't even put her underwear on right?"

Before I could answer, the council chamber doors swung open and we saw Peters's head. "Come in, please."

Burns had gathered up her notes and Peters had shut his briefcase. Clearly, a decision had been reached while we were outside. The more I looked at their faces the more convinced I became that I wasn't going to like it. And when it was Peters who started speaking, I was certain.

He spoke slowly and formally, a public official speaking for the record. I wondered if the meeting was being recorded. "Mr. Garrett, Snyder County takes homicides very seriously. You're not from this area, and what we've been able to learn of your background gives us cause for concern. First, you may not have told us all you know about this homicide. Second, whether you have or not, you may not decide to make yourself available for the eventual trial of this case. For both of these reasons, and after consultation with the district attorney's office, a decision has been reached to hold you in custody as a material witness. You will now accompany me to the station for processing."

His words were so illogical, so out of step with the urgency of the situation, that I thought I was having another of my sleep-deprivation hallucinations. But when he pulled my hands behind me and I felt the cold metal of the handcuffs go around my wrists, I knew.

I wasn't going to give them the satisfaction of a show of temper. I'd given them everything I had when I thought their minds were still open, and it hadn't been enough. As Peters led me away, I just turned to Lisa. "Find McMahan and see how much money he has. Then get me the best criminal lawyer in the county. And fast."

Chapter Twenty-Four

Friday 9:00 A.M.

It was only a hundred-foot walk from the council chambers down the stairs to the police department, but I thought it would never end. I kept my head down and looked at my shoes on the polished red linoleum and thought of how each step was taking me farther from Kate. The knight in shining armor was just one more arrestee being booked. And then what? I'd go into a holding cell while the detective did the paperwork, then a trip to the local district justice for the preliminary arraignment and the setting of bail. Being from outside the area I had no expectation of an ROR bail—I guessed I'd be needing around five thousand dollars, cash. If I was lucky and Lisa could get her hands on the money without having to go back to Philadelphia, I might be out by the end of the afternoon. If not I'd probably have to spend the night in the Snyder County Jail. I wondered if a county this small had any provisions for posting bail after office hours. The idea of the lockup didn't bother me—I'd once done ten days in the brig for threatening an officer—but I'd be ten hours out of the case, maybe even twenty-four, and I couldn't afford to waste even a minute.

Inside the police station, we went down a short corridor with yellow cement block walls on either side. Near the end the corridor broadened to the left. I saw a camera on a tripod and a fingerprinting table. I was in the booking area.

Peters took off the cuffs. "Stand over there while I get the camera set up," he said, and pointed across the corridor toward a small cell with a sliding barred door. It was clean enough, and the yellow walls made it about as cheerful as such a place can be, but when I thought of going inside all I could think of was Kate being shoveled into a grave.

I leaned against the bars while he fiddled with the height of the tripod and made sure the camera had film. Then he motioned me over for the front and side shots. The flashes dazzled my eyes.

"Now it's time for the prints. Ever had it done before?"

"In the marines, and when I got my PI license."

"Then you know the drill. Keep your fingers relaxed and let me do the work. Otherwise this will take all day."

He took off his suit jacket, revealing an automatic in a shoulder holster. He did my left hand first, inking each finger and then rolling it out. We did two cards for each hand. One for the state, he explained, and one for the FBI. When he was through he gestured toward a sink with a liquid soap dispenser. It was hard work getting the ink off, and I wasn't in any hurry.

When I was finished he handed me a towel. I dried my hands and handed it back. "Okay, Garrett, into the cell." He raised his arm and pointed, exposing his gun.

I turned toward the open door and took a step. Then a thought appeared in my mind, as clear and stark as if someone had said it out loud.

If you go in there, Kate will die.

I slammed him into the wall and went for the gun.

I'd caught him by surprise, but he had fifteen years on

me, and he wasn't exhausted or hurting. He bounded back off the wall, pulled down his shoulder to protect his gun, and rushed me. I hit the wall behind me, my head snapping back so hard I saw stars. But I found the grip of his gun and held on. I yanked as hard as I could but it was caught in his holster. He had both hands free, and he threw a fast one-two at my solar plexus. Keeping my right on his gun, I sideslipped enough so that the punches landed on my ribs. It hurt like hell but I was still standing. I threw a weak left that glanced off his jaw, and he responded by gripping the top of my left shoulder, searching for the pressure point. He found it in a hurry; my entire left arm went numb and fell uselessly to my side. He followed up with a right cross to my breastbone that sent me flying. I went backward into the wall again and slid to the floor. He stood over me, his legs apart and his arms at the ready, waiting for me to try again.

And then a very strange thing happened. His eyes widened, he backed off, and raised his hands. I followed his gaze. In my right hand was his gun, pointed up right at his belly.

"Back into the cell, Vic."

"Don't do anything stupid," he said.

"Funny. I was going to say the same thing to you."

He backed in, his hands high. I didn't know if the safety was on or if there was a round in the chamber, but as long as he did what I said, neither one of us had to find out. I kept the gun on him while I picked myself off the floor.

"All the way to the back of the cell. Good. Now where are the keys?"

"Dispatcher keeps them. Garrett, you'd better think about what you're doing. This is aggravated assault. With a mandatory firearms enhancement. We're talking serious state time here. Play it smart. Give me the gun."

"The department have an unmarked car?"

"Why do you want to know?"

I raised the pistol and gave him a good look at the muzzle. I repeated the question.

"Yeah, it's the one I usually drive. You know, it's not too late. I can just put in my report that we had a struggle. Charge you with simple assault, plead it to disorderly conduct—"

"Where's it parked?"

"Right out front. Look, this isn't the way to get your girl back."

"So now you think she exists after all."

"Give us more time, put in a wiretap maybe—"

"Time's the one thing she doesn't have. Anybody else in the station now?"

"Just me and the dispatcher. But you take her, that makes it two counts of aggravated—"

"You got any more clips? Toss them out here, real slow, with your left. If you've got a backup gun leave it where it is. I don't want to have to shoot you."

He reached awkwardly into his left armpit and tossed two clips through the door to me. They clattered on the bare concrete over to my feet. I kept my eyes on him while I knelt down and felt around till I had them.

"The car keys."

"Dispatcher has them."

"Bullshit."

"No, really. We turn them in when we check into the station."

I decided to take him at his word. The prospect of getting close enough to frisk him, as young and fast as he was, didn't appeal to me. I slammed the cell door shut on him. "Get out your handcuffs and cuff one wrist. Now throw me the keys. Good. Now sit down, facing the bars. Put both hands through the bars and keep them there." When he had complied I snapped the other cuff onto his left wrist.

"Garrett, you're crazy, you know that? You're going to go to jail for a long time. Ever been in an SCI? It's not—"

"I'm going to put the keys to the cell and to the cuffs on the fingerprint table. I expect somebody will be by within an hour." I went to the front of the station, where a stout woman with a gray bun was sitting in front of a radio. I pointed the gun at her and motioned with the muzzle for her to stand up. Her eyes widened but she didn't give me any trouble. Inside of two minutes I had the keys to the unmarked car and I was locking her into the other cell.

"Garrett!" the detective yelled. "Listen to me. Please."

The last word got my attention. I knelt down just outside his cell. "Yeah?"

"Don't do anything stupid," he said earnestly.

"I already did. You told me so yourself."

"Look, you've bought yourself an hour with this stunt. Two, maximum. But you know we'll be coming out there after you."

"That's exactly what I was counting on."

"Then at least wait until dark. I don't care about you, but I'd hate to have a cop get shot doing something in broad daylight he could do as well in the dark."

"You don't think I'd shoot a cop, do you?"

"I didn't say that."

Despite everything I had to smile. "So you really *are* worried about the make-believe drug dealers holding my imaginary girlfriend, aren't you?"

"You're a jerk but you're not crazy."

Before I stepped into the street I shoved the gun into my belt in the small of my back. I didn't know what kind of special security precautions they had, and for all I know I could be walking out into a semicircle of rifles pointed at my chest. I looked out: I was the only one on the street. I took a deep breath and kept going.

The car turned out to be a chocolate late-model Plymouth. Only the municipal plate gave it away as a police car. I popped my last two Fastins as I roared out of Selinsgrove and threw the bottle out the window. A littering rap was the least of my problems.

Traffic on 522 was light. In the twenty miles I covered on the main highway, I only passed three cars, and one of those was in Middleburg itself.

I would be lying if I said I wasn't frightened. I couldn't think of a way for all this to work out. The day would most likely end with me either in jail or dead. I had enemies in front of me and behind me, and except for Lisa, no friends at all.

I kept it at forty once I reached the gravel road and headed south, thankful that the rain would keep down the dust. The cruiser was a lot more car than I was used to, and I had some trouble with the tighter corners, but by ten I was a quarter of a mile past the farm lane. I parked there, getting as far onto the berm as I could. A quick search of the car revealed a police radio in the glove box, and a first aid kit and a fire extinguisher in the trunk. No carbines, no riot guns, not even any extra pistol ammunition. I tried to take comfort in the observation that, by the time I'd fired off the three clips I probably wouldn't need any more, one way or the other.

I headed due west into the woods and then cut to my right until I was going northwest, climbing the southern slope of the hill I'd seen earlier to the south of the farmhouse. The trees were bare but the underbrush was thick, giving me lots of cover. It was impossible to move silently in the tangle of vines and brush, and I didn't try. Every couple of minutes I stopped to listen, but that was the extent of my precautions. The odds of someone being so far away from the farmhouse were pretty remote.

Unfortunately, they weren't zero.

I was about three-quarters of the way up the hill when I stopped to listen again, and this time I heard something. It was an odd noise, regular but not mechanical, and I couldn't tell where it was coming from. I lay down on my belly and listened. Then I pressed my ear to the ground. It was louder now, although I still couldn't get a sense of its direction. It was a soft sound, but heavy, like something was being struck over and over. As I listened I noticed two variations. Sometimes the sound was metallic, and sometimes it stopped for a few seconds. It didn't sound like any animal I could think of. What the hell could it be? The rhythm was right for someone chopping down a tree, but none of the trees I could see would have withstood half the blows I'd heard, and the sound didn't seem right, somehow. An ax on a tree ought to make a sharper sound. Okay, so someone is doing *something*, over and over again, with some kind of hand tool. A sound that's louder through the ground than through the air.

Digging.

Cautiously, I worked my way a few yards farther to the east and listened again. The sound was the same, no louder. So going east wasn't getting me any closer. That meant the sound was either coming from the north or the south. I looked behind me, to the north. The hill fell away fairly rapidly in that direction, and flattened out not more than forty yards away. From that point north, the ground had been cleared for farming. I was fairly high up on the hill, and I had a view of at least half a mile in that direction. Checking as carefully as I could without binoculars, I couldn't see a sign of human activity. That meant it was south, over the top of the hill.

I wriggled forward on my belly, pausing every few feet to listen. It was slow going, made harder by the need to move silently. Fortunately the twigs and brush were too damp to snap as I slid over them. The sound slowly grew louder as I approached the crest.

The hill came to a steep summit, more like a ridge than a hill, and curiosity and impatience told me to crawl straight to the edge and get a look. But the crest right in front of me was bare, and I hadn't come that far, that carefully, to hurry. I stopped again to listen just short of the crest. The noise was coming from dead ahead this time. If I'd kept going straight I would have blundered right into it. I crawled a few yards to my left, until I'd placed a small stand of saplings between the noise and me. Then I inched my way to the top.

Dead ahead was the farmhouse, with a big gravel parking area occupied by a red pickup truck. The farmhouse was two stories, with a tin roof and white siding. Behind and a little to one side was a large, one-story building, also with white siding. The garage I'd been in last night was to the left. This time the door was shut. If the van was inside there was no way to tell from here.

To my right, not ten yards away, a man was digging a hole. His back was to me and he was bent over, but I could tell he was big, and that he was working hard. He was wearing jeans and a brightly colored shirt of red and yellow. And, I saw, a pistol in a holster on his belt. The hole was nearly six feet long and about half that in width, and he was waist-deep in it. A big pile of red dirt slowly mounted behind him. Farther back, I noticed that he'd carefully cut out the covering of weeds, grass, and wildflowers into neat squares, like sod. He was going to a lot of trouble to make sure the hole was invisible once it was filled.

I could only think of one reason why someone would want to dig a hole and not have anyone know it was there.

I moved back, away from the crest, and moved toward him. I remembered what Bonowitcz had said about these operations not having many people. If I could take out this one quietly, there might only be a couple left. I might even be able to get into the farmhouse without being detected.

I reached the crest directly opposite him and peeked over. It was a perfect setup. His back was to me, not more than ten feet away, and his head was at the level of my waist. The ground between us was bare of twigs, vines, or branches. I pulled out my gun, checked to see that the safety was off and that the chamber was empty, and held it by the muzzle.

I got to my feet and made my rush, keeping low. I covered the distance in three big steps and leaped into the pit. As I came down I brought the butt of the pistol down onto his head as hard as I could.

He never heard me, I'm sure of that. But just as I made my leap he started to straighten up. I don't know if he'd decided to take a break or whether he was just hefting a particularly heavy shovelful of dirt. Whatever the reason, I connected with his shoulder instead of the back of his head.

He was stunned and hurt, but he wasn't out, and he had a shovel. We went to the bottom of the pit together, but I rolled off him and he was on his feet before I could get up. He took a grip midway up the shaft of the shovel and swung at my head. I rolled to one side and the blade buried itself in the soft dirt. He tried to pull it out but it was stuck. He kicked me in the side, hard, and I dove for his feet before he could kick again. This time I took a boot in the face that sent me sprawling.

I pumped a round into the chamber and raised the muzzle to his face, giving him a good look. That should have been the end of it, of course. If he moved he was a dead man and we both knew it. For a moment our eyes met and it hung there between us. But then he went for his gun. It was a crazy chance and he should have known better, or cared. He got his own gun free and it started its arc toward my belly.

I pulled the trigger. There was no other way.

Chapter Twenty-Five

Friday 10:00 A.M.

The echo of my shot rolled around the valley. Before it died away I heard a door slam in the direction of the farmhouse. I thought of heading for the lane, but then I realized it wasn't a car door I'd heard. Someone was either going into the farmhouse or heading out a rear door. Then, one by one the blinds on the farmhouse windows snapped down.

I knelt by the man I'd shot. One round, that caught him in the throat and exited behind his right ear. I kicked away his pistol, just to be on the safe side, and started moving toward the farmhouse. I kept low but I didn't bother to crawl. Now that they knew I was out here, speed was more important than stealth.

I moved from cover to cover as quickly as I could, pausing each time to keep an eye on the house. Except for the blinds being pulled, it looked just the same. No one visible, no windows broken open, no noises at all.

I stopped when I reached the pickup truck about twenty yards from the front door. Being careful to stay behind a tire, I tried to catch my breath. My headache was worse again, so bad I was starting to see tiny lights. Closing my eyes helped—at least until I had to open them again. The back of my head hurt so badly I was sure I'd burst open my wound somewhere along the way. I put my hand back and it came away covered in blood.

I thought about the farmhouse, from the top down. No dormers, at least not in the front. Five windows upstairs. On the first floor there were two windows on one side of the door, and one big picture window on the other. Some remodeler must have combined two of the older, smaller windows somewhere along the line. The front door looked pretty solid, and I had to assume it was tightly bolted and probably reinforced. There was no cover between me and the house, but there were no positions for anyone to catch me in a cross fire, either.

I'd talked to many of the marines who'd fought at Hue, during the '68 Tet offensive, and I knew how they'd storm a building like this. You have to expect that the doors and windows will be covered by fire, or mined, or both. So the best entrance to use is the one you make yourself. In Hue they'd used 105s firing at point-blank range, M48 tanks, and bazookas. When none of those were available they used antitank rockets and satchel charges.

And what if you had nothing at all? Just a stolen pistol and no time?

I opened the door to the pickup on the passenger's side. Instantly I heard the sound of breaking glass and a rifle shot. The windshield and the passenger's window shattered, and I tried as best I could to keep the flying glass out of my eyes. I felt shards ripping through my sleeves, and spots of blood began appearing on the ground underneath me. A second shot came a moment later, and then a third, but they passed harmlessly through the cab. The shots were coming too fast for a bolt-action rifle. The man inside had either a semiautomatic or a full-blown assault rifle.

I didn't feel brave. Or afraid, either. Being afraid involves the luxury of enough time to consider the danger. My only thought, aside from the necessity of caution, was that Kate might still be alive, only a few feet away, and that unless I acted quickly it would all be for nothing.

I crawled inside the truck, lying on the floorboards of the cab with my head near the parking brake and my feet sticking out the passenger's side. My luck was back; the keys were in the ignition, and it was an automatic transmission. I pumped the gas pedal once with my right hand, then reached up and turned the key. It cranked for a moment, then caught. I pressed the pedal with my hand to get a good flow of gas going. With my left hand I released the parking brake. Then I reached up and dropped the transmission into reverse.

The truck moved backward drunkenly, bouncing as it left the parking area and moved into the field. I pulled the wheel to the right so that the truck described a quarter of a circle and wound up facing toward the house, but moving away. I had traveled about fifty yards when I was jolted so strongly I hit my head on the underside of the steering wheel and the truck came to an abrupt halt. It came to a stop tilted sharply to the left, which put my head lower than my feet and increased the pain in my head to the point where I was afraid I was going to pass out. I shoved it into drive, then reverse, then drive again and managed to rock myself out of whatever I'd been stuck in.

The moment I stopped again there was a string of rifle shots, so fast they almost sounded like one. So it was an assault rifle after all. He was firing full auto, short bursts. I felt the rounds strike home and heard the hiss of coolant running out of the radiator.

I shoved the gas pedal all the way to the floor. The truck hesitated, then leaped forward across the field, gathering speed as it went. I wasn't sure of my exact direction except that I was heading in the general direction of the house. Of course, I had to hit just right or all I'd do was just kill myself in the impact. I heard another burst, closely followed by two more. I was sure they struck home, but the truck was bouncing too much for me to feel the impacts.

If he was any good he'd know what I was going to do and what it involved. He'd know I was going to have to stick my head up over the top of the dash to see where I was going, and he was waiting for his chance. I could imagine him, his finger tightening on the trigger, the muzzle firmly braced, waiting for me to show myself.

If I don't do this everything's been for nothing.

My head popped up. No more than half a second, but enough for me to see that I was too far to the right, that I was headed for the door rather than the picture window. And enough time for him, too. As my head went back I felt a blow and a searing pain across my forehead. Blood flooded down over my eyes. The truck rocked under the impact of dozens of high-velocity rounds at point-blank range.

Blinded, I pulled the wheel to the left and made sure the gas was all the way to the floor. Then I just pressed my head to the filthy floor and shut my eyes.

The truck crashed through the picture window like the end of the world. I was thrown in six directions at once and slammed into every projection in the cab. Glass and bricks rained in through the open windshield. Another tremendous bounce, and then the truck slammed into the far wall. The passenger door flew open at the impact, but I was too busy being thrown forward and backward to be flung outside. I could feel the entire house reeling and swaying under the impact.

I tried to get up, but I was covered in bricks and my hands slipped in the blood when I tried to push myself up. The impact had thrown blood all around the inside of the cab. Mixed in with dirt and brick dust, it looked even worse. I heard a single set of footsteps coming rapidly closer. Shit, I wasn't going to have time to get out. Or even get up. After all this, I've just moved my place of dying a little bit. And Kate . . .

One chance left.

I stopped moving and just lay there, face down. I turned my head to one side so he'd see the blood coming out, and snaked my right hand into the small of my back and put it on the pistol. Slowly, keeping my hand under my coat, I eased the gun out of my belt and closed my eyes. I felt blood in my mouth and opened it; a rivulet of blood ran down my chin. I heard his footsteps in the broken glass and debris as he approached the truck. A bit of luck—he approached from the passenger's side. Another bit—he didn't empty the rest of the magazine into me the moment he had a clear shot. Had our positions been reversed I wouldn't have bothered to shoot, either. Most corpses on the battlefield looked better than I did at that moment.

I couldn't be sure he was standing right at the passenger's door by my feet. He could be almost anywhere, especially if he was being careful. But if he wasn't there, it didn't matter anyway. It was a lousy chance, but it was the only one I had.

I raised the muzzle enough to clear my own legs and started blindly pulling the trigger as fast as I could.

The noise of repeated rapid firing was deafening, but over the sound of my own gun I heard the ripping sound of his weapon on full auto, and a scream.

I tried to listen, but my ears had already been too punished. Painfully, I moved the bricks off myself one by one and worked my way out of the cab. I didn't bother trying to stand up; I just let gravity take me down to a sitting position on the floor, with my back against the side of the truck.

I wiped the blood out of my eyes with my sleeve and looked around. I was in a large room, probably a living room, although it didn't seem to have much in the way of furniture. A few feet away was the gunman, barefoot, wearing a T-shirt and briefs. He had probably been sleeping, or getting himself some breakfast, when he heard the first shot. A couple of feet away was an M16 with a curved thirty-round clip. The smell of gunpowder and hot oil filled the room.

On my hands and knees, I crawled over to him. He was Hispanic, no more than mid-twenties, perhaps younger, with a slender build. In better circumstances, he was probably a handsome young man. I'd hit him once, in the chest, and the front of his T-shirt was covered with blood. He was tough—he kept one hand on his wound and was trying to reach his rifle with the other. He was too badly hurt to make much progress but he kept trying anyway.

I moved the M-16 well out of reach. Then I put my pistol to his head. "How many more of you?"

He looked at me with half-closed eyes. *"Un hombre, señor."*

"What about the woman? *El señora?*"

He tried to speak but nothing came out. Then he closed his eyes and his head lolled. I touched his face; it was cold. He was going into shock.

I checked the magazine in my pistol, shoved it into my belt, and picked up the M16. Except for the bigger magazine, it was the same weapon I'd used as my service rifle in Vietnam. The round it fired was four times as powerful as my pistol's, and the M16 fired at full automatic. I pulled back the M16's bolt and checked the clip; there were at least a dozen rounds left, maybe more. Enough for the moment, anyway.

I pulled myself up with the help of the door handle. The first-floor layout was simple; a big room and a small room in the front, and two small rooms in the back. I worked my way through, which didn't take long. None of the other three rooms showed much sign of use. In the kitchen, one of the small rooms to the rear, two plates were on the table, but no food or utensils. I took a minute to wet a dish towel and tie it around my forehead to keep the blood out of my eyes.

I hesitated before taking the stairs, which was a mistake. A stairway is a natural ambush point anyway, and these were particularly steep and narrow. I could feel my will draining out of me. A man can be so tired that he can literally fall asleep standing up, and I could feel myself falling into it. How easy it would be to curl up in the corner and just get some rest. Not for long, just for a minute . . .

I felt myself move. Surprised, I looked down and saw that my right foot had made it up onto the first step. I grasped the banister and dragged up my left. Then the right again. I remember each one of those steps, how it looked, whether it creaked under my weight, and how far it was from the top. Finally I reached the top landing. It opened onto a small hallway with four doors, two on either side, all closed.

I should have stopped to work out a plan, but I was afraid that if I hesitated at all, I'd never get moving again. Anyway, my ability to plan anything worthwhile was in doubt. I opened the first door on the right. Just storage. The second door on the right was a makeshift bedroom; three mattresses on the floor, three cardboard boxes full of clothes, and a couple of small suitcases.

The first door on the left led to a room with a mattress on the floor. But this mattress had sheets and a pillowcase. There was a suitcase in the corner. I was getting ready to search the suitcase when heard a noise.

I moved into the corridor and looked at the door of the fourth room. Unlike the other doors, this one had a lock, a sturdy one, clearly new, set a few inches above the doorknob. I heard the noise again, a little louder this time. A thumping sound was coming from inside.

I stood to one side, reached over and tried the knob. It turned easily, but the door wouldn't budge. I braced myself against the opposite wall, set the rifle for single shots, and started pressing the trigger. The noise in such an enclosed area shook my head like a blow from a two-by-four. My shooting was terrible—three rounds missed the door and buried themselves in the wall and one blew the doorknob off, which was the last thing I wanted. But one landed just where I wanted it—just to the left of the face of the lock. I took a step and kicked at the door. It rattled and then sprang open. I jumped back out of the way, but there was no return fire. I set the rifle back to full automatic and stepped inside.

The room held a single kitchen chair, facing away from me, and a TV tray table. Someone was in the chair, ankles bound to the front chair legs. The chair was bolted into the floor and the window was crisscrossed with lengths of pipe forming a crude set of bars. I hurried forward, thinking it might be Kate, but before I'd taken two steps I realized it was a man. He was about fifty, with thick hair and a deep tan. The sports shirt and slacks were familiar.

After all my searching, I'd found Frank McMahan again.

I put up my gun and moved closer. He was straining to look at me over his shoulder, but a loop of rope around his waist held him fast. His lower face was covered with a thick gray slab of wrinkled duct tape, and his wrists were tied behind him.

I ripped off the tape in one quick motion. Fortunately for him, he'd shaved recently. "Jesus Christ," he said, "am I glad to see you!"

"What are you doing here?"

"You warned me not to mess with this detective shit." He shook his head. "I should have listened."

"Make it fast. What happened?" I bent down and started fiddling with the ropes on his wrists. They were held by some kind of complicated nautical knot I had trouble figuring out.

"I was up late last night, sittin' in my room, thinking about what to do when all of a sudden my scanner went nuts. First there was all these calls about this body. It must have been around two. I was scared it was Kate, but the description was all wrong. Every volunteer ambulance and emergency crew in the county was talking about it like it was a big deal. Hell, we get more homicides in Miami in a day than they get here in a year, I bet. Anyway, later on there's reports of gunfire out this way. I followed the calls on my map. The cops looked but nobody found anything. I figured it just might mean something, so as soon as it was light I got dressed and drove down here."

"By yourself?"

"I tried your hotel, neither one of you was there."

"We were meeting with the police."

"They here, too?"

"They wouldn't get involved."

"Jesus Christ."

"I know," I said. "I know."

"I came out this direction, drove around for a while, just driving around where the scanner said all the shots came from. Then I tried this lane. Some big spick points a gun at me and tells me to get out. So here I am. This is the place we're looking for, isn't it?"

"I think so." I worked the knot on his wrists free. He started working on the rope around his waist while I did his ankles. "Have you seen her?"

"No. Just the one big guy. What the hell is going on out there?"

As I worked, I told him what had happened last night. By the time he was free I had covered the story through my escape from the police station. He stood up, shrugging off his ropes. "I never thought I'd be glad to see you, Garrett," he said.

"The same goes for me, if you want to know the truth."

"So where is she?" he wanted to know.

"If she's here at all, there's just two places left. The garage and the shed."

"You choose," he said. "My guesses haven't been too good lately."

"We have to start somewhere. I say the shed."

"You can see it from here."

Cautiously, we moved to the window, each of us staying to one side. Outside, through the bars, we looked down at a one-story metal shed. The front door wasn't more than twenty yards away. From my viewpoint there were no other buildings in sight, and no people, either. *Un hombre,* the boy had said. I wondered if I could believe him.

"Whoever is in there, they're ready for us. We need help."

"You mean, wait for the cops? Hell, this far out, they could be an hour."

"Got a better idea?" I asked.

McMahan rubbed his hand across his jaw. "We can't quit now. Rush 'em. Right now they're surprised. Let's not give them time to think of a way out."

That was the trouble with McMahan—as difficult as he was, a lot of the time he was right. "If we're going to do something on our own, without waiting, I'm going to need your help," I said.

"I figured it that way."

"You ready to take a chance on getting killed for a woman who's left you?"

"I already did, coming here."

"So why tempt fate?"

He looked away. "You screw up a lot, Garrett. You screw this one up, I've got to go back and tell my kids what I did to rescue their mom. I've got to be able to look them in the eye."

I pulled the automatic out of my belt, made sure the safety was on, and handed it to him, butt first. "Know much around guns?" I asked.

He inspected the pistol gravely. "I shot a .45 in boot camp in the navy." He didn't bother to say how many years ago, and I didn't want to know.

"The safety's on," I said. "But keep it pointed at the floor anyway. Don't point it at anything you don't want to shoot. This won't kick as much as a .45 and it won't make as much noise. Use two hands when you shoot."

He hefted it, his mouth drawn in a thin line. "Okay."

"Frank, you really think you can shoot somebody? Up close, I mean? A lot of people freeze, and that gets them killed."

"I can do it."

"You mean it? I've got to be able to count on you."

"Come on, let's get this over with."

I started toward the door, carrying the M16 by its handle. I hadn't taken more than a couple of steps when I heard the click of the safety on McMahan's gun.

"Garrett?"

I turned and found myself staring down the barrel of his gun. "Drop it," he warned. "Give it a good toss or I'll blow you away right now."

My gun clattered into the corner and I held up my hands.

Chapter Twenty-Six

Friday 10:30 A.M.

Frank lowered the gun to his side but kept it trained on me. "What else you carrying?"

I swallowed. "Nothing."

"Bullshit. Turn around and keep your hands up."

He frisked me, clumsily but thoroughly, all the while keeping the gun in tight at his side. Then he stood back, keeping the chair between us. "Why the hell did you stick your nose where it didn't belong?"

"If you wanted her dead, why did you go to all this trouble?" I asked.

"It wasn't 'cause of you and her, I'll tell you that."

"Drugs?"

He nodded. "She tried to turn me in to the feds, but they weren't interested."

"Why not?"

"Because the guy she talked to, he's one of ours. By the next day my people knew all about it."

"But having her killed in Miami was too obvious," I said. "Especially after she'd been to see the government."

"My people told me she had to go. At first I didn't know

what to do, until she tells me she's running off with you. Now I can have it done a thousand miles away."

"So why keep her alive?"

"Just one reason," he said. "You. I was going to have her held just a few hours, enough to be sure that nobody was snooping around. Sure enough, the same damn night, you turn up. I call and tell them to hold off a little bit. The next thing I know you're popping up all over the place. Even filing a missing persons report."

"So you told them to hold off a little longer."

He nodded again. "The cops being involved, that changed things. I needed a new plan. I figured the cops would be looking at me pretty close, so I'd better show how concerned I was."

"So you came up here and stomped around and made all your speeches in front of Lisa and me. Fine. Great alibi. So then why keep us looking in the county where Kate was? Why not send us on a wild-goose chase?"

"I thought about it, believe me. But if the body was ever found, it would look funny if I'd thrown you off the track. I couldn't have it both ways. I could be in Florida, or be up here making like I was trying to help."

"If you didn't care about Kate and me, why did you want to kill me?"

"I didn't." He looked down at the gun and then up at me. "I still don't. The guys who do the jobs, they got their own ideas sometimes. For myself, I thought you were safe, that you'd never find the place. But you got lucky. Too bad for you. Anyway, I've still got your assistant to cover for me."

"She never trusted you."

"Don't matter. She's still got to say I helped look."

"Where is Kate?"

"They've probably done her already. I don't get involved in the details. With you sneaking around here last night we decided to clean up this morning and pull out."

"You're a pretty cold bastard, if you don't mind my saying so."

He shook his head. "It's not a choice. She was toast the day she walked into the federal building, no matter who takes care of it."

He raised the gun until all I could see was the big black hole of the barrel trained at the middle of my face. I watched as he gently squeezed the trigger, watched as his finger curled back, watched as the hammer rose to full cock.

Nobody made any speeches. He just pulled the trigger the rest of the way, and the hammer dropped.

Chapter Twenty-Seven

Friday 10:45 A.M.

We both heard the flat metallic click as the firing pin dropped on the empty chamber, but only I was expecting it.

As soon as I heard the sound I was making my move, dropping low and racing for the corner where the M16 lay. He was fast, but the room was small and even a two-step lead made it no contest. I dove for it anyway, rolling as I grabbed it, and came up with the stock set securely under my arm.

It was good that I did. He was charging toward me, holding the empty pistol like a club, screaming at the top of his lungs. My finger found the trigger and pressed down as the muzzle swung up toward him. The rifle bucked and the room exploded with noise as I sprayed the rest of the magazine in McMahan's direction. He landed heavily on top of me, and for a moment I wondered if I could have missed. But he didn't move, and then I felt a warm, sticky wetness.

I let go of the empty rifle and rolled him off me. He clutched at his belly with both hands. "You goddamn son of a bitch!"

I picked up the pistol, put in a fresh clip, and jacked a round into the chamber. Then I looked down at him.

"If you'd been tied awhile, they would have made the ropes tight enough so that you would have rubbed your hands to get the circulation back. You didn't, because you'd only been in the ropes a couple of minutes, right? You tied yourself up when you were caught up here without a gun. Am I right?"

"I'm not saying anything," he gasped, "till I talk to my lawyer."

"You're the kind of guy who has to shave every few hours. If your story was right it's been at least six or seven hours since you could have shaved, but your face looks like a baby's ass."

He glared at me. "Go screw yourself, Garrett."

"You know what really got me thinking, though? The call from Kate, right after you left the hotel. Lisa thought it was funny, but she didn't realize exactly why. It was the timing. Why did the call come just then? Because when you left you set it up."

"Get me a doctor, damn it."

"Don't worry, they'll all be here soon enough."

I picked up the piece of duct tape and held it under his nose. "This was already wrinkled when I pulled it off you. How come? Were they using this on Kate?"

"Go to hell."

"Fine." Before I left I patted him down, just to be sure. No weapons, just a large wad of cash which I stuck in my pocket. He looked at me accusingly while I tied his hands behind him.

"Sorry, but this is my fee."

"For what?" Surprise crossed his face, along with the momentary hope I was willing to cut a deal.

I bent over and put my face close to his. "For not beating you to death real slow with the butt of that rifle." I stood up and headed for the door. The case wasn't over until I saw her body myself.

"Garrett! You're not going to leave me here?"

I didn't bother to even turn around.

I went downstairs. The front door was heavily barred from the inside, so I decided to go out the picture window. I stepped through the gap where the window had been and worked my way around to the side of the farmhouse. Cautiously, I put my head around the corner. I glimpsed the shed, about the size of a big mobile home, to my right, about fifty feet away. It stood completely by itself, with no buildings or any other cover nearby. I saw a door, and was starting to count windows when I heard the sharp crack of a pistol shot. A piece of brick chipped off and flew by just above my head.

I pulled back and flattened myself against the side of the house, but no more shots came. Aside from the farmhouse, there was no cover for a shooter within a hundred yards. Unless whoever had shot at me was very, very good, he was up ahead, in or around the shed.

I ran to my left, around to the other end of the farmhouse. Getting down on my belly, I inched my way to the corner and slowly extended my head. I could see the side of the shed. No door on that side, and only one window. I judged the window to be eighty feet away, and in between there wasn't enough cover for a field mouse.

I pulled back and lay on the ground with my back propped against the house. If my friend with the M16 was right and there was only one man left, the odds were that he'd stay where he was, at one of the front windows, waiting for me to show myself again at the same spot. But if he had a partner, the logical place for the second man was the side window, since it commanded the only other line of approach. I hadn't drawn fire, but that didn't mean anything. If he was smart, he'd wait till I was halfway across and take me at his leisure. And even if I faced only one man, he might decide to rotate around the windows and check out both sides. I had no idea of the shed's internal layout—maybe it was one big room where one man in a central spot could keep an eye on the front and the side at the same time. The only certainties were that there was no cover, that at least one man in there was a good shot, and that whoever was inside was waiting for me.

Against all that was the possibility that just maybe Kate was inside, and still alive.

I turned the corner and started running toward the window as fast as I could. I don't know where the energy came from—some mixture of fear and hope kept me moving. My footsteps on the muddy ground seemed incredibly loud, and I was sure I'd be detected by noise alone. For all my effort I seemed to be standing still. With every step I expected the shot that was going to drop me like a felled steer. Would they finish me off right away, or leave me there for a while, gut-shot and bleeding, to see if someone came to rescue me? I could feel my knees shaking as I ran, and I fought the urge to just lie down and hug the ground. I'd seen men do that, in Vietnam, just lie down and assume the fetal position in the middle of a battlefield. It was the last thing a lot of them ever did. If I could make it to the shed, I told myself, I had at least some chance. Out here I had none at all.

Ever so slowly, the shed became larger. The window, I saw, was large, old-fashioned, and double-hung, with six panes of glass in each of the upper and lower parts. But mainly I saw how low it was—the sill was no more than two and a half feet above the ground. I could only see inside dimly, but there was enough visibility to tell me that there was nothing—and no one—standing behind the glass.

I put on a kick of extra speed and covered the last few yards. My chest felt like it was going to explode. Then I crossed my hands over my face, lowered my head, and leaped through the window.

My head hit the top of the frame and splintered it. Glass flew everywhere, and over the sound I heard a string of gunshots, close by, and the sound of a ricochet even nearer. I hit a concrete floor and instinctively tucked into a shoulder roll. Before I could complete it I crashed into something rigid, but soft, that brought me to a stop. After a moment I realized it was the back of a sofa, covered with a tarp.

"Give yourself up!" I shouted. "This is your only chance!"

I counted at least five shots, closely spaced, that tore into the sofa. But I kept myself pressed hard against the floor and they all passed overhead. Each one ricocheted off the floor and walls, and the noise was deafening. You could work at staying out of the line of fire, but there was nothing to do about ricochets but pray.

I didn't want to return fire without knowing where Kate was, but I wanted to let him know I was still alive. I rolled over, pointed my gun at the roof, and fired twice.

"Give up! This is your last chance!"

The response was three more shots, so close I could barely tell them apart. And then, just after the third, a faint metallic sound, the click of steel hitting something. It could have been anything—the muzzle knocking against a pipe, a spent casing striking something just right and making a noise, or just somebody's foot glancing off something metal. But just maybe it was an empty clip being ejected. And if it was, I had maybe three seconds to do something about it.

I stuck my head out from behind the right side of the sofa and steadied the elbow of my gun arm on the floor. There wasn't much to see. The sofa blocked my view to the left. Right in front, about fifteen yards away, was a big wooden table, turned on its side so that I was looking at the top. Farther to the right was a jumble of oil drums, boxes, and broken-down furniture.

I didn't like it. The sofa prevented me from getting my left hand onto the gun for a good two-handed grip, and I wasn't much of a shot with a pistol anyway, even starting from a good stance. But at least I was the one who had his head up.

Before I could think through my next move he made my decision for me. He popped up just above the center of the table and started spraying the sofa. His first two shots were wild as he tried to line up on me and shoot at the same time. I was ready for him. Aiming at the table, just below his head, I started shooting as fast as I could. I fired six or seven shots in a couple of heartbeats. Suddenly his head disappeared below the tabletop. A moment later a dot of light appeared a couple of inches down; and a moment after that, a second and then a third. Some of my shots had drilled right through the tabletop. Perhaps he was lying low, perhaps he was really disabled; but one way or the other, he was on the ground and light was coming through the holes.

I waited. Even if I'd hit him, the bullets would have lost a lot of energy going through the wood. Lots of people have been shot several times with pistols and kept fighting.

I counted to a hundred, then crawled back to the left-hand side of the sofa before I stood up. Shards of glass fell off me and onto the floor. I was bleeding some more, and the towel had come away from my head. I wiped away the blood as best I could. I walked toward him, my feet crackling on the glass.

Keeping my sights trained and both hands on the grip, I worked my way around one side of the table. The first thing I saw was his feet, in heavy work boots, the toes pointed at the ceiling. Jeans and a white pullover sweater with a splotch of blood on the chest. I stood about ten feet away, too far for him to make a move and yet close enough for me to be sure of a hit. I could see now that he was Hispanic, and that his hands sported some crude tattoos. From prison? He was still holding an empty clip in his left hand. Then I saw his gun, a good five feet away. I moved in and gave him a quick kick in the knee, but there was no response. I rolled him over and saw that his side was covered in blood. I checked for a pulse and couldn't find one.

Then I head something. A soft, urgent moaning noise.

I looked around. Facing the window, tied to a kitchen chair, her mouth taped, was Kate.

Chapter Twenty-Eight

Friday 11:00 A.M.

Her face was in shadow and she was gagged with a piece of cloth that tied behind her head, but there was no doubt, this time, that it was her. Her ankles were handcuffed to the legs of the chair and her hands were behind her. I crossed the room on numbed feet and stood over her for a moment. Then I put out my fingers and touched her shoulders. She was wearing dark slacks and a clingy green turtleneck top that felt like silk. And through the fabric I could feel her, warm and alive.

I stuck my gun into my belt and untied the gag. I was watching her eyes, those marvelous wide emerald eyes, and they narrowed for a moment when she realized it was me. "David!" she gasped. "Thank God. I knew you'd come for me. Are you all right?"

I touched the side of her face with a finger, tentatively, afraid she would vanish into thin air. Suddenly I thought I was going to cry. "Are you?" I asked.

She swallowed. "They haven't hurt me. What about you?"

I realized how I must look. "I'm fine, really I am."

She closed her eyes and took a deep breath. "Thank

God. It's been such a nightmare. But look at yourself—you're bleeding!"

"It's nothing." I moved behind her to get her hands and found them handcuffed.

"He's got the keys in his back pocket," she said.

I rolled over the corpse and found two sets of keys, one for the wrists and another for the ankles. In a few seconds her hands were free and I was working on the ankle cuffs.

I paused and ran my hand up and down her calf. "I can't believe you're really here," I said.

She rubbed her wrists and then ran her hands down both sides of my face and pressed them against my cheeks. "I'm here, darling. I really am." I put my head against her knee and she stroked my cheek. Her slacks were a smooth, thin material, like silk, and the texture of her body came right through. I pressed my cheek against her leg, and for the first time in three days I didn't feel tired anymore.

I freed her ankles and helped her to her feet. She pressed against my chest and I felt her arms go around me. She was thinner than I remembered, and she seemed to nestle in my embrace. Some moments, no matter how short, are so weighted down with importance that they seem to last forever. I remember everything about that moment, how the room smelled of gunpowder and oil, how drops of my blood dripped onto her blouse, how her fingers felt on my spine. She had her hands spread wide, and I could feel each one of her fingers separately. Mostly I just remember how good I felt.

When we pulled back she put her arms around my neck and kissed me long and hard. I responded once, and then again.

"God, it's good to see you," she whispered.

"I never thought I'd see you again."

We stood for a while like that, saying nothing, just enjoying the moment. It had been a long, long time coming. At last we disengaged a little, afraid to let go.

"Frank was behind all this," I said. "For what it's worth, he didn't want to do it. His bosses knew you'd been to the police. He couldn't figure any other way out."

"You think you know what people are capable of. . . ." She shook her head.

"You don't seem completely surprised."

"Tuesday night I wouldn't have believed it. I've had three days to think about it."

"How did it start?" I asked.

"He let them use his company as a cover for shipments, and he laundered some money for them. It started back in the early eighties, when interest rates were so high. It was either work for them or go bankrupt. I told him he was crazy but he paid no attention. I never had a thing to do with it—for all the difference that makes. I knew about it and I kept my mouth shut."

"What went wrong?"

"Frank started drinking too much. He boasted about how important he was. Then he made threats about how much he knew and how they'd better start treating him better. It only happened when he was drunk—when he was sober he kept his mouth shut."

"What did they do?"

"They sent a man around, back in January, warning him to shut up. That's when I went to the police. It was only a question of time till he shot off his mouth again, and then they'd kill us all. Not just him, but Annie and Frank, Jr., and me. That's the way they work, you know."

"So you decided to take a February vacation."

"When I left I didn't expect to ever see him again. I was wrong. He kept a lid on it, for a while at least, but I knew it wouldn't last."

I let go of her. "You should have told me about this, you know."

"I know. I started to, but . . . I never did. And anyway, it wasn't your problem."

"If you were going to be part of my life, then it was my problem, too."

"It wouldn't have made any difference."

"I could have been killed relying on Frank," I said.

She closed her eyes. "You're right. I'm sorry. For that and a lot of things."

"Damn it, how could you not trust me? If I'd been in your shoes I would have told you."

"Trust comes to you easier than it does to most people. Easier than to me, anyway."

"If I'd known, I could have met you in Miami. You never would have been alone."

"So you could be killed, too?"

"I'm pretty good at staying alive. Anyway, I would have taken the risk for you and you know it."

Her voice was very small. "Now I do."

"You never really knew me, Kate," I said slowly. "You never really believed in me." She just looked at the floor. All the weeks we'd talked about her coming to be with me, she'd kept this to herself. It was between us now, sharp and broad as a wedge.

I took a breath and stood by the chair; it was time to talk business. "You might as well start by telling me what happened in Harrisburg."

"There were two of them, a man and a woman. They paged me, told me they were from airport security, that there was a family emergency and they had to get me to a telephone. I didn't know what was going on till they had me outside. Then the man put a gun in my back and they put me in the van. The woman took my ticket and went back to the town and I guess she went on to Philadelphia."

"And led me on a merry chase." I gave her the bare bones of what had happened in the past three days. I left out most of the corpses, which made the story go a lot faster. "Are you sure you're not hurt?" I asked.

"No. They never hurt me, just kept me locked in a

room upstairs in the farmhouse. They fed me and even let me take a shower. They brought me out here just this morning."

"They were digging a grave for you up on the hill."

"When they moved me out here this morning I was afraid it was something like that." She looked around. "David, we've got to get out of here. All the bodies? And all the drugs? They must be around here somewhere. And there's probably a lot of cash we can't explain, either."

"I've spent the last three days lying to the police, but that was only so I could stay on the street. If we take off they'll be looking for me on more felonies than I can count."

"It's crazy to stay and wait."

"It's crazy to *leave*. The police will assume we're drug dealers and murderers. I can think of one cop in particular who won't need much prodding. Besides, it won't be long. The police know I'm here."

"What?" Her eyes widened and she looked around. "You told them you were coming?"

"I begged them to help and they wouldn't. So I stole a police car and came myself. They can't be far behind."

She went to the window and looked out. "So they'll be after you, too."

"Once they see the farm, they'll see that I was right."

She turned to face me. "But what about me?"

"Huh?"

"David, you have no idea how dangerous this is. These people—they'll be after me, and they're never going to give up."

"All the more reason to get police protection."

She spoke slowly, thinking it through as she spoke. "Right now, if we put out the story I was killed here, they'll stop looking for me. But if the police find me it's all over. I'll never be safe if they know I'm alive. They'll watch you in Philadelphia to see if you'll lead them to me."

"Frank's alive, you know," I said. "Back in the farmhouse."

"Oh my God. Now I know they'll never give up."

"But he thinks you're already dead."

"He does?"

"That's what he told me when he had no reason to lie. And if I'd been here an hour later, he would have been right."

"You know what that means, don't you? They'll believe him. Not just the police, but the Colombians, too."

"Yeah," I agreed. I felt something well up in my chest, something that had nothing to do with any of my physical pain. "If the police don't find you."

She put her hands on my shoulders. "Then you see what we have to do?"

She was touching me, close and warm and alive; and slipping away even as I watched. Falling back into the shadows. "Yeah," I said. "I do."

She nodded her head, slowly, mechanically. Her lips started to form words but nothing came out. Then she put her head down on my chest and cried. I just listened, not moving. After a while she pulled back and dried her eyes. It was time to get to work.

"You have any changes of clothes?" I asked.

"Just what I have on."

"Are you wearing anything under that top?" I asked.

"A little silk shell. Why?"

"Would Annie or Frank recognize it?"

"Annie would. It's one of hers from years ago."

"Get it off. We need it."

She pulled her top over her head, revealing something white and sleeveless with a high neck. It was sheer, and through it I could see the outline of her bra. She pulled off the shell and handed it to me. The morning sun played on her bare skin and on the lacy wisps of turquoise that crossed her chest.

"That's the same bra you were wearing the first night we went to bed," I said.

"I'm glad you remembered."

"Remembered? I'll never have trouble remembering you."

I turned away, conscious of her eyes on me. I draped the shell over the bullet-riddled couch and fired three shots into it from just a couple of feet away. The holes were rimmed with black power marks. Then I turned it inside out and set it down in the pool of blood by the gunman. The silk turned pink and then dark red as the blood seeped into the fabric.

I picked it up and tore it in half. After all, someone stripping a dead body wouldn't be fussy. Then I rolled it up and tossed it into a remote corner behind an old dresser.

"What if they ask about the rest of my clothes?"

"Maybe they'll think this just got dropped. You have your purse?"

"On the sofa."

"Is there anything in there you absolutely *have* to keep? This will play better if they find your purse intact."

"There's nothing I can't live without." She paused. "There's a couple of hundred in cash."

"The more you leave in there, the better." I pulled out Frank's roll of bills and did a rough count. I handed her about a thousand and kept a wad about twice that thick for myself.

"David, I can't take this from you."

"If you want to stay alive, you will. You've got to get out of here and you don't dare use checks or credit cards. Besides, it's found money anyway."

She folded the bills and put them into her back pocket. "David, you know, this just might work."

I tossed the purse on top of the shell. "It's not original. I learned it from your niece Amy."

"If it worked for her it might work for me." For the first time she was allowing herself to sound hopeful. "But the blood isn't going to match."

"There's a dozen technical reasons it might not work, and none of them matter unless somebody pays attention to them. You're missing, presumed dead, and the people that killed you are dead. With a little luck you just fall through the cracks."

"We may not be together again."

"I know."

"What you said a minute ago, that you're going to remember me? That was a wonderful thing to hear. Even now." She took a step toward me. I saw how the delicate straps of turquoise molded themselves to the curves of her shoulders, and how her belt rode, just below her navel. Her thumbs were hooked through a couple of her front belt loops, pulling her slacks even lower. I could see the bottom of the curve of her belly, almost to her bikini line. She was close enough to touch.

"David?"

"Yes?"

"How long till the police get here?" she whispered.

I hesitated a long time and then I shook my head. Her emerald eyes met mine and held them. If she saw deeply enough, she knew that turning her down had nothing to do with how much time we had.

She turned away, put on her top, and ran her fingers through her hair. I looked out the window and tried not to think about anything at all.

When she was ready to go she took my hands in both of hers. "I'm sorry, David."

"Now you'd better get out. My story isn't going to be very convincing if you're standing here."

"So what should I do?"

"Get off the East Coast and go talk to the FBI again. If Frank rolls over, this will be a huge case and they'll want your testimony against the higher-ups. If he doesn't, they'll want to know what you can tell them about him. Either way, the government will be interested."

"How does that help?" she asked.

"They'll put you in witness protection. I can't protect you, but the U.S. Marshal's Service can."

"I have family in Seattle."

"Good. Then you'd better go to Oklahoma or North Dakota or New Mexico. Anywhere that nobody would expect you to go. Don't tell me and don't tell anybody else. I'll take care of telling Annie that you're all right."

"David, I just wish that—"

"You can take one of the vehicles around here but the police will be watching the roads. You're better off going cross-country to a road and hitchhiking out of here. The main road is about two miles north of here. Nobody's going to be looking for you anyway."

"I want you to know—"

"Kate, just go."

"David—"

"There's nothing you can say that's going to make it any easier. So just go."

It was a heavy door, but she shut it softly behind her.

Chapter Twenty-Nine

Friday Noon

I was still sitting there on the sofa when I heard a noise. It came from above, a rhythmic, thumping sound. Helicopter blades. The sound grew louder. At the same time I heard other sounds—car engines and voices, then footsteps. Lots of them.

I thought about going to the door, but what was the use? What had kept me going for the last four hours, the last three days, was gone, and I was just myself again, tired and middle-aged and hurting. Even when they announced, "Police! Open up!" I stayed where I was.

After a count of three the door splintered and a steel I-beam came through. It withdrew, struck again a little lower, and came through again. The third time the door flew open and I found myself looking at half a dozen armed men, all in full riot gear and all pointing weapons directly at me. "Freeze! This is the police! Keep your hands in plain sight and don't move!"

That was easy enough. My hands were already in sight and I didn't feel much like moving anyway. They moved into the room smartly, covering the windows, while two more men approached me, laid me face down on the floor, and patted me down. I felt them lift Peters's gun from my belt. They left me that way for several minutes while the room was secured. I sensed many people moving past me.

When they rolled me back over I was looking at Detective Peters. He was wearing pants from a business suit, a white shirt and tie, and a flak jacket. He helped me to my feet. "You look like hell. You all right?"

"Some cuts."

"Then what's this?" He touched my forehead.

"Crease from a bullet." It didn't seem very important anymore.

"We have a medic along. We'll have him take a look at you."

"There's a man in the farmhouse, first floor."

"We have someone with him already. The man on the second floor, you know him?"

"Frank McMahan. He was behind the whole thing."

"He hasn't been very forthcoming so far," Peters admitted.

"He will be. He's just waiting till he can see his lawyer. Then he'll be playing 'Let's Make a Deal.' "

"Any idea about his wife?"

"Dead. McMahan told me so himself."

He dropped his voice and tried to sound sympathetic. It didn't work. "I was hoping you'd wait, like I tried to tell you."

"That was the plan. It changed when I found the grave."

"Grave?"

"They were digging one on the crest of the hill to the south. When I saw that I decided I couldn't wait any longer. Oh, by the way, you'll find a body in there, too."

"Mrs. McMahan's?"

"The gravedigger's. He tried to take my head off with a shovel, then he went for his gun. Once I started there was no way to stop."

"So where's her body?"

I indicated the corpse by the table. "Before he died he said something about *el rio*. You might want to drag the river." I decided to let them find the purse and the clothing for themselves.

"So why a grave *and* the river?" he asked, puzzled.

I looked him straight in the eye. "I guess you'll have to ask him. We didn't get around to discussing it."

"I think it's time for you to hear your rights, Mr. Garrett."

"Hold on a minute. I need to make a telephone call."

"You'll have plenty of time for that later."

"No, this isn't for me. I mean, calling the McMahan family. Their daughter's waiting by the phone and she's scared to death."

"I don't have authority to allow you to make long-distance calls on our equipment."

"Jesus Christ," I said. "All right, forget it. I'll do it myself."

"Sorry. And I'm especially sorry I have to do this at a time like this." He reached into his breast pocket and pulled out a folded multipart carbon form and handed it over. He didn't look sorry at all. It was an arrest warrant for me, for two counts of aggravated assault upon police officers, theft of a firearm, and unauthorized use of a motor vehicle. I looked at it with mild interest. "Think you can make any of this crap stick?" I asked.

"Of course I do."

There was no judicial seal at the bottom, and no preliminary hearing date set. "This hasn't been filed with the magistrate yet, has it?"

"No."

"Then I'm going to offer you a chance to save your sorry little ass. I bet you found enough drugs to get the whole county high and keep it there for a month."

"Why should I tell you?"

"Because in an hour you'll be telling every newspaper and radio station and TV station in the state. And by tomorrow you'll be working on a TV movie deal. How big a haul?"

"You're a pretty presumptuous guy, Garrett."

"So tell me I'm wrong."

"This isn't a media circus."

"Then if I go out that door I won't see any cameras or reporters?"

He swallowed. "Well, it's certainly newsworthy—"

"How much have you found, damn it?"

"Roughly a quarter million dollars' worth of cocaine."

"And you're still looking. There could be more."

"Yeah."

I lowered my voice. "This can go down one of two ways. One, I can tell the truth. That I was trying to rescue my girl, over your violent objection, and stumbled into all this. You'll look like an idiot, which is what you are. But there's another way."

"I don't know why, but I'm listening."

"My role is minimized, maybe I'm just a confidential informant. The drug raid was your idea. We work it out later, if there has to be a trial, exactly what the hell I was doing out here. You take the credit and you're halfway to being a county commissioner."

"That could never work."

"It's only a problem if there's a trial, and after McMahan cuts his deal the only one left to try is a shot-up kid who's probably an illegal alien anyway. Whoever he is, he's not a Snyder County voter. You've got firearms and assault charges on him without bringing the drugs into it. Any way it happens, the story is still that you broke up a major drug distribution operation."

"I don't make deals."

"There's a second part to this if I tell the truth. Kate McMahan's kids sue the ass off you, the county, and the borough for negligence concerning her death. I brought you information and you refused a specific request for assistance. Since the authorities wouldn't help, I was forced to act on my own. And look me in the eye and tell me that Ettinger wouldn't be a good witness against you."

"Come on, Garrett."

"She had a chance and you took it away from her."

"You can't make that stick." He was close to being right on that score. As a government official he probably had immunity from suit. And even if it got past the immunity issue, it was on the very edge of the law. But I knew that and he didn't. More important, he had something to lose and I didn't.

I pressed on. "You want me to try? To have this whole story come out? Think about the publicity. You'll be lucky to be allowed to direct traffic."

He jabbed a forefinger at the warrants. "You're the one who should be worried, not me."

"I'm not the cop who lost his gun."

He gave me his blandest look. "I've got it back now. I'll deny it."

"Nice try, but there's three drug dealers with slugs from your gun in them. Going to call them hunting accidents?"

His face reddened and he made a fist. "Garrett . . ."

"I don't give a damn what happens from here. But you should."

"You're bluffing."

I handed him back the warrants. "Then arrest me and find out."

He looked at me glumly. "I don't trust you, Garrett."

"I don't trust you, either, and I don't like you, besides. But we can still do business."

"How do I know you won't change your mind?" he wanted to know.

"Because you have five years to file those charges. I have more to worry about than you do."

"What about the assistant DA?" he asked.

"I never met one yet who didn't want to be a judge. Big drug raid, there's some glory in it for everybody. She'll play ball."

"And Ettinger?"

"He'll keep it to himself. You're not worth risking his pension."

He gave me a nasty look, but he didn't follow it up. Instead, he squatted down and studied the holes in the table. "For the record, Garrett, tell me about this." He didn't look at me.

"What about it?"

He looked the corpse up and down. "If you tell me you struggled for the gun, he threatened to get control of it, and you killed him in self-defense, there wouldn't be any charges."

"Is that what your report is going to say?"

He looked at me. "Yeah."

"What about the others?"

"Self-defense, too."

"Put in whatever you want and I'll sign it."

"You'll probably be getting a citizen's commendation from the governor out of this. Might even help you get your law license back."

I thought about what Kate had said about the Colombians. "If it's all the same to you, I'd just as soon not have my name in the papers."

More publicity for him. He didn't look too unhappy. "There's going to have to be a coroner's inquest in a few days. Make yourself available."

"I guess that means we have a deal."

He didn't answer, or even look at me, but he ripped the warrants in half and stuck the pieces in his pocket. "Let the medic take a look and then go home and get some sleep."

"The hell with the medic. Just let me out of here. I need to call my partner."

"No you don't. She's been at the station the whole time, raising hell about you. She was part of the reason we came when we did—she swore that you wouldn't wait. She insisted on coming along. I made her stay in the back, but she's here. But you ought to get yourself cleaned up. You've got blood all over you."

I had to agree, about the blood. It had been a bloody trail, and it led through Maggie and Ashley and Joe and Elsie. And the man in the grave and the man behind the table. The end of the trail, six deaths later.

I started to ask him where Lisa was, but I was interrupted by her voice at the door, shouting my name. She came in slowly, taking in the scene as she went.

"David, are you bleeding?"

"Only a little. Most of this belongs to other people." I was getting tired of reassuring people about my health.

She knelt closer so I could whisper to her. "I cut ourselves a deal with Peters. Let's get out of here before he changes his mind."

I started to get up and began losing my balance. She caught me as I was about to slide back down to the floor.

"Come on," I said. "There's nothing for us here, and I need to get to a telephone. I need to call Florida." I wondered what I was going to tell Annie. I couldn't tell her anything on her home phone, it might be bugged. . . .

I leaned on Lisa and she walked me to my poor ruined car. The passenger's seat had never felt so comfortable. Even with the seat back upright, I could feel myself falling asleep.

Lisa started the engine, but she left it out of gear.

"She's alive, isn't she?"

"Why do you say that?"

"Because you're sad, not angry."

I rubbed my temples to stop my headache. It didn't help, and my fingertips were numb. "She's safe."

"So what happened?"

I closed my eyes and leaned back. I allowed myself the luxury of a long, deep breath. "Eurydice screwed up."

She put the car in gear and let me sleep.